MORE THAN YOU KNOW

JAZMINE HARRIS

Cover illustration by Serena Connell
Dustjacket design by April Richelle

Hardcover ISBN: 979-8-9886838-1-0
Paperback ISBN: 979-8-9886838-0-3
eBook ISBN: 979-8-9886838-2-7

To Angela,
I often thought of you when I needed the motivation to finish this book.
"Angie's waiting on the finished result!" I'd say.
Your friendship has been greatly appreciated.

MORE THAN YOU KNOW

CHAPTER 1

They said high school was about losing friends, making new ones, and finding yourself. They also said it would be the best four years of your life. It took me all four of those years to realize that it wasn't about what other people said; it was about what *you* said…or didn't.

I'd spent so much of my time in high school imprisoned by feelings of unrequited love—except I wasn't even sure if they were unrequited; I had just assumed. I was too chicken to confess my own feelings, so I went through each and every day wondering if there was the slightest chance he felt the same way I'd felt about him from the moment we first met.

I know what you're probably thinking. *Who's talking right now, and who is "he?"* I'm getting there, don't worry.

Let's start with *him*: my best friend, Ryan. He's kinda the center of this whole story, anyway. I was the new kid at school when I first met him. What's better than moving away from all your childhood friends to a new school in the middle of freshman year? Anything. Anything is better. Thanks to my mom's new job as a creative director at a local brand development agency, she'd finally had the opportunity to move into her dream home after years of nine-to-fives at a job that didn't appreciate her but "paid the bills," so I couldn't blame her—but it still sucked.

My first day at my new school wasn't bad, though, because somehow, out of the 468 freshmen there, Ryan was chosen to show me to my classes.

At first, it was dreadful. Students and faculty bustled around me in the front office as I waited for someone to show me around. I sat in a secluded corner by the door, watching people walk in and out without so much as giving me a glance. I felt nonexistent and irrelevant, but then, suddenly, my view went from nerve-racking to breathtaking. Someone was finally acknowledging me.

I looked up from his ID, which dangled from his neck in front of me. It read: *Ryan Alvarez*, and I couldn't decide on what to say: "oh shit," or "marry me." This guy was beautiful.

"Are you…Gabrielle Perkins?" he asked, pausing to read my name from a sheet of paper he had folded in half.

"Yeah," I confirmed, getting up from my seat, "but you can call me Gabby," I finished.

"Gabby," he smiled. "I'm Ryan. I'll be showing you around," he explained, opening the door for me as we left the front office.

"Sorry for the wait, by the way. I was caught up in a meeting with my coach this morning." He was walking me down the main hallway, which was lined with trophy-filled showcases and spirit posters advertising the next basketball game.

"Ah, so you're an athlete," I commented. This didn't surprise me since he towered over me. Granted, I was only 5'4", so everyone seemed tall to me, but I knew above average when I saw it. "Which sport do you play?" I asked.

"Golf," he smirked.

"Golf," I repeated. It wasn't what I was expecting, but tall people golf, so it wasn't unbelievable.

For a moment, Ryan was silent. I looked up to find him red in the face, withholding laughter. "What?" I asked, to which he finally released his amusement with a contagious cackle.

"I play basketball," he told me, moving his lanyard slightly so I could read the "Men's Varsity Basketball" t-shirt he was wearing. It was perfectly visible, even without him moving his lanyard, I just hadn't noticed.

I smiled in embarrassment. "I guess I walked into that one, huh?" Ryan certainly had the frame of a basketball player, standing at about six feet with toned arms and shoulders. His complexion was golden, like that of a glazed donut, and his hair was an assortment of very short, dark curls that lay neatly at the top of his head.

"Nah, you're nervous. I get it," Ryan reasoned, stopping in front of an inconspicuous door right between two of the showcases. "Here's our first stop." He swung open the door and waited for me to enter, following closely behind me.

"This way." He led me through what appeared to be a breakroom, and I quickly gathered that we were in the teachers' lounge. After following him through what felt to me like an endless maze, we approached a printing room with a classic blue backdrop and a camera set up against one of the walls. *It* screamed "school photos," and *I* screamed internally. I was far from camera ready, especially if Ryan was taking my picture.

"What's this?" I asked, hoping it was anything but the obvious.

"I'm taking your ID-slash-yearbook picture! This is what you get when you arrive in the middle of the year: a random basketball player taking your portrait," he teased.

"Lucky me!" I cheered sarcastically, taking my place against the backdrop.

"Point guard, point-and-shoot, it's all the same," he said, bending over to look through the camera viewfinder. "Say cheeeese!" he sang.

"WAIT!!! How do I look? I wasn't expecting to take pictures today," I admitted, adjusting my struggle-bun. My four-day-old wash-and-go was in its *wash-and-no* phase, and throwing it in a high bun was the last stage of my hairstyle progression before my next wash day. I would have attempted to look better for my first day, but my mom and I had just finished settling into our new house the night before, so I was too tired to be bothered with my hair.

Ryan stood up straight and looked at me, dropping his playful demeanor. "You look good, Gab. Don't worry."

There was something about the sincerity behind those six simple words that helped him gain all my trust in that moment. I relaxed, smiled for the camera, and then blinked away the flash-induced blindness until I could see again. I walked over to Ryan, who was still looking at the camera, and peered at the LCD screen, which had my photo on the display. I gasped in surprise at how great it had turned out.

"See. What'd I say?" He stood straight up again, looking down at me with satisfaction. "The front office will call you to pick your ID up when it's ready. I bet yours will come out way better than mine, see?" he said, showing me his.

I had no idea what he was talking about. How could anything get better than his? He was extremely photogenic, but I had to admit, his face in the photo had nothing on the real thing—live and in action. I glanced back and forth between him and his ID, marveling at how one guy could be so ridiculously attractive.

"You okay?" he asked, lowering his ID and waving his hand in front of my face. Maybe I had spent longer than I'd thought memorizing his features.

"Yeah!" I nodded in embarrassment. "What's next on the agenda?" I asked.

"Follow me." He led me out of the teachers' lounge, back into the main hallway, and then stopped in the middle of the floor, where the main hall split into a four-way.

"Okay. We can do this one of two ways: I can do the tour the *'right way'* and show you where your classes are with a long, boring speech about what our school has to offer, *or* I can do the tour *my way* and show you every nook and cranny of the school so that we don't have to be in class," he offered.

"I'll take nook and cranny for four-hundred, Alex," I affirmed.

"Only nerds watch *Jeopardy!*" He rolled his eyes, though I could see him fighting the urge to smile at my comment.

"I guess we're both nerds, then, since you know where the reference comes from." I crossed my arms with a bit of cockiness.

He nodded in defeat and looked at me with a smirk, as if making a mental note about me. "Back to the tour," he continued, turning abruptly to the left and proceeding down the hallway. I laughed quietly to myself as I followed him.

"This is my favorite part of the school. The athletics wing," he said, spreading his arms enthusiastically like Rose at the front of the *Titanic*. If this was the start of our love story, there was no way I was about to play Jack. (He deserved better. Justice for Jack.)

"What do you think?" He smiled like a kid at a candy store as he turned to face me.

Before I could answer, a large group of guys poured out of a nearby door, and from the way they perked up when they spotted him, it seemed like they all knew Ryan.

"Hey, look, y'all, it's Mr. Varsity!" one guy yelled. Ryan flashed a smile at his comment.

"Congrats on getting moved up, my guy. Don't forget about us now that you're playing with the upperclassmen," another guy said, dapping him up.

"Never that. I'm kinda in the middle of something, though, if y'all don't mind," he explained. The boys looked at him with confusion for a split second, and then seemed to notice me.

"Ohhhhhh," they all said in unison in much quieter voices, like realizing an infant was sleeping.

"She's cute, bro. That's all you?" one of them asked quietly, nudging Ryan in the arm. They were horrible whisperers.

"You not gon' introduce us?" another intervened, making himself more visible.

Ryan smacked his teeth and stepped aside. "Gabby, these are my nosey ass teammates. Nosey ass teammates, this is Gabby. She's new here, and I'm showing her around."

"*Ex*-teammates," one clarified, extending his hand for a shake. "Ryan broke up with us this morning, so we're officially on the market—I mean, *I'm* officially on the market—"

"She's good, bro," Ryan interrupted, slapping his ex-teammate's hand away and putting his arm around my shoulder. "I saw her first," he asserted, winking at me.

With that, almost as quickly as they'd been made aware of my presence, they seemed to forget it, engaging Ryan further in conversations related to the meeting they had just walked out of. While Ryan wrapped up his discussions, he kept is arm around my shoulder like it belonged there—like *I* belonged there—and as he spoke, I got to admire more of him: his confidence, his muscular build, his cologne.

He glanced down at me every now and then to check on me, and each time I could feel my face get warm from embarrassment as I fought the urge to smile. I could tell Ryan was the kind of guy who could have any girl he wanted based on his looks alone, so that attention, whether he was assigned to show me around or not, felt special. I almost couldn't believe someone as blatantly attractive as him was speaking to me, much less had his arm around me. As a matter of fact, I was sure a guy like him had to have a girlfriend, but time proved me wrong.

Freshman year? Single.

Sophomore year? Single.

Junior year? You guessed it.

Each year, my feelings for him grew, and each year, I bit my tongue.

Three years later, when we were seniors, Ryan's beauty was more captivating than ever. He'd grown into a smarter, more mature, 6'2" teddy bear with abs and a jawline. He was easily the Puerto Rican heart throb on campus. Maybe it was puberty, maybe it was basketball, or maybe he was just that damn perfect, but he became more to me than just the guy who showed me around when I was the new kid. Even so, he was less than what I craved of him.

Best Friend, noun.

1. A favorable companion.

2. Usually a guy some girl doesn't want to admit her feelings to.

3. Not my boyfriend.

That's right. I, Gabrielle Perkins, was stuck in the friend zone.

I had no one to blame but myself for my position—it's not like Ryan put me there. I was always too scared to tell him how I felt about him. You know the trope: one friend catches feelings, tells the other friend, and the whole friendship crashes and burns, or it's just never the same again. My feelings were like venom; if I released them, I risked killing the friendship, but when I kept them inside, they ran through my veins, killing me slowly.

At least, that's what I'd convinced myself of. Ryan had never given me any reason to believe he wouldn't feel the same, but something in me didn't believe I was good enough for him. He was so popular with everyone. Not in a cliché, *he's the cool jock* way, but in a, *he's genuinely a good guy* kind of way. People sincerely liked Ryan, and with him being as handsome as he was, you already know the girls were all over him. I knew it was only a matter of time before one of them actually earned his attention in return, and I was right. Someone *had* won over his heart.

You know the saying, *"you don't know what you've got until it's gone?"* I say, you don't know what you've got until it's someone else's. I'll never forget the moment I was blindsided by the news that Ryan had made things official with Indya Chavez, the school track star.

It was the first day of senior year, and my other best friend, Melanie, and I were hanging out in the senior section of the parking lot, looking at the paintings everyone did for their parking spots.

"Why did you paint a chicken on yours?" I questioned, tilting my head as I analyzed Melanie's parking space.

"That's not a chicken! That's Guapo!" she argued, hitting me on the arm. Guapo was Melanie's Yorkie.

"Aren't dogs supposed to have four legs?" I laughed, taking a picture with my phone as Melanie got back into her car and pulled forward into her spot.

Melanie, Ryan, and I were more or less like the three musketeers, with them connected through me. Symbolically, my parking spot was between theirs; Ryan's was on my left, and Melanie's was on my right. For three years, we'd had a routine: park, wait for each other, and walk to class together. So, imagine our surprise that day when Ryan pulled up and Indya got out of his passenger's seat.

I was so busy wiping tears from laughing at Melanie's chicken-dog that I hadn't realized that Ryan had pulled into his parking space.

"Ryan," I snickered, walking toward his car to show him the picture of Melanie's parking spot. "Tell me this doesn't look like a chicke—" I stopped, taken aback at the sight of his passenger door swinging open. I looked at Indya in confusion, while also trying not to be rude.

"You guys know Indya, right?" Ryan smiled, getting out of the driver's side.

"Yeah, uh…I guess we just…weren't really expecting her," I admitted, glancing at Melanie, who looked just as confused as me.

"Indya and I are together, now," Ryan explained, throwing his arm around her shoulder and my heart into a blender with one swift move.

"*'Together,'* like, you guys are partnering on a school project, *'together'*?" Melanie asked, trying to lighten the blow. I could feel her softly rest her hand on my back in consolation.

"*'Together,'* like, I'm his girlfriend," Indya asserted, wrapping her arms around Ryan's waist to make her point.

"We're gonna be late for class," I said, abruptly walking away, dragging Melanie behind me.

"But we still have like twenty minu—"

"WE'RE GONNA BE LATE FOR CLASS," I repeated, walking faster to discourage Ryan and Indya from following us. I could feel myself falling apart the farther we got from the parking lot, but I couldn't let Ryan see that.

Ryan's announcement put my heart on ice, but seeing Indya wrap her arms around him made my blood boil. *That could've been you,* I thought, realizing my own fault. I was pissed at myself and hurt that Ryan hadn't considered me in that way. I'd had three years to make my move—confess how I felt—but I still couldn't help but feel betrayed. Shouldn't I have been next in line for a chance at having his heart? What was wrong with me? What was right about…*her*?

Was my skin too dark? Was my hair too thick—too kinky to admire? Indya was half Black and half Filipino, but her skin had the same light, sun-kissed complexion as Ryan's, and her hair had a looser assortment of curls than mine. Ryan had never made me feel less than because of my Blackness, but seeing him choose someone whose Blackness looked different than mine led me into a game of comparison.

My point is, seeing Indya wrap her arms around Ryan was like watching everything I'd ever wanted with him slip away, and it lit a fire under my ass. I wasn't the *"as long as he's happy, I'm happy"* type. Why do girls feed themselves that lie when they know it's indigestible? I wanted him to myself, but I was too late.

So, what's the point of the remaining thirty chapters, then, right? It's obvious I was just a weenie who choked on her feelings and missed out on love—or at least the possibility of it.

But what if I told you that's the exact opposite of what happened? That I had made up my mind to tell Ryan how I felt, only to get side-tracked by a guy I didn't see coming. A guy who made this story a lot more complicated than the one I expected to tell you.

Put on your seatbelt; it's a long ride.

CHAPTER 2

Everyone has that one friend who just…gets it. For me, that friend was Melanie. She balanced me out with her outspoken and unapologetic personality. I was the thinker, and she was the doer. I kept things inside, and she blurted them out…a little too much.

Melanie and I became friends shortly after I arrived freshman year. I'd gotten called to the front office to pick up my ID a few days after Ryan's "orientation," and when I got there, a girl I'd never seen before was standing at the desk in front of me.

"Okay, Miss Reyes, here you go…again," the secretary was saying to her as she handed her an ID. "Try not to lose it this time," she added.

"Thanks, Carol. Fourth time's the charm!" the girl—Melanie—chimed. "Loving the top, by the way." She grabbed her ID and turned toward me to leave, and I remember being taken aback by how beautiful she was. She had dark, wavy hair that gracefully decorated her shoulders, gorgeous cheekbones, long, beautiful eyelashes, and curves women often paid for.

Carol seemed less than impressed with Melanie's charm, however, and I had to hold in laughter at her reaction to a student calling her by her first name. The tag on her shirt read *Carol Stripe*, but I was almost certain she and Melanie weren't on a first name basis. Of course, that was only an assumption based on the fact that Carol was a middle-aged White woman who likely had kids older than we were.

"May I help you, sweetheart?" Carol asked, turning her attention to me.

I approached the counter and wrote my name on the sign-in sheet. "I'm here to pick up my ID card," I informed.

"Oh yes! You must be Gabrielle," Carol said, scanning her desk, "I know I had it here somewhere, I must've misplaced it—"

"Carol! There was another ID stuck to the back of mine," Melanie said, swinging the office door open as she made her way back inside.

"Yes, that belongs to Gabrielle, here," Carol confirmed.

"Thank you," I said as Melanie handed it to me. I scanned it and smiled at how nice it had turned out, just as Ryan said it would.

"Miss Reyes?" Carol called out as Melanie made her way back to the exit.

Melanie stopped in the doorway. "Yes?"

"Please, from now on, call me Mrs. Stripe," Carol asserted.

"Aw, but I thought we were getting close, Caro—I mean, Mrs. Stripe," Melanie whined playfully.

"That's because you keep losing your ID, Miss Reyes."

"Well, why do we need to wear these things, anyway? My teachers should know my name by now!"

"I don't make the rules, hon. Have a good rest of your day," she finished, taking her seat again at the front desk.

Melanie stepped aside and held the door for me, and I awkwardly brushed past her.

"Thank you," I said.

"You're welcome," Melanie replied, joining me at my side as we proceeded down the hallway. "Your ID picture came out really good, by the way."

"Thanks! Ryan took it for me a few days ago," I explained, analyzing it again.

"Ryan? Ryan Alvarez?!" she asked in disbelief.

"Yes?" I confirmed, looking at her in confusion.

"Oh my god, *you're* the new girl I've been hearing about! Come on," she said, taking my hand and pulling me into a nearby women's restroom, barely taking a breath before she started again.

"So, how was it?! I need all the details. I heard people saying Ryan was with a new girl, but it didn't make sense to me because Ryan's always been single, but now I see they literally meant a *new* girl. You're new, right? Or did you lose your ID like I did?"

I chuckled at how fast and energetic Melanie was when she spoke. It was almost overwhelming. "Uh, yeah, I just transferred here a few days ago. Ryan showed me around the school for my orientation and took my ID photo for me," I explained. "What were people saying?"

"Oh, nothing bad! Don't worry! It was mainly just the guys on the basketball team talking about a new girl who was with Ryan when they got to class the other day. When the freshman girls got wind of it, it started circulating like crazy, but no one knew who they were talking about," she explained.

"Oh." I sighed in relief, leaning against the sink counter. "Well, it was me," I confirmed nervously. "He must be pretty popular then, huh?"

Melanie joined me against the counter. "Are you kidding? The girls here have Ryan fever, I swear. I mean, obviously he's cute, right? But I think the fact that he's not a man-whore and plays hard to get makes them want him even more. So, yeah. He's *definitely* popular."

"Oh *god,* I feel like I just walked into Animal Kingdom. Please don't tell anyone I was the one with Ryan. I don't need girls making me their enemy before they even know me."

"I won't," Melanie agreed, sticking up her pinky for a pinky promise. I giggled and interlocked mine with hers.

"I'm Melanie, by the way. I just realized I never introduced myself."

"Gabby," I replied.

From that point forward, we stuck together, and the restroom became our safe haven. It was where we debriefed one another on events and confessions that simply couldn't wait until after school. Eventually, during one of our restroom sessions, I confessed to Melanie that I liked Ryan, and ever since, she'd become my biggest advocate for telling him how I felt.

When Ryan started dating Indya, Melanie became even more adamant that I tell him. She saw first-hand what seeing them together did to me. I ate less, slept less—I was overcome with heartbreak and anxiety. When I progressed past my sad phase, I hit denial. I convinced myself that it was just a fling and it'd all be over, soon, but Melanie didn't care, fling or not. *"That could've been you and you know it,"* she'd tell me. The further senior year progressed, the more she brought it up. She wanted nothing more than for me to have the chance to be happy with Ryan—or to at least say I'd tried. Her newest tactic was to narrate Ryan's actions in the halls of the school to emphasize that he was often doing things without me or with Indya instead.

"Oh, look! There goes the love of your life, living his best life without you because he doesn't know how you feel," she narrated dramatically to me one day as Ryan walked by with his basketball teammates. The varsity team had a tournament that was pretty far away, so they were leaving before our last class period. The bad news was, I wouldn't have him next to me in Sociology to talk to. The good news was, he wouldn't be there to hear me scold Melanie for loudly narrating my love life for all to hear.

I pulled Melanie into our Sociology class and dragged her to our seats. "You've really got the *keep it a secret* thing down pact, Mel, congrats," I scoffed, referencing my feelings for Ryan.

"Yeah, yeah. You know this is nobody's fault but your own, right? It's January, now! Five more months and we're all graduating and heading our separate ways, Gabby! Are you gonna hold onto this forever or finally tell him how you feel?" she asked, taking out her pencil pouch.

We of course had had this conversation a million times, but now that senior year was half-way over, it actually started to sink in. *Five* months left? It hadn't really occurred to me that high school was almost over. I hadn't even thought about what I wanted to do after we graduated. I mean, I knew I was gonna go to a community college and knock out all my core classes, but that wasn't until the fall. Melanie would be starting a pre-nursing mentorship at our local hospital this summer, and Ryan would most likely be busy with basketball like he usually was. But me? Well, I didn't know what I would do with the rest of my life, yet.

During class, I sat there, ruminating on our inevitable graduation and what was to come after that, hoping that my future plans would spontaneously present themselves to me. It wasn't until a nudge from Melanie ripped me from my thoughts that I realized that the entire class period had gone by—I hadn't heard a thing.

"Okay, so to close out, I'll be introducing your final projects, which will be due at the end of the school year. I want you to attend a social event for a group of people you aren't familiar with, analyze the group's culture and customs, and document your experience. Simple, but it must be structured according to the rubric that's being passed around," Mr. Nicholson explained, handing out a stack of papers to the first person in each row. I made sure to grab an extra rubric for Ryan, as was our routine whenever one of us missed class.

I was pretty apathetic to all my teachers, but Mr. Nicholson was my favorite for the simple fact that he didn't take himself too seriously; he was laid back, nice, and made things simple to understand. But still, no matter how much I liked the teacher, there was one thing I would never like: projects.

♥ ♥ ♥

"Wow, I should've known my day was too good to be true. I had no homework from any of my teachers, and then the very last one drops a whole project!" I complained as I threw my backpack on Melanie's bedroom floor and collapsed into the beanbag chair next to her bed. Guapo quickly jumped into my lap and took his usual position. I would often spend the afternoons at her place or Ryan's. Sometimes all three of us would pick a house and get our work done together, but during basketball season, it was usually just Melanie and me.

Melanie sat on her bed, glued to her phone. I glanced at her, waiting for a response. Nothing.

"Mel?"

She finally spoke. "Is it something to worry about if Marcus randomly starts following a new girl on Insta? It's probably nothing. It's nothing, right?"

"Did I ever tell you how great of a listener you are?" I said sarcastically.

"I'm serious, G!" Melanie whined.

"Girl, you and Marcus have known each other for so long—why are you worried about who he follows on Instagram all of a sudden? You know that boy has only had eyes for you since he learned how to *spell* 'eyes,'" I told her. Marcus was Melanie's boyfriend. They'd been dating since the end of junior year, but had known each other since pre-K. One day, he finally mustered up the courage to admit how he felt about her, and it worked in his favor. (Maybe I should've taken notes from Marcus.)

Anyway, Marcus didn't go to the same high school as us; he went to a fancy charter school a mile down the road. They technically shared athletics and extra-curricular programs with our school, so he often went to sporting events and dances with us, but I think the distance was starting to get to Melanie.

"It's not just some random girl that he followed, Gabby. He followed Lynsey, from the dance team," she explained.

I stared at her plainly, trying to figure out Lynsey's significance. She was the captain of the dance team and very pretty…but also very shallow. Being pretty was basically her personality.

"You know who Lynsey is, Gabby!"

"Well, yeah, I know who she is, I'm just trying to figure out why you said it like she's a threat to your relationship." I sat up in her beanbag chair and propped my elbows on my knees; Guapo adjusted himself accordingly. It was honestly shocking to see someone who was so confident and bold to the rest of the world turn around and question her worth over a boy. I'd never seen her like this.

"I'm just saying, she's pretty—scratch that—*gorgeous*, and he just followed her on Instagram. He probably wants her instead of me, but he saw me first and now he's stuck with me," Melanie sighed.

"You know who else is *'pretty—scratch that—gorgeous'* that he follows on Insta?" I asked, pointing across the room to her reflection in her vanity. "*You!* And you're way more interesting than her! You're beautiful, smart, funny…good at painting chickens! The list goes on, Mel!" I smiled as I watched her crack up at my chicken joke, but I was very serious. Melanie was an amazing girlfriend and an even better best friend. I refused to let her think otherwise.

"Why are you worried about this now, anyway? You've been dating each other since last year," I pointed out.

"I just get worried that things are going *too well*, sometimes, you know? Like maybe it's too good to be true. It's like…I'm so attached that I'm scared to lose him, especially with senior year winding down. What if we don't last past graduation? There's so many other beautiful women in college," she admitted.

"I know the feeling," I sighed, "well, not exactly. But…I understand you." We fell silent for a moment. I knew breaking her insecurity would be way harder than telling her to "love herself." That was usually easier said than done and not very helpful to tell someone, anyway.

"What's kept you from telling Ryan how you feel all these years, Gabby? I mean, I understand being nervous that he doesn't feel the same, but has he ever made you feel like he'd reject you?" Melanie finally asked.

"I haven't told him because I don't want to lose the only guy I've ever created a bond with. I know there's a chance he feels the same, but it's the chance that he *doesn't* that I'm scared of, you know? What if I tell him, and it messes up the friendship? I thought for sure being friends was a guarantee that we'd always be in each other's lives, but I'm scared I've started to lose him to Indya. I guess I've just felt hopeless, like no matter how tightly I cling to someone, I can't control if I lose them in the end. Like how I lost my dad," I explained.

"Damn, Gabby. I didn't even think about the situation with your dad. I'm sorry," she said, throwing herself back onto her bed. "That's tough," she followed, staring at her ceiling. Another small silence fell between us.

I had lost my dad when I was very young—too young to remember. My mom told me he died in his sleep, and the doctors couldn't figure out the cause of death, so I knew from an early age that sometimes losing others was beyond our control. I just…hated the feeling that losing Ryan to Indya might've been another thing I couldn't control.

"You know what?" Melanie started, raising herself back up. "Losing your dad may have been something you couldn't control, but losing Ryan doesn't have to be. The only thing you *can* control is you…what you do or don't do…and what you do or don't say."

"But what if—"

"If you lose Ryan because you dared to have a crush on him, then FUCK Ryan!" Melanie exclaimed, causing me to clutch my invisible pearls. That was brutal, even for her.

"Melanie!"

"Okay, that was harsh, but seriously, G, I can't think of anything more ridiculous than for Ryan to know you have feelings for him and decide that he doesn't want to be your friend because of it. Ryan is honestly too sweet to be that guy, and deep down you know it. Besides, you don't know if you'll lose Ryan because of his relationship, or because you drift apart after high school, or whatever else, but if you do lose him, don't you want the peace of mind of knowing you left it all on the line? Nothing unsaid?"

Melanie had a very strong point. And she was absolutely right. Deep down, I knew Ryan wouldn't ditch me for having feelings for him, but I was clinging to every possible fear for dear life just in case. "You're right," I admitted.

"I know I'm right!" she chimed. "So are you gonna tell him, now, or what?"

"I—"

Just as I started to answer, I got a text from my mom, and rather than finish my sentence, I grabbed my phone, leaving Melanie in suspense.

I need more fruit for my smoothies! Stop by the store on your way home. Surprise me this time.

"Sorry, Mel, I gotta go. My mom wants me to run an errand," I said, getting up. I grabbed my untouched backpack and hugged her before I left. The truth was, even after her amazing speech, I still wasn't sure if or how I would tell Ryan how I felt.

"This isn't over!" she called out as I left her room.

On my way home, I stopped at a nearby store to get my mom her surprise fruit. This wasn't my first time fetching her groceries on my way home, but I always felt so clueless in the produce section. Was this what being an adult was like? Walking through food aisles, saying "ooo, that looks good," and throwing it in your basket? Because if so, I had it down pat. Adulthood, here I come!

All jokes aside, though, the more I thought about growing up, the more I realized I wouldn't know what I was doing. Like, what the hell was a mortgage? How does one pay taxes? And cooking? Psh. I couldn't even cook Ramen noodles without forgetting about them boiling on the stove.

"The tangerines are really good."

My thoughts were interrupted by a dangerously handsome guy who was smiling down at me—most likely in amusement. He had glowing, chocolate skin, a muscular build, and a beautiful smile.

"I'm sorry?" I said nervously.

"The tangerines are really good. I come here after almost every game to get some," he explained. "You looked sorta lost, so I thought I'd give a suggestion."

I took a second to analyze his attire, only to realize he played basketball for my—*our*—school. Which meant his glow was probably just sweat from his game, but Lord knows this boy was fine, glowing or otherwise.

Why haven't I seen you before? I thought. "Thank you, uh…"

"Daniel," he said, reaching out for a handshake. "We haven't properly met."

"Daniel," I repeated as I shook his hand. There was something about him that scared me; maybe it was how easily he talked to me, even though I was a stranger, or maybe it was that I wasn't used to cute guys talking to me at all—besides Ryan, of course. "Well, um, thanks for the suggestion, Daniel. Hopefully my mom likes them." I smiled shyly as I placed the tangerines in my basket. He smiled back and then made his way down the aisle. I couldn't leave with just one kind of fruit, but I had no idea what paired well with tangerines.

"Strawberries? No… Blueberries? Eh… Raspberries…? I don't even know what those taste like…" I muttered to myself. I looked around to see if anyone was watching me struggle and caught eyes with Daniel again. I gave an awkward lip-smile and quickly turned away. "Fuck it," I sighed, snatching a bag of mixed berries from the shelf. When in doubt, pick them all.

As I made my way to my car, I spotted a piece of paper on my front windshield. *Oh shit!* I thought. It *had* to be a ticket. I…may or may not have double-parked in two spots reserved for motorcycles, *but* I was only going to be in the store for like two seconds, anyway! "Mom's gonna kill me," I said to myself, only to breathe a sigh of relief when I realized my guilt had fooled me. It was a flyer.

JESUS FREAKS PRESENT:

THE HOLY LIT-UATION: A BIBLE STUDY LIKE NO OTHER

GET LIT BY THE LIGHT OF JESUS CHRIST

MARCH 16TH FROM 8-10 P.M.

1112 Church Ave.

"So corny," I laughed, tossing the flyer onto my passenger's seat. I could barely go five sentences without cursing. The last thing I needed was to send someone's saved-and-sanctified grandmother into cardiac arrest with my vocabulary.

CHAPTER 3

"Did I tell you what happened when I left your house yesterday?" I asked, blocking out the sound of Ms. Redlich's lecture as Melanie and I sat in Advanced Health the following day.

"No, what happened?" she whispered, staring intently at the game of tic-tac-ignore-the-teacher we had started on a random sheet of paper.

"Well—"

"Gabby, nice of you to volunteer! Tell me what oxytocin is," Ms. Redlich interrupted.

"It's a hormone produced when we have sex and stuff like that," I replied.

"You're on track, but stop the side conversations." She turned back toward the white board and continued teaching.

Advanced Health was my least favorite class. Melanie and I liked to talk; Ms. Redlich liked to talk, too. How were we supposed to talk without her constantly interrupting our interruptions? I was considering a student-teacher conference so we could work out our talking schedules.

"Ms. Redlich?" someone asked. That voice. I knew that voice. Barely—but I knew it.

"Yes, Daniel?"

My head shot up. It was him. Tucked in the corner seat at the opposite side of the room. How the hell did I go that long without— actually as little as I paid attention in that class, it made sense that I hadn't known he was there. Maybe that's what he meant by "properly met;" he knew I existed long before I knew he did.

"MELANIE!!!" I yelled in a whisper.

"Shhh, I'm about to beat you, I just don't know how yet!" she replied, her eyes never leaving our piece of paper. She had yet to beat me in a game, not since we first started at the beginning of senior year.

"That's him! That's Daniel!"

"Who?" she asked.

"The guy from last night!" I whisper-yelled again.

"What guy from last night?!" she asked a little too loudly, finally looking up.

"LADIES!" Ms. Redlich yelled. I looked over at Daniel, who was now laughing to himself, and quickly buried my face into my hands, hoping I would magically disappear. I guess this was *my* version of a proper introduction. Gabby, the delinquent student.

After class, Melanie pulled me into a restroom on our way to lunch. "You met that guy last night? Like…as in a hook-up?" she asked.

"What! No, he told me which fruit to pick!" I clarified—or so I thought.

"Is that what they're calling it now, Gabby?!" she said, pulling out her phone. "Fruit...to…pick," she said aloud as she typed. I looked at her screen, confused, only to find her on Urban Dictionary.

"Oh my gosh, Melanie, NO. He literally helped me pick out fancy oranges for my mom last night at the grocery store," I explained.

"The one down the street from my house? You know, they never have the potato chips I like. I always have to go all the way across town to get them," she babbled on.

I stared at her in disbelief. "FOCUS, Melanie!"

"You're right. Sorry. Continue," she nodded.

"ANYWAY… He introduced himself and told me to get the tangerines, and that was it. I noticed he was wearing our school basketball uniform, but I had no idea he was in our health class! I was so nervous that I didn't even tell him my name. I got out of there as soon as I could."

"GOOD. You have googly eyes for Ryan, remember? The last thing we need is another guy for you to *not* tell your feelings to. I'm stressed enough with one," she replied, walking to the restroom door and holding it open for me. I was shocked yet again. Was Melanie passing up the opportunity for *"good chisme,"* as she'd call it? I slowly walked to the door in protest.

"*Vamos!* It's Taco Tuesday, girl. The only *'cultural'* food the lunch ladies don't mess up," Melanie declared as she rushed me through the door.

Ryan and Indya had already beat us to our table by the time we made it to the cafeteria. Even though I loved to eat, lunch period had been less than favorable lately. Indya was a Ryan-hog, taking most of his attention every day with her endless gossip about the track team. He was the type to give you his undivided attention when you spoke, which was one of the many things that made me fall for him. Clearly Indya enjoyed that about him, too. I glanced his way occasionally as Melanie and I talked, but he was always focused on his *precious* motor-mouth girlfriend.

"I'm going to the bathroom," I told Melanie. I needed a quick break from the Indya and Ryan show.

"Damn, girl, again? What, now!?" She started to get up with me.

"NOT one of those bathroom visits, Mel," I clarified. "Save my seat, please."

I really didn't even have to use the bathroom. I just needed an excuse to get away. As I ventured farther from the cafeteria, I contemplated Melanie's question about telling Ryan how I felt.

"Hey, Gabby, wait up!" Ryan jogged toward me in the hallway. "You texted me yesterday saying you grabbed a paper for me in Sociology?" he asked.

"OH! Yes," I remembered, "it's actually in my locker. I can go grab it real quick."

"I'll go with you," he smiled, joining me at my side. Walking down the empty hallway with him took me back to my first day at the school.

"I remember taking you on a tour down this hall freshman year," Ryan mentioned, as if he'd read my mind.

"That's still one of my favorite memories of us." I looked up at him and met his gaze.

"Oh yeah? That's one of mine, too." He put his arm around my shoulder the way he had on my first day. He smelled so good—then and now. "I had to keep my arm around you so the basketball team wouldn't harass you. They were like a bunch of vultures," he chuckled.

"I'm glad it was you who gave me the tour. I don't know if we'd be friends if you hadn't." We approached my locker and I began turning the dial on my combination lock.

"Really? What makes you say that?" He leaned his left shoulder against the locker next to mine and put his hands in his jacket pockets.

"Well, you got a lot of attention once it got around that you were promoted to varsity. Freshman guys wanted to be cool with you, freshman girls were all over you, and then there were the upperclassmen who started to take you under their wings." I shuffled through my bag, looking for his paper. "If it weren't for you showing me around, I don't think you would've ever noticed me." Finally, I found the paper, slightly wrinkled from being shoved in my bag, and handed it to him.

He smiled, seemingly amused at the sight of the crumpled paper. "I would've noticed you." He returned his focus to me. "You're smart. A lot of people think you don't care about school, but I've noticed how intelligent you are. You just get bored easily, like I do."

I was shocked at his observation. "You're giving me way too much credit." I shook my head and closed my locker door, leaning against it with my right shoulder so that I faced him.

"Am I? Because I haven't met too many people who watch *Jeopardy!* for fun. And from all the times we've done homework together, I've seen that the stuff is like second nature to you, always." He crossed his arms and gave me his signature *"you know I'm right"* smirk.

"Okay, fine. You might have a point. I don't know what it is about school, but, I just zone out. The work is easy, I just hate it— the structure, I mean." I shrugged.

"You just need an environment that teaches the way you learn best. Sometimes it's in a traditional classroom, sometimes it's not," he suggested.

"Maybe," I sighed. He reached forward and moved a tress of hair from my face so that it was no longer separated from the rest. It was little, sweet things like that that made me so fond of Ryan—that made me wonder if any ounce of him had feelings for me, too.

"You did something new with your hair. What do you call this? A twister? A twisty?" he asked genuinely. "It looks really good on you."

I laughed at his description. "Thank you! It's called a *twist-out,* but yeah, I tried something new this time. I'm surprised you noticed," I admitted.

"Of course I noticed." He furrowed his brow. "Why wouldn't I?"

I tilted my head to the side and gave him a look that told him he knew *exactly* what I meant. Indya made it hard to get any time in with Ryan—let alone a conversation at lunch.

He laughed and playfully rolled his eyes. "Yeah, okay. Indya can be…a little clingy. But I haven't forgotten my promise." He stood up straight. "I haven't replaced you," he said warmly.

The memory echoed in my head.

"Ryan, promise me you'll never replace me!"

"I promise."

I'd been so naïve to ask for such a hard commitment. I'd even used that promise as my excuse to hold out on telling him how I felt. It was the only feeling of hope I could hold onto at the time, but I couldn't have him forever. Hell, I didn't even *have* him to begin with.

In truth, I was surprised that he even remembered that conversation. I'd made Ryan promise not to replace me during spring break of our junior year. Our men's basketball team had just played the last game of the season, and a large group of students had gone out to a drive-in movie afterward to kick-start the break.

Ryan and I got out of his car and made our way over to the concession area. The smell of his cologne blew gently in the breeze. To me, it smelled like a warm hug—the kind of hug you got from someone much taller, much stronger than you—the kind that made you feel safe enough to fall asleep—the kind you didn't want to let go of—the kind you got from Ryan. Before the drive-in, he had gone home to shower and then he'd picked me up from my house. Melanie and Marcus had started dating at this point, so she'd caught a ride with him, though we'd meet up with them later. I remember this night so vividly because it was probably the closest Ryan and I had ever gotten, both physically and as friends.

The drive-in was so packed because of the excitement of both spring break and the release of yet another film in a popular, fast-driving movie franchise. Teens were everywhere, and traffic was congested as people looked for spaces to park.

"Gabby, watch out!" Ryan said, pulling me out of the way by my waist as a guy blasted past us to catch a football. I stumbled back against his chest and steadied myself in his arms.

"Are you okay?" he asked into my ear, his hands still on my waist as I turned to face him.

"Yeah, I'm good," I confirmed. He grabbed my hand and then took the lead as we pushed our way through the crowd and avoided cars on our way to the concessions area. I caught glimpses of girls who would see Ryan first and light up, then see me attached to his hand and look at me in disappointment. I'm sure to them we looked like a couple, and even though I knew we were just friends, I reveled in the appearance that we were more than that. I felt special, in a way. That is, until a group of girls spotted Ryan in the concession line.

"Oh my gosh, Ryan, you did so good tonight!" Thirsty Number One beamed. She was a strawberry blonde cheerleader from our school, something I only knew because she was still wearing her cheer uniform at the drive-in like she needed to tell the world *"Look! I'm a cheerleader!"*

"Totally. You guys are gonna make it to finals next year, for sure!" Thirsty Number Two added. She had a caramel complexion and her hair was in a high bun with a ribbon in it. The ribbon made me guess that she was also a cheerleader, but she, at least, had enough dignity to wear normal clothes outside of school grounds.

"Are you here by yourself?" Thirsty Number Three asked as she twirled her hair around her finger. I did the biggest eye roll and turned to look at the menu. I already knew what I wanted, but I needed something interesting to look at.

"No, I'm not. I'm here with some friends." I felt Ryan throw his arm around my shoulder and then pull me closer to his side. "Gabby and I are just grabbing some snacks, first." I was so close to him that

I had to wrap my arm around his waist or else my shoulder would be awkwardly smashed against his torso.

"Aw that's nice!" Thirsty Number One cooed, though she didn't bother looking at me for more than a second.

"I guess we'll see you later, then," Thirsty Number Three said. She had finally stopped twirling her hair. Maybe the look I was giving her killed the mood. Tragic.

"Enjoy your spring break!" Thirsty Number Two waved. She was the only one who seemed to be speaking to both Ryan and me this time.

"You too." Ryan waved back as they walked away.

"It never fails that when I'm with you we get approached by your fan club. It's like I don't even exist. We'll literally be talking, and they'll still interrupt to get your attention like I'm not even there." I shook my head in amusement. It happened so often that I couldn't even get mad anymore.

Ryan chuckled and nodded. "I've noticed that, too. They never really have anything to say, either. It's always small talk and hair twirling."

"Yeah, well, it's only a matter of time before you fall for one of those hair twirlers. Just watch," I teased.

"That'd be your worst, nightmare, huh? Being replaced by a hair twirler?" He looked down at me in amusement. His arm was still around my shoulder, and my arm was still around his waist. I was so comfortable that I hadn't realized until then.

"Yeah, but it'd be their dream come true," I said seriously, returning his gaze. For a moment, there was a silence between us. Still wrapped in one another's arms, it was the perfect position for a kiss—the perfect moment. I caught his eyes move briefly from mine to my lips and then back to my eyes again, and then—

"Next in line?"

We snapped our heads toward the concessions counter, coming back to reality and seeing it was our turn to order. For the rest of the night, we didn't speak about that moment, or get close to reliving it again. I would occasionally feel his arm brush against mine as we sat in the bed of Marcus' truck, and I would sometimes test him and rest my hand near his, but neither of us made it past our passive aggression.

The thought of him one day replacing me lingered throughout the night. That was indeed my worst nightmare. I didn't want to lose him, especially not after the night we'd had and the tease of what could've been. When the night was over, he took me home, walked me to my front door, and hugged me. It was that warm, safe hug I came to love so much. I still didn't have the courage to talk about what had happened earlier that night, and apparently neither did he. As he walked back to his car, though, I thought about the hair twirlers and I called out to him as he reached for his driver's side door.

"Ryan, promise me you'll never replace me!"

He didn't hesitate. "I promise." He grinned, getting back into his car.

Standing face-to-face with Ryan against those lockers gave me the same nostalgia from the drive-in, but of course, moments like those were always short lived with him.

"You okay?" He waved his hand in front of my face. "You look like you're in deep thought."

That snapped me out of it. "Yeah! Sorry, I just—sorry," I laughed, deciding not to explain my trip down memory lane.

"Please, don't do that," he protested.

"Do what?"

"Act like there's nothing wrong when there is. Indya does that all the time and then it turns into a much bigger issue than it has to be."

"Wow, you mean you're not the perfect couple?" I asked sarcastically.

"I'm serious, G," he insisted. "Are you alright?" He stepped closer, and my heart began to race.

"Yeah," I breathed. "I was just thinking about the night I made you promise not to replace me," I confessed, avoiding eye contact.

"Why the sad face, then? Was that not a good night?" he asked, leaning his head to the side in an attempt to re-capture my gaze.

"No, it was! It was a great night, actually." I looked back at Ryan to find a satisfied smirk on his lips.

"Good. Aside from your first day here, that's my favorite memory of us," he said, pulling his phone out of his pocket as he spoke.

"Really? Why?" I felt a spark of hope rise in my chest. I wouldn't have to confess how I felt if he did it first.

But the moment was broken when Ryan looked up from his phone. "Indya's wondering what's taking me so long. We should get back to the cafeteria so you can finish eating," Ryan suggested. "I'll tell you after school, though!"

"Fine," I sighed. Of course Indya had interrupted at the worst possible moment. Sometimes it felt like my life was a fiction novel being written solely for someone else's entertainment. Why couldn't they write Ryan with feelings for me? Or me with more courage? Or, better yet, un-write Indya's existence?

As we made our way back to our lunch table, I noticed someone sitting in my seat. *I thought I told that girl to save it, not donate it*, I thought. Melanie's face lit up when she spotted me. Before I could try to figure out why, the seat-stealer turned around—it was Daniel.

"Hey, G, Daniel was just telling me about our class assignment for Advanced Health," she explained.

"Class assignment?" I asked.

"That's what I said! You know, we should probably start paying attention in that class," Melanie laughed.

Daniel cracked up at Melanie's comment, but never took his eyes off me.

"What's up, bro?" Ryan dapped Daniel up before taking his seat next to Indya.

"Not much, man," Daniel said. "You okay? You look uneasy," Daniel asked, returning his attention to me.

"I just feel bad that I didn't know you were in my class until today," I admitted nervously.

"Wait, y'all have a class together?" Ryan queried.

"Yeah, but she didn't even know it until today," Daniel teased, flashing his beautiful, perfectly straight teeth at me once again. There was no doubt he'd worn braces with a smile that pristine.

"I mean, you *do* sit all the way in Timbuktu—you're at the farthest seat away from me and Melanie," I defended. Melanie raised an eyebrow at me from behind Daniel, and I suddenly realized how hard I was cheesing.

"Even if I sat closer, it probably wouldn't change anything. You're always passing papers back and forth instead of paying attention," Daniel challenged playfully. In my periphery, I could see Ryan's head bounce back and forth between Daniel and I as we bantered with one another.

"You must not be paying attention either if you know what Melanie and I are up to." I moved my verbal chess piece and awaited his rebuttal.

"True," Daniel nodded, "but which one of us knew about the homework assignment?" he flirted. Checkmate.

Everyone looked at me for my response. I had nothing. I hadn't had banter that well-matched with anyone but Ryan up until then.

"*Touché.*" I squinted my eyes at him in defeat. "A worthy opponent, for now." I extended my arm for a handshake. "Gabrielle Perkins," I introduced.

"Nice to properly meet you, Gabrielle Perkins." Daniel shook my hand sweetly, getting up from my seat. We watched awkwardly as he walked to his own table.

"Ooo, I see you, Gabby!" Indya cheered.

"See what?" I asked as I sat down.

"Girl, don't try to act like you weren't flirting with him just now. We all saw it! Right, Ryan?"

"Yeah, that was uh…something," he answered, looking at me in confusion.

"Psh. We just met. That's crazy," I refuted.

"That's exactly what I was thinking," Melanie interjected, tilting her head as she looked at me. "Very crazy."

I took a bite from one of my gone-cold tacos and forced myself to chew. It was the most eventful lunch period I'd had in a while. First, a moment alone with Ryan, and then joking around with Daniel? Taco Tuesday was now my favorite, too—but unlike Melanie, it wasn't because of the tacos.

CHAPTER 4

I managed to escape Melanie's burning curiosity after lunch, but it was only a matter of time until it caught up with me again. First, I left her hanging about if I would finally tell Ryan how I felt, and now, I'm sure she was wondering what was going on between me and Daniel.

There was nothing between us, though. We had literally just met the night before, and she knew that. Indya's comment didn't help at all, either. I wasn't *feeling him*. I was just returning his energy. I can't help it if *he* was the one flirting. Right?

"Gabby!" Melanie jogged up to me in the hall. "What the hell was that?" she asked as we walked into Sociology.

"What the hell was what?" I questioned. It had only been two class periods since lunch, but I was playing stupid. I knew exactly what she was referring to.

"You flirting with Daniel at lunch. And why were you and Ryan gone so long?"

We got to our seats at the back of class and sat down. Ryan wasn't there yet, which wasn't like him. He usually beat us there.

"I was *not* flirting!" I argued.

"Yeah, okay, Miss *Colgate*, they could probably see that big ass smile you had on your face from across the cafeteria!"

We immediately cracked up at her remark. "Okay, I *was* smiling kinda hard, wasn't I?" I laughed.

"Kinda?!" she teased.

"Well, *anyway*…I was hanging out in the hall with Ryan, that's why I took so long to come back."

Melanie gasped dramatically and leaned closer to me. "Did you do it?" she whispered.

"Well…" I trailed.

"UGHHH. Well then, what took you so long, Gabby?"

Before I could respond, Ryan took his seat next to me, and I could immediately tell his energy was different than it was at lunch. "Hey," I greeted, trying to figure out his mood.

"Hey," he replied plainly, pulling paper from his backpack.

"You okay?" I asked.

"Yeah." He still hadn't looked at me, and I wasn't going to let it slide.

I turned sideways in my seat and stared at him until he returned my gaze. *"Please don't do that,"* I mocked.

He nodded to himself in amusement. Of course I was using his words against him. If I had to be open, so did he. "What's up with you and Daniel?" he finally asked.

Melanie swung her legs around in her seat to face us. "THAT'S WHAT I WAS ASKING!" she yelled.

I shook my head in annoyance. "Why does everyone think something is going on between us?! I literally just met him last night."

"Last night?! As in a hook-up?" Ryan seemed way more concerned than I'd anticipated.

"That's the same thing I said!" Melanie exclaimed from the other side of me.

"NOT like that. I ran into him at the grocery store after I left Mel's house. I literally had no idea he existed until then, and he was teasing me for it. That's all," I asserted, looking back and forth between Melanie and Ryan.

"Hmph," Ryan said to himself, "good to know."

"What was that?" I asked.

"What was what?" he repeated.

"Hmph," I mimicked. "Why'd you do that?"

"I just never would've expected you to start talking to Daniel, that's all," Ryan laughed.

"Is that a bad thing?" I questioned.

"Alright, class! Let's get started," Mr. Nicholson sang as he entered the room. If someone interrupted us one more time that day, I was going to scream.

"After school," Ryan mouthed.

I pouted in my seat as Mr. Nicholson began his lecture. Luckily for him, I liked his class. But still, I thought a little bit about what Ryan had said during lunch about how sometimes we need environments that teach us in the ways we learn best. Sitting still for fifty minutes with minimal interaction between myself and my teachers was just not my style. It was too easy for my mind to wander. What would classes be like if teachers held discussions rather than lectures? What if they let us ask questions back and forth instead of shoving information at us and expecting us to remember it all?

"How many of you have met someone new, recently?" Mr. Nicholson asked.

Melanie and Ryan looked at me without hesitation. I awkwardly raised my hand along with a few others.

"Great! One of the first things we notice when we meet new people are their patterns. What makes them different from us? What makes them similar? How do they talk? How do they dress? Et cetera. In Sociology, our goal is to evaluate these patterns. We'll ask questions like, what makes a group of people function the way they do? What are the environmental and social influences to their behavior? How do their behaviors affect the people around them? And so forth. My goal is for you all to become experts at societal evaluation as the semester progresses…" Mr. Nicholson elaborated.

So, basically, we were going to overanalyze the behavior of a new group of people? I'd overanalyzed everything about me and Ryan for long enough to know I had this Sociology thing in the bag. I just had to figure out who that new group of people was going to be. I wasn't exactly in the business of seeking out new people to be around. My circle was so tight-knit, it was basically a dot.

♥ ♥ ♥

When Ryan wasn't gone for basketball, we had an after-school routine of walking out together before going our separate ways. Ryan would go into the gym for basketball practice, and Melanie and I would continue outside to the parking lot. (The track was too far from the gym for Indya to tag along, but we all know I wasn't complaining.) That day, Melanie lingered at a distance so Ryan and I could finish our conversation from lunch.

"Tell me what he says," she whispered before hanging back.

"Duh," I whispered back.

"You're doing more walking than talking, Ryan, spit it out!" I whined once we were alone. Time was of the essence.

"Okay, okay!" He chuckled, stopping in front of the gym.

"Which one do you want first? The favorite memory or the Daniel thing?" he asked.

"The—"

"Favorite memory," Melanie coughed from a not-so-far distance. We slowly turned our heads and looked at her. She was pretending to scroll on her phone, peaking up at us.

"Really, Mel?"

"Fine!" she whined, scooting one foot farther away.

We looked at her still.

"Damn! How much space do y'all need?!" she argued, walking a few more feet away.

I rolled my eyes and Ryan shook his head. "Let's start with the favorite memory," I said.

"Right," he agreed, fidgeting with the bag strap on his shoulder, "well, that was the closest I've felt to anyone in a while. Basketball season is always a very stressful time for me, and that night I'd never felt more relaxed. I don't think I would've felt that way without you around," he admitted. He had a flustered look on his face—the kind guys get when they're not used to being vulnerable. It was both awkward and sweet.

"I never knew that, Ryan! Thank you for telling me," I gushed. My cheeks were getting hot, and my face was starting to hurt from fighting back the so-called Colgate smile I'd displayed with Daniel earlier that day.

"I guess I would've told you before, but I just never knew how. And then I started dating Indya, and, yeah…"

"Right…" I followed. I guess I couldn't blame him. It's hard discerning what's okay and what's not when you have a girlfriend and a girl best friend. It was admirable that he cared enough about his relationship to err on the side of caution.

"But back to Daniel!" Ryan cleared his throat. "I was just surprised to see you two talking. Daniel is—" He glanced up and stopped speaking.

"Daniel is what?" I asked.

"He's coming this way, and I'm gonna be late," Ryan explained, looking back at me. "I'll tell you another time," he threw out, pulling me into a hug.

"Promise?" I sighed as we released one another.

"I promise," he confirmed as he shuffled to the gym door. I turned around in search of Melanie, only to crash right into the chest of someone else.

"Whoa, if this is payback for earlier, I didn't mean it!" Daniel laughed, grabbing my arms to keep me from falling backward.

"I'm so sorry! I didn't see you—" I cut myself off, realizing the trap I had set for myself.

"No surprise there," he smirked. I laughed at the role of invisibility I'd unintentionally given to Daniel.

"I just meant I didn't mean to run into you, that's all," I tried pathetically.

"That's okay. I was looking for you anyway, so it worked out," he said, handing me two sheets of paper. "It's the homework assignment for Advanced Health. I went back and grabbed a couple extra sheets for you and Melanie."

"Oh wow, Daniel, thank you! That's so nice of you. Ms. Redlich usually passes these out, I'm not sure why she switched it up, this time." I spun my bag in front of me and slipped the papers inside.

"She was probably banking on the fact that you weren't listening." Daniel winked.

"Yeah, she might have it out for us, now, huh?" I chuckled. "Thanks again."

"Don't mention it." He shrugged. We looked at each other awkwardly for a moment, not saying anything, until he spoke again. "Well, I, uh…I gotta get to practice, so I'll…see you tomorrow?" We slowly walked around each other until we'd switched places.

"Yeah, I'll see you tomorrow," I confirmed.

"Really? *The* Gabrielle Perkins is actually going to see me tomorrow?" He put his hands over his heart sarcastically. "How'd I get so lucky?"

I rolled my eyes playfully and waved him off. "Bye, Daniel!"

"Bye," he grinned, backpedaling to the gym door. He had such a suave and charismatic nature, never taking his eyes off me until the moment he got to the door. I was so flattered by his overt flirtation that I'd nearly forgotten that Melanie was still in the distance, watching.

Sure enough, though, as soon as I turned around, I spotted her a few feet from me, and it was abundantly clear that she'd seen the entire interaction between Daniel and me. She had a suspicious smirk on her face—she clearly thought there was more to the situation than what met her eye.

"It's not what it looks like!" I threw my head back as she walked toward me with judgement in her eyes.

"We'll see about that, *'Gabrielle Perkins',*" she teased, mimicking Daniel's voice. "Now, start from the beginning…"

CHAPTER 5

Over the next couple weeks, I was itching to finish my conversation with Ryan, but between basketball, class, and homework, it never felt like the right time. If I'd learned anything about Ryan, it was that he wasn't one to forget a promise, and he'd promised we'd finish talking about it, so I was taking him for his word.

But before I knew it, it was February, and with playoffs around the corner and college commitments becoming more important for star athletes like Ryan, Daniel was the last thing I wanted to bother him about. The only issue was, the less I tried to think about Daniel, the more he seemed to show up.

I would see him between nearly every class, now, and he'd smile at me every time. There was something about that smile that made me feel…chosen—like it was a smile he'd reserved for me and me only. It was starting to become more and more apparent to me how attracted I was to him, and not just in a superficial way. I mean, yes, he was handsome, I've made that pretty clear, but there's a difference between seeing a handsome face, and feeling a magnetic pull to that face. There was more to him than just his looks drawing me in, and I couldn't put my finger on it. At first, I barely knew him, and that was okay, but soon enough, I *wanted* to know him.

Before you say anything, yes. I know this entire story so far has been me going on about my feelings for Ryan and how I hated seeing him with Indya and so on and so forth, but hear me out—what if I just needed to drop the Ryan thing and move on? What if Daniel was that push I needed to move forward? That way, I didn't have to confess my feelings for Ryan; he could be happy with Indya, and I could be happy with Daniel. Even though I knew shifting my focus to Daniel wouldn't get rid of my feelings for Ryan, I couldn't help myself. Each interaction with Daniel was like a seed of interest planted in my mind, and I was curious about what would bloom if I decided to water it.

♥ ♥ ♥

"Did you remember to do the homework assignment?" Melanie asked as she pulled hers from a folder in her backpack. Advanced Health was wrapping up for the day, and Ms. Redlich was finally taking in the assignment from a couple weeks before.

"As a matter of fact I did!" I smiled, holding it in front of me with pride.

"Wow, look at us being responsible in her class for once," Melanie sniffled, wiping away an invisible tear.

"Are you guys ready to hand in your work?" Daniel cut in, causing Melanie and I to jump in our seats.

"Uh, yeah." I looked up at him standing in the aisle, already holding a few papers, "how long were you standing there?" I asked, handing him our homework.

"Long enough," he smirked as he continued his way up the aisle, collecting papers along his way. I could smell the faintest hint of his cologne as he passed. It was too faint to describe, but I'd caught enough to want more than just a sample.

The bell rang, dismissing us for lunch, and I watched as he handed our homework to Ms. Redlich as I made my way to the door.

"Is it me, or is Ms. Redlich only nice to Daniel?" I asked.

"She's nice to everyone but us, Gabby," she said matter-of-factly.

"Yeah, but she's EXTRA nice to—"

"OW!" Melanie exclaimed as I crashed into her suddenly-stopped body in the classroom doorway.

"My bad, I didn't know you stopped!"

"Yeah, well, there's hallway traffic. I didn't want to get trampled!" she exclaimed. We stepped aside by some lockers so Melanie could fix the shoe I accidentally took off when I ran into her.

"It's not even Taco Tuesday! How'd they get out here so fast?!" Melanie complained as she got herself together.

One of the downsides to attending a large Texas public school was the enormous crowd of kids brushing past one another in the hallway, especially when it was time for lunch. We were never really in a rush to get to the cafeteria (except Melanie on Tuesdays), but the less time we spent being bumped into, stepped on, and pushed, the better.

"Hey, Gabby!" I heard someone call out over the noise of the crowded hallway. I looked to my left and saw Daniel, who was just leaving our classroom. "I was wondering what you and Melanie were doing this Friday," he continued as he approached us. "A couple of my friends are throwing a party at my place, and I was hoping you could make it?" he asked. I was so caught up in how fine Daniel was that I almost forgot Melanie was next to me. That is, until she nearly broke my damn ear drum.

"A PARTY?!" Melanie squealed as she popped up from tying her shoe.

"I know it's loud, Melanie, but we are RIGHT HERE," I yelled back, covering my ear.

"My bad," she apologized. "You know I love a good party, though, girl," she explained.

"Really? I couldn't tell," I said sarcastically.

"I'll give you the details during lunch," Daniel chuckled as we drifted toward the cafeteria.

By the time we made it to our lunch table, Ryan and Indya still weren't there, so I invited Daniel over to fill us in on his party. He sat across from me, where Ryan usually sat, which wasn't awkward at all until Ryan and Indya finally showed up.

"Uh, hey," Ryan said, staring at Daniel.

"What's up, man?" Daniel greeted, getting up. "I just finished giving Mel and Gab the details about our party on Friday," he explained.

Our? Melanie and I looked at each other. Ryan was involved but hadn't told us about it first? I mean, I know Melanie didn't talk to Ryan as much as I did, but the least he could've done was fill *me* in. I bet Indya knew, though.

"Oh, thanks, man! Less work for me," Ryan smiled, dapping Daniel up before he walked away.

"You knew about this party?" I asked Ryan when Daniel was gone.

"Yeah, it's a basketball thing. We won our tournament last Friday, so the team decided to throw a party this weekend to celebrate since it's our bye week," he explained.

"Why didn't you tell me about it during Sociology yesterday? Or literally any day before that?" It was Wednesday, so he'd had five days since the tournament to share the details with me or Melanie.

"It wasn't on my mind, honestly. You know I wouldn't leave you out, though, right?"

I looked at Indya, then back at him. "Actually, no, I wasn't sure about that, but thanks for the affirmation."

Ryan stared at me with a *what's your problem?* face and I ignored it with an *I'm really enjoying this mystery meat* face. He turned to Indya, whispered something in her ear, and then got up.

"Gab, can we talk?" he asked.

I got up and followed him into the hall, lingering several feet behind him.

"What was that about?" He spun around and faced me once we were out of anyone's field of view.

"I don't know, Ryan, I just wish I would've heard about this party from my *best friend* and not someone else, especially since it's a party *you* helped plan." I crossed my arms in frustration.

"Okay, but you know I'd never leave you out, right? I still would've told you," he asserted.

"When? The day of? The party is in *two* days, Ryan. You KNOW my mom hates last-minute plans," I argued.

"You're not being fair right now, Gab." Ryan shook his head, glancing toward the cafeteria behind me.

"How am I not being fair, Ryan?"

"Because you're being selfish! Not once have you asked me why I haven't told you. If you did, I would've been able to explain myself. You still found out about the party, right? And who's to say I wasn't going to tell you today at lunch or in Sociology? I've been a little more busy than usual, lately, and I'm balancing everything the best I can. And honestly, Gabby, you should be a lot more busy, too!"

I brought my hand to my chest. "*Me?* What's that supposed to mean?"

"Yes, you! Did it ever cross your mind that *we* have college in the fall? Or that *we* have scholarships to apply for? Or that *we* have work to do so that we can graduate?" I looked away from him. He made a good point, but he was ignoring *my* point.

"I'm sorry, okay, Ryan. You're busy. I didn't ask because that's been abundantly clear, lately. I just don't want this to become a habit—you not telling me things, or me finding out from someone else. Over the last couple weeks, it feels like every time I want to hang out or talk it's *'not a good time.'* So finding out you had enough time to plan a party kind of hurts," I explained.

Ryan looked as if a wave of understanding washed over him. "I see," he began, "I'm sorry. I get where you're coming from, now. I guess I've been a little selfish, too, then…" He paused, looking down at me sympathetically. I averted my eyes from his gaze. This was not a moment he could charm his way out of with those gorgeous, dark brown eyes or his ridiculously pretty eyelashes.

"But, truly, Gabby," he resumed, "I do care about you and I would never intentionally leave you out."

I nodded once in acceptance, still a little too prideful to accept his apology verbally.

"You know what's funny?" he chuckled a little.

"No, but I'm sure you'll tell me," I said, confused at the sudden change in emotion.

"I literally just had a similar conversation with Indya before we got to the cafeteria. I haven't been spending much time with her, either, and she thought I was losing feelings for her," he elaborated.

"You haven't?" I was shocked. I thought for sure he'd been with Indya when he wasn't with me.

"No, and I'm the common denominator in these conversations, so clearly I need to fix something," he commented.

"Glad you figured it out," I smirked. "I could've been less passive aggressive, though, so I'm sorry."

"I'm sorry, too," he smirked back, holding his arms out for a hug. I playfully rolled my eyes and obliged.

"You said that already," I teased as I wrapped my arms around his torso. A wave of nostalgia washed over me as I took in the familiar scent of his cologne. It was the warm hug smell I'd always loved, but almost as quickly as I began to enjoy it, the reality of what could have been versus what was ripped me from his chest.

"What's wrong?" he asked.

You belong to someone else, I thought.

"Nothing," I lied, "let's go eat."

CHAPTER 6

You know, for a girl who didn't care much about school, you would think I'd been to quite a few house parties, but I hadn't. This wasn't the first I'd been invited to, but it was the first I'd decided to go to.

My mom was surprisingly chill about my attendance at Daniel's party. I was expecting her to go overboard and demand to talk to his parents, look up his criminal record, find his social media pages, the whole nine yards. But it was simple.

"Don't come back with anything you ain't leave this house with," she said. I stood in her bedroom doorway in shock, waiting for the hassle. That was it? No curfew? No excessive questions? In typical Black mom fashion, she looked at me like: *get out my face before I change my mind,* and I walked away like: *you don't have to tell me twice.* Black telepathy; it's a beautiful thing, really.

Come Friday night, I didn't even take the risk of asking her if it was still okay for me to go. As far as I was concerned, if she'd said yes once, that was a yes for eternity.

"Um, it's still winter, you know, Mel!" I said as she got into my car wearing ripped jeans and a crop top. Granted, we lived in Texas, so we rarely experienced a real winter, but anything lower than sixty degrees Fahrenheit was cold to us.

"We're going to be inside the whole time! Chill, G," she smiled.

At that, I began to question my own outfit as I drove to Daniel's house. I wasn't exactly dressed to impress; I had on leggings and an oversized sweater hanging off of one shoulder. Melanie, on the other hand, looked amazing. She was blessed with what I call the steal-your-man package: an *hourglass*, and *class*. Now, ask yourself, what do those two words have in common? Don't make me spell it out.

As for me? You know how they say, *"shake what your mama gave ya?"* Well, my mama was a liiittle stingy. I mean, I had a little something, don't get me wrong, but this was the era of Instagram models. All I ever saw was praise for hourglass figures and voluptuous bodies. Part of me wished I was receiving that praise, too. Skinny women were still sought after, but in my mind, if you were to ask a guy if he wanted a curvy body or mine, he'd pass me up in a heartbeat.

"Will Marcus be there?" I asked. I had a feeling Melanie was dressed that way to keep his attention. There was a strong chance Lynsey would be there, and, well, you remember how she reacted about Marcus following Lynsey.

"Is it that obvious?" she whined.

"What? I'm just asking!" I exclaimed.

"No, you can tell I'm trying to impress him. That's why you asked," she said.

"Well…yeah. I just feel like you shouldn't have to try this hard to impress your own boyfriend. He chose you for a reason, and you weren't even trying when he met you!"

"It's just—if Lynsey is there I want to make sure I'm the only one he wants to look at," she sighed.

I wanted to tell her again how beautiful she was and how she didn't need to compete for his attention, and maybe I should've, but it's hard for someone to hear you when their insecurities are louder than you are. Plus, I understood her. I had gone through the same thing when Ryan and Indya started dating. I would put more effort into my outfits, wear elaborate hairstyles, and walk past him in the hallways, hoping he'd see me and think *"wow, Gabby looks good today."* So, trust me, I resonated with her feeling like she had to compete—but the difference between her and I was that I was competing for a guy I *couldn't* have, and she was competing for a guy she *did* have.

I pulled up to the address in the text Ryan had sent me, and quickly double-checked to make sure I hadn't gotten the street name wrong. The house before us was far from anything we'd expected. In fact, to call it a house would be an understatement. With its elaborate architecture and long, elegant walkway, it was practically a mansion. I drove past car after car parked along the arced driveway pavement, finally finding a spot that was closer to the front door.

"Dannnnggg I didn't know Daniel was living like *THIS*," Melanie marveled as we approached his front door.

"Girl, I didn't even know this neighborhood was zoned for our school!" I added. We could feel the music pulsate through the house from outside.

Simultaneously, I pulled up my hand in a fist to knock, and Melanie reached out her hand to grab the doorknob. She looked at me in disappointment and sighed, "Have my family parties taught you nothing, *mija?* When you show up to a loud party, don't knock. Just walk in." She pushed the door open like she was letting me into her own home.

"*Touché.*" I nodded as I introduced myself to the interior of Daniel's home.

Walking into that house was like entering the set of an unrealistic movie about a suburban high school kid at a ridiculous house party that could pass as a college rager. We walked past every party trope possible: the beer pong jocks in the kitchen, the oblivious couple making out in the corner (there were plenty of those), and even a random dance circle in the middle of the living room with people battling it out to choreography they *had* to have practiced beforehand. In the midst of all of it, though, I still hadn't found Ryan or Daniel, and Melanie still hadn't spotted Marcus.

"Maybe they're upstairs?" I wondered loudly. At this point we had spent nearly ten minutes wandering around and pushing ourselves through throngs of hormonal teenagers.

"How do we even get upstairs? There's so many people blocking the way!" Melanie asked in my ear.

"Gabby! You made it," someone said suddenly, approaching us from behind. I spun around and made eye contact with Daniel as he emerged from behind the last few people in his way. This was one moment where it was impossible not to notice him. He cleaned up very nicely, if I did say so myself. His polo t-shirt was a pristine white that shone in spite of the dim lighting around us, but even that couldn't out-do the gleam of his smile.

"Is the entire school here, dude?" Melanie asked.

"Seems like it, huh?" he confirmed.

"How did you even find us? We've been walking around forever and haven't spotted you or Ryan once!" I asked.

"Well, we know you don't have a track record of being observant, so…" he joked.

"Fair enough." I rolled my eyes playfully. Clearly, he wasn't going to let the *"I didn't see you"* thing go.

"No, but seriously, Ryan and I were kicking it in the loft upstairs, so I was able to spot you guys from up there and come get you. That is, if you wanna come chill with us?"

"Absolutely, there's no way I'm staying down here in this sea of hormones," I laughed, looking at Melanie, who was busy scanning the room for you know who. "Mel," I called, waving my hand in front of her face.

"Hmm? Sorry, what?" she semi-yelled over the music.

"Do you want to go to the loft with Daniel and Ryan?" I repeated.

"Uh, you go ahead, I'm gonna go look for—"

"Marcus, I know. Call me when you find him," I interrupted.

Daniel took my hand and led me through the crowd, and my heart fluttered with nervousness. I knew it was only so he wouldn't lose me, but holding his hand made me feel special—protected even—the same way I felt when Ryan led me through the drive-in the year before.

"Look who I found," Daniel announced as we approached Ryan and Indya, who were sitting on a couch laughing at something when we arrived. Or should I say, *Ryan* was sitting on the couch. Indya was sitting on his lap.

"Hey! You get lost on the way here?" Ryan teased, getting up to hug me.

"Yeah, actually. Getting to the house was easy; getting to you was a different story. It's like High School Musical on crack downstairs," I explained.

"I should've warned you ahead of time. That's my fault," Daniel said. "Is it okay if I get your number so that we can avoid the lack of communication from now on?" he asked sweetly as he grabbed my hand. My heart was beating in a frenzy again at his touch. I was so caught off guard that I couldn't even speak. I could feel eyes watching us and the room began to shrink.

Say something, I thought. Instead, I nodded like a little kid and fumbled to get my phone from my back pocket. *Stop shaking, hand, you're embarrassing me*, I commanded myself.

Ryan turned to Indya in amusement, the both of them seemingly impressed. "That was smooth, bro," Ryan laughed, "I didn't know how you were gonna do it, but that was good. I can't even lie."

"Wait—so, you planned on getting my number anyway?" I asked Daniel as we traded phones.

"This guy wouldn't stop begging me for your number, but I told him to ask you himself," Ryan explained.

Daniel rolled his eyes. "I wouldn't say I was *begging*, but yeah, I did ask a few times. Ryan was acting like I wanted his social security number or some shit," he laughed.

A few times? I wasn't used to the feeling of a guy actively pursuing me in some form. It all felt…oddly validating—but imaginary. There I was, in front of one guy, who made me feel special but probably didn't feel the same about me, and another guy, whose interest in me was becoming more apparent, and yet it didn't feel like real life. I'd spent so much time feeling hopeless about the one guy that I realized that even when a guy *did* show interest, I didn't quite know how to receive it.

"Oh, um…I think Melanie needs you," Daniel said, handing me my phone, which was now ringing.

"Hello?" I answered.

"I found Marcus! I'll catch up with you a little later. I'm gonna chill with him for a bit," she explained.

"Okay, cool. I'll find you later, then," I agreed, ending the call.

"Is everything okay?" Daniel asked.

"Yeah, she's hanging out with her boyfriend." I shoved my phone in my back pocket.

"Where's yours?" Daniel tried.

"Oh please. You wouldn't have asked me for my number if I actually had one," I said.

"I know, but it never hurts to be sure," he flirted.

I looked up at him pathetically, unsure how to return his energy. The confident, playful Gabby that went toe-to-toe with Daniel in the cafeteria was nowhere to be found. There, I'd been standing and he'd been sitting—an even playing field—but in this moment, he towered over me, and I didn't know what to do with myself. That smirk of a smile, his chill demeanor, and his perfect face almost made me forget that Ryan was there. Daniel was attractive in a literal sense, and I wanted to be closer to him, but another part of me was frozen in place.

"Hey, Daniel, there's some guy on the roof trying to jump in the pool," a group of girls yelled, rushing up the stairs.

"What?! Alright, I'm coming." He rushed to the staircase, with Ryan, Indya, and a few others following behind.

"Don't move! I'll be back," Daniel yelled out to me as he descended the stairs.

♥ ♥ ♥

I felt so awkward without Melanie with me. She'd been to a ton of big family parties and knew how to maneuver her way around intoxicated bliss. I, on the other hand, looked painfully out of place as I stood at the railing of the loft and people-watched.

Downstairs, everything had looked so much better. Everyone was dancing. Everyone was having fun. It seemed cohesive. But from upstairs, I saw the truth. Everyone was glued to the people they knew or to their phones.

It was more realistic than I'd originally thought. In real life, no one actually goes to these parties wanting to socialize with new people. No, we ignore the strangers around us while we have our own fun with our own friends, but we do it at the same time, creating the illusion that we're all in it together.

I was guilty of this, too. There was no way I'd be there without Melanie, and I probably would've left thinking I'd had so much fun if we were actually hanging out at the party. But now that I was able to see everything as an outsider looking in, I saw how dangerous it could all be.

Since Daniel and Ryan had left, no one had even glanced at me. No one had said anything to the girl standing alone. It was like being the new kid all over again. Everyone was absorbed in their own experience.

I wondered how many people around me were actually unhappy. A selfish crowd is the perfect hiding place for those in pain. How many people were drunk off their asses because of something more than just "having fun?" How many people were depressed? How many were dealing with abuse? How many were raising themselves? I definitely wouldn't know who's who in an environment like this. So how much worse was it every day, when we weren't partying, when we were at school, or when we were walking past strangers on the street? Why the hell would anyone create a world where it's so easy for people to suffer and not be noticed?

"You look more stressed than me, and I just talked someone off my roof," Daniel said, pulling me from my thoughts as he leaned against the railing next to me.

"Yeah, I guess I kinda zoned out. " I turned to see that his head was rested on his folded arms, and he was looking at me kindly, like he were admiring a sleeping baby. "How'd it go, by the way?" I asked.

"Crisis averted." He stood up. "Someone paid him to jump off the roof, so I had to pay him even more not to."

"Kids," I scoffed sarcastically.

"Right? Who raised these animals?" Daniel chuckled. "What's on your mind, though?" He nudged my arm, and then leaned on the railing again, this time a little closer to me. "You really did look stressed when I walked up to you."

"Nothing worth talking about in the middle of a party," I insisted, adopting a more cheerful tone. "Why don't we go downstairs and join the rest of the *animals*'?"

"And do what? Dance?" Daniel looked amused.

"Don't tell me the party host is too cool to dance?" I challenged.

He stood up, smirking at my sudden boldness. "Actually, I've been turning down dances all night. I just wanted the right person to ask." He stood up and extended his hand, and I was absolutely flabbergasted. Did he just pull an Uno-reverse on me?

"Hey!" I heard Melanie yell from the staircase. Daniel and I swiveled our heads to look at her, and I noticed that she had Marcus attached to one hand and a red plastic cup in the other. "Why are you still up there? Let's go dance!"

Daniel turned back to me, his hand still out. "Don't make me beg you like I did Ryan," he chortled.

"So you *did* beg," I laughed, taking his hand.

We scaled the wall, squeezing past people as we descended the stairs to the living room. A Drake song was playing that no one could resist dancing to, and I mean no one. Everyone was moving—tough-guys and wallflowers alike. Whether it was an offbeat bounce or a simple two-step, I couldn't find a single person who wasn't enjoying the music. The Afro-beat begged for hip movement and rhythm, and even though my hips were almost pre-pubescent in width, I at least had rhythm. Melanie and I bopped to the music, gracefully brushing against other people in the crowded room. I faced her, too nervous to look at Daniel.

"Dance with him," Melanie mouthed to me.

"I'm scared," I mouthed back.

"Turn around," she asserted, quickly spinning to face Marcus so that I had no choice but to do the same.

"I was starting to think you forgot about me," Daniel said into my ear.

"Looks like you've got plenty of company, anyway," I rebutted, because there were girls all around us passively trying to dance with him, and I saw right through it. You know how it goes. You act like you're dancing with your friends, but you dance close enough to a guy to "accidentally" brush against him every now and then. I only peeped what was happening because I was Mrs. Passive Aggressive herself.

"Like I said, I've been waiting for the right person." He looked me directly in the eyes, but I felt it right in my heart, which was pounding in my chest, and I was rendered speechless. "May I?" He hovered his hands near my waist.

I nodded, still speechless. *Where's that energy you had before, Gabby? Get it together!* I thought. But I couldn't. My knees felt like they belonged to a baby deer learning to stand for the first time, and the only thing keeping me up was the secure grasp of Daniel's hands. Whether he knew it or not, he had control of my body, and I was surprised at how well he handled it. If he wanted to move left, we moved left. If he wanted me closer, I was closer—all by a light pull at the waist. His touch was possessive, like I was his and no one could rip me from his hands, but it was also gentle, like he'd let me go the minute I felt uncomfortable.

"I never would've expected you to be a good dancer," I finally spoke.

"I'm full of surprises," he smiled, taking my hand and pulling my arm around his neck. I followed his lead and put my other arm around him as well. Slowly but surely, we got closer and closer, until we got just close enough to build tension.

Do I rest my chest against his? Do I not? I went back and forth with myself until suddenly the DJ switched to a Latin song whose name I couldn't remember but I ironically knew every word to. It was Melanie and I's favorite song to dance to at her family parties. We immediately spun around to face each other and hit our routine as if it were just us in Melanie's back yard. Before I knew it, *we* were those kids in the movies in a dance circle who'd undoubtedly rehearsed their dance before the party. We ended the routine in the middle of the crowd and were met with whoops and applause. When the song finished, I turned outward and spotted Daniel and Ryan standing together, both clapping, and both visibly impressed.

"A'ight, y'all, my boy Daniel ain't pay me to be here all night, so you know the drill. Y'all ain't gotta go home, but…"

"Y'all gotta get the hell outta here!" We all finished the DJ's sentence and laughed collectively as the lights cut on. Finally, the great exodus.

"I never would've expected *you* to be a good dancer," Daniel admitted as I approached him and Ryan.

"I was hoping you'd do the dance," Ryan confessed. "I begged the DJ to play that song before he finished his set."

"Oh, so I'm not the only one begging around here!" Daniel laughed, roughhousing Ryan.

"Wait, how did you know about that dance?" I asked.

"You guys did it at Melanie's birthday party last summer. I was running late, but I walked in while you two were in the middle of it," he explained.

And there I was again, speechless, conflicted. Every time I felt myself being pulled in Daniel's direction, Ryan showed me just how observant he was when it came to me. Yes, Melanie danced, too, but why was he looking at me when the song finished and not the both of us? Why did he remember one dance he saw us do *months* ago? Why did he beg the DJ to play the song just to see us do it again? …If I were just a friend to him?

Outside, I sat against the hood of my car—next to Daniel, who was on his phone—watching Melanie say her last goodbyes to Marcus. Ryan and Indya were still inside, helping clean up with the rest of the basketball team. As people walked by, I wondered what lives they were returning home to now that the party was over.

Daniel's irritated tone took me out of my head. "I heard you, Dad… Alright," he said, breathing a sigh of frustration as he hung up. He shook his head and fixed his glance in front of him, avoiding eye contact. "Sorry about that."

"Oh, don't be, parents will be parents," I said.

He looked at me with a soft, half-smile. "Thank you for coming. I didn't get to talk to you as much as I wanted to, but I had fun dancing with you."

Melanie finally let Marcus go and started walking toward my car. "Well," I said, unlocking my doors so Melanie could get in, "if I recall correctly, you have my number, now. You know, so you can fix the *lack of communication*," I mocked as I opened my door.

He laughed and nodded his head. "Good night, Gabby."

CHAPTER 7

"Nice work, Gabrielle," Ms. Redlich said, handing me my assignment the following Monday.

"Gabby, you got an A?" Melanie gasped.

"It's not the first time I've received an A in this class, thank you very much."

"G, the last time you got an A in this class was when we turned in our signed permission slips for extra credit to watch an R-rated movie in clas—"

"OKAY, WE GET IT, DANG. Spilling my business all loud and what not," I interrupted.

My phone buzzed in my lap, and I giggled as I glanced across the class at Daniel. We had been texting the entire weekend since his party. I looked back at Melanie to find her staring at me with suspicion. I kinda sorta most definitely had been texting Daniel the entire class, and she kinda sorta most definitely had noticed. The best part about having a best friend is that they know you better than anyone else. The worst part about having a best friend is that you can't get anything past them. Then again, I wasn't necessarily trying to hide the fact that I was texting him.

"Who's that?" she asked in an *I already know* voice.

"Hmm?" I replied. Suddenly, I was hard of hearing.

"You've been on your phone the entire class. I didn't even get my rematch in tic-tac-ignore-the-teacher because you've been too busy making googly eyes at Daniel's messages!" she exclaimed. The bell rang, and I immediately started packing my things to avoid responding. I really didn't feel like being judged; this was the first time I wasn't stressing over Ryan since senior year started. When I got up from my seat, I spotted Daniel hanging around the door. He was looking at me, waiting.

"How'd you do?" he asked as I walked up to him.

"I got—"

"'Scuse me, Daniel, we need to use the bathroom," Melanie said, pulling me past him and out of the classroom.

♥ ♥ ♥

Melanie checked under the stall doors to make sure it was just us and then turned to face me. "Spill it," she demanded. "You like him, don't you?"

"How could I not, Mel! He's so sweet and funny. I've been talking to him since the party, last Friday," I explained.

"I don't know how to feel about this," she admitted, pacing past me to one of the sinks.

"Just feel happy! Pleeease? I mean, at least I'm not sulking about Ryan, right?"

"Yeah, but you still haven't dealt with the Ryan thing—you've just distracted yourself from it. I don't want you to fool yourself into thinking you're over Ryan if in reality you're just projecting the feelings you have for Ryan onto Daniel," she said.

"I promise it's not like that, Mel. We're just getting to know each other," I replied.

She was quiet for a second, then walked toward the door. "Fine, but promise me you'll slow down on all the texting," she said, opening the door, "it's like you're not even here because you're always smiling at your phone like a weirdo," she finished.

"Alright. I'll slow down," I promised.

I never slowed down. I texted Daniel every second I could: in the morning, in class, in-between class, after his practices. Within two weeks, I practically knew his life story—where he was from (Texas, born and raised), his favorite color (black), his favorite number (six, also his jersey number), his family dynamic, all the good stuff. He was an only child (like me), he bumped heads with his dad a lot, and his mom spoiled him with nice things to make up for working all the time. Both of his parents made good money; his dad was a prominent real estate agent for one of the biggest agencies in Texas, and his mom was a linguist, so she was often away in foreign countries translating messages between global ambassadors. Pretty lavish life if you ask me, which explained the enormous house he lived in.

He was so incredibly sweet, complementing me any chance he got. Usually, I saw through those things, but he had a way with words that was so luring that I couldn't help but develop feelings very quickly. The only problem was, we spoke more via text than in person. Our only class together was Advanced Health, and we sat with our own friends at lunch. On top of that, we only had five minutes to get from one class to the next. Despite all of that, I contemplated what life would be like if Daniel and I were more than…whatever we were.

♥ ♥ ♥

"How fast is *too fast* to start dating someone?" I asked Melanie as we hung out in her bedroom one day after school. Ever since she'd called me out about texting Daniel so much, I'd held off on texting him when I was with her, and the urge to pick up my phone was killing me.

"Well, it depends on how long you've known the person. Why? Is this about who I think it is?" she asked, carefully applying a coat of pale pink polish on her second toe.

"IDK, I just feel like I've gotten so close to Daniel these past couple weeks, and I kinda want to see if there's more to it. At first, we were genuinely getting to know each other, but now we flirt so much that there's no way we're just being 'friendly,' you know?" I admitted.

Melanie stopped painting mid-stroke, put the top back on her nail polish, and looked at me. "Tell me you're joking," she demanded.

"What?" I sat up.

"Tell. Me. You're. Joke-ing," she over-enunciated. "You've only been talking for what? Two weeks? And you're already thinking about being his girlfriend?! Not to mention all you do is text and you've barely gotten to know him *in person*."

"That's not true," I pushed back.

"Really? Give me *one* example of a face-to-face conversation you've had with him other than at his party a few weeks ago," she challenged.

"Okay, fine! This week at lunch, for example," I began my recap, swinging my legs off the side of her bed, "while you were in the taco line, Daniel and I were in line for hamburgers…"

♥ ♥ ♥

At first, I didn't realize he was behind me, but then I felt someone touch my hair and turned to see who it was. "Sorry, you had something in your hair," he said, showing me a white piece of lint on his fingertips.

"Thank you! It's probably from my sweater," I reasoned, tugging on my sleeves to show how easily the lint came off. Texas was having one of its random cold fronts, and I had thrown on the warmest thing I could find, forgetting the trail of lint it left every time I wore it.

"Your hair is really pretty, by the way. Is this a twist-out?" Daniel asked. He twirled a clump of my hair around his finger and then let it bounce perfectly back into place. My eyes widened with shock. The last thing I was expecting was for him to know what a twist-out was.

"Yeah, it is, actually," I smiled. "I think I've finally perfected it."

"How long does this usually take you?" He placed his hands on my shoulders and quickly spun me around, as the line had started moving without me realizing.

"Oh gosh," I let out a sigh, moving ahead. Even the thought of doing my hair made me tired. "If we're just talking about the process of twisting my hair—maybe thirty minutes. If you count washing my hair before that… Mmm, I'd say maybe two or three hours, total," I explained.

"Can't rush perfection," I heard him say above me. I fought a smile but ultimately cracked as his next comment came with perfect comedic timing.

"Mine takes two hours, too."

I cackled out loud and turned around to face him again. "Two hours? Doing what?" I raised an eyebrow.

"Girl, you don't see all this fine-ness?" Daniel asked, flipping his nonexistent hair. Don't get me wrong, he had gorgeous waves in a neatly edged up bald fade, but it was far from two hours' worth of hair.

"Oh, I see it! I just don't see how it took two hours," I answered, taking a step backward as the line progressed behind me.

He licked his bottom lip and smiled slyly. "So, you think I'm fine?"

"What?" I asked, not realizing he'd set me up.

He raised his hands like he was innocent. "You said it, not me."

"I—you asked me a question!"

"And you answered it, did you not?" he smirked.

"Next in line?" a lunch lady called from the service counter. I quickly turned around and grabbed a food tray, eager to escape any form of admission. Yes, I *absolutely* thought Daniel was fine. I came to that conclusion when I first laid eyes on him, but I didn't need him to know that yet.

♥ ♥ ♥

"…And that's when we met up and walked back to our table," I told Melanie, finishing the flashback of my *"face-to-face"* conversation with Daniel.

"That's it?" she asked, clearly unimpressed.

"You told me to give you ONE example, Mel. That's your one example!"

"You hear that?" She stuck one finger up, like she wanted us to be quiet. I looked around in confusion.

"If you listen close enough you'll hear the crickets snoring, because they were too bored to chirp," she continued.

"Oh, *ha, ha*. You're a comedic genius," I said sarcastically, chucking a pillow in her direction.

"No, seriously, though, Gabby! You even said in your little recap that you avoided admitting that you thought he was cute! You don't see a pattern here? You avoided telling him he's cute *just* like you avoid telling Ryan how you feel—"

"Ughhh, why does it always have to be about Ryan?" I interrupted, throwing myself back onto her bed.

"Because YOU'VE made it about Ryan every day since the moment you found out he was dating Indya!!!!" Melanie all but yelled.

"YES!" I sat up again and crossed my legs in one swift motion. "And finally it's not about him, Melanie! Why can't you see that and be happy for me?! The more I talk to Daniel, the less I think about Ryan. Being around Ryan and Indya at lunch doesn't bother me anymore. Ryan's busy schedule doesn't bother me anymore. Everything finally feels okay—*I* finally feel okay. Stop acting like you've never liked a guy, Mel. Seriously."

"No one is *acting* like anything. I'm just trying to keep it real with you!"

"Really? Because it seems like no matter what I do, whether it's with Ryan or with Daniel, you don't approve unless I do what you tell me to. Did I tell you how to process your feelings when you were talking to Marcus? No. I was happy for you."

"The difference between me and Marcus and you and Daniel is that Marcus and I had been friends for forever before we started dating. *YOU* just met Daniel last month! And you hadn't even started talking to him like that until his party!

"When Marcus and I realized we had feelings for each other, we put on our grown-up pants and had a conversation about it, but you and me both know you have a problem with confessing your feelings. So, EXCUSE ME if I'm trying to keep you from stringing Daniel along and digging yourself a hole you can't get out of," she snapped.

"How am I digging myself a hole, Mel? I haven't done anything but like the guy," I asked.

"Let's say you *do* start dating Daniel. Don't you think, as time progresses and he gets to know you better, that he'll eventually notice your feelings for Ryan? How do you think that'll turn out? Because your feelings for Ryan haven't magically disappeared, and I don't think it's smart to develop new feelings for someone else when you still have strong feelings for Ryan. Plus, like I keep saying, you *just met* Daniel. You like all the good things about him, but you've never gotten to experience the bad. Have you ever seen him when he's angry?"

"No," I said reluctantly. "Why does that even matter?"

"Because anyone can put their best foot forward to make you like them! I saw the good *and* bad in Marcus before I *ever* considered dating him, Gabby."

"If that's the case, then what exactly is it about him that you like, Melanie? Because from what I've seen, you don't even trust him! Every five minutes you're worried about if he's interested in a different girl, liking another girl's pictures on Insta, or if he's losing feelings for you because he hasn't texted you back right away. At Daniel's party, you ditched me for him just so you could make sure he wasn't looking at Lynsey!"

"You don't understand," she insisted.

"Then help me understand, Mel, please! You can't possibly feel okay with as much as you worry about him. It's not good for you! There are some days at lunch when you're too busy to eat because you're looking through his social media or babysitting your phone waiting on him to text back. I feel like I can't even talk to you about what I notice because you get so defensive and emotional, and I hate feeling like I hurt you! It's not fair!"

Melanie got quiet. I watched as she re-opened her nail polish and resumed painting her toes. We rarely argued, not like this. I knew she meant well, but I was starting to feel attacked. I didn't want to think about Ryan, not right now. I just wanted to cling to what felt good, and at that moment, it was Daniel. To be honest, the argument had nothing to do with Melanie, and even though I meant what I said about her and Marcus, it wasn't the right time or the right way to talk to her about it. I realized that as I sat on her bed under a cloud of pride and regret.

Melanie finished painting her unpolished toes before speaking again. "I'm not trying to invalidate your feelings for Daniel, but you caught them fast—really fast—and I just want you to be careful. I can't make you deal with your feelings for Ryan, that's up to you, but at least give it more time with Daniel. Make sure you're not projecting the way you feel about Ryan onto Daniel. Make sure you actually like him for him," she suggested.

"Fine," I surrendered.

"As for Marcus and I, you're right, okay? I'm just scared that I'm not enough… You may look at me and think *at least you have someone*, but the way you're scared of losing Ryan if you confess how you feel is the same way I'm scared I'll lose Marcus if my feelings aren't enough."

Damn, I thought, sinking back into Melanie's bed. It really didn't matter whether Ryan was more than my friend or not, whether he knew how I felt or not—the fear of losing him was all the same. Even if I had him, I would dread the thought of losing him for the simple fact that he meant a lot to me. Did it even really matter anymore, then, if I told him? If I *"left it all on the line"* as Melanie had once put it? As much as I wanted to say *no, it didn't,* something in me was saying it did.

CHAPTER 8

On Monday, I walked into Sociology to find Ryan and Melanie already sitting on either side of my empty desk. It was the first week of March, and there were only three months left of us being…us: seeing each other five days a week or more, eating lunch together, talking to each other in class. There was simply no guarantee that we'd have it this good in college. So, why, with the little time we had left in high school, were we wasting it being mad at each other?

"Hey," Melanie said dryly.

There was still tension from our argument over the weekend. Ms. Redlich had even asked if we were okay in Advanced Health because we were actually paying attention. This wasn't our first time being at odds, but I had a lot of pride, and she hated being the first to apologize, so things were just flat-out awkward. At lunch, we talked indirectly to each other by joining Ryan and Indya's conversation. Do you know how hard it was to nod and smile while Indya talked, just to avoid Melanie? We looked ridiculous because neither one of us would swallow our pride, it was just this big, silent game of

You break the ice first.

No, you.

No—YOU.

As I sat down at my desk, I glanced at Ryan and remembered him calling me selfish, and I thought about how unfair it was to let Melanie feel bad for being a good friend, even if it hurt my ego.

"Hey," I finally said back. "I'm sorry for getting so upset on Friday. You were just being real with me, and I can't be mad at you for that—I'm *not* mad at you for that," I explained.

"Thanks, G. I really didn't want to hurt you in any way; I'm just worried about you," she said. I could see the relief wash over her immediately and her normal personality return like nothing had ever happened. "It was so hard paying attention in Advanced Health today, girl," she added.

"Man, tell me about it! They really pay Ms. Redlich to talk; can you believe that?" I laughed.

"About time…" Ryan said to himself. Melanie and I paused our reunion and looked at him; he was still facing forward like he hadn't said anything.

"What was that?" I asked, leaning over with my hand by my ear.

"It sounded like Ryan, but with no balls," Melanie teased, making both Ryan and I crack up.

"Do you know how awkward I felt at lunch today? I mean, I don't mind you two bonding with Indya, but I really could've gone my entire life without listening to you all rant about your…times of the month," he explained.

"What can we say? Nothing brings us girls together like a good ol' period rant," Melanie smiled sarcastically.

"Although, that probably wasn't lunch appropriate," I said apologetically. "Sorry, Ry."

At the end of class, Mr. Nicholson reminded us about our final projects, and I guarantee you, the entire class had a *damn, I forgot about that* expression plastered across their faces. I probably looked normal compared to everyone else because…well, I used that expression a lot.

"Have you started on yours, yet?" Ryan asked me as he packed his things.

"No, have you?" I said.

"Nah, but practice was cancelled today, so I was wondering if you wanted to go grab something to eat and catch up? Maybe we can give each other ideas on what to do for our projects," he offered, standing up.

I looked up at him in awe, like my first day of school all over again. His senior ID dangled in front of my face the way it had back then, and the picture was even better than the one from freshman year; his face was more mature, and he was actually smiling.

I hadn't had the opportunity to hang out with him outside of school in so long that I couldn't completely believe what he was saying. I could hear Melanie clear her throat playfully beside me as she packed her things.

"Whew," she coughed, "I am…rather parched. I'm gonna go get some water. See you tomorrow!" she said as she walked out of the classroom, giving me a look that screamed *"you better do it!"*

"I'd love that!" I smiled. I was trying to play cool, but I couldn't hide my excitement.

I loved spending time alone with Ryan. Though there'd been plenty of times since, I still remembered the first time we hung out by ourselves. It was the summer before junior year, and I had gone to one of his basketball tournaments. In-between games, we'd chilled near his team and talked—nothing special. During his games, I'd sat awkwardly in the bleachers, cheering him on with his parents—that was actually the first time I'd met them, and like all parents who meet a friend of the opposite sex, they'd assumed I was his girlfriend.

"What? No, we're just friends, dad," Ryan laughed back then. I laughed with him because it really was funny how precious parents could be, but it was still kind of awkward.

By that time, I was well aware of my attraction to him, not just physically—I had a full-blown crush. He was so gentle and kind with me, and I guess I'd gotten attached. The thing is, he never did anything extravagant, just simple things, like holding the door for me, asking me if I was okay, and keeping me on track in school (Lord knows I needed that). But when you like someone, those things mean a lot more to you than they do to them. For him, it was probably just treating a girl with respect. In my mind, though, he was proposing soon.

In all that time, our alone moments hadn't gotten old. Especially now that Indya was in the picture and it happened far less than it used to.

♥ ♥ ♥

"Where do you want to go?" Ryan asked as he got into his driver's seat. We'd decided it'd be easier if we just rode together.

"Let's go to that new burger place down the street. I heard it was bomb," I said. He looked at me without saying anything, nodding with approval.

"…Why are you looking at me like that?" I asked.

"You finally know what you want to eat. I never thought I'd see this day," Ryan laughed. I wasn't the most decisive person at lunch, and that's all I'm going to say. No further questions, I don't need you laughing at me, too. This is *my* story. I do all the laughing, here, got it?

When we got to the burger place, Ryan was the same gentleman he'd always been. He opened the door for me, let me order before him, and even paid for my meal. How could I *not* like him? Honestly, tell me how. Somewhere along the way, though, I thought about Indya. Where was she, and would she be okay with this?

"Hey, so uh, where's Indya?" I asked as we sat down at a spot near the window, where all the table-for-two seats were.

"Probably at home, why?" he asked before realizing what I meant. "Oh… Yeah, this might seem a little weird… Me, here with you and not her on my day off from basketball," he finished.

Technically, he answered my question, but at the same time, he didn't. Is it bad that I secretly hoped he would tell me they got into a big fight and broke up? That he never wanted to see her again and that she was the worst person he'd ever met? Yes? Okay, but like…on a scale of one to ten, how bad? If it's less than ten, I'm gonna assume it wasn't that bad, just saying.

"Wouldn't she be upset about us hanging out alone?" I asked.

"Mmm-mmm!" He shook his head no. "She thought this was a great idea, actually. She knows I promised we'd catch up soon."

Unbelievable. Who was this chick? Cinderella? Why was she so freaking nice and understanding? "I see why you like her," I said, taking a big gulp of my soda to keep from vomiting. I needed to face the fact that aside from our run-in on the first day of senior year, the only reason I didn't like Indya was because she had something I didn't, and that was…well, childish.

"Man, that girl is…amazing," he started as he watched people walk by through the window. I was glad that he wasn't paying attention to me *act* like I was comfortable. "We have our moments, don't get me wrong. But—" He paused after looking at me. I guess my discomfort was more obvious than I'd thought. "Are you okay?" he asked.

This was a great chance to finally come clean and tell him how I felt, but I couldn't. I didn't want to make him feel bad for liking his own girlfriend. Plus, I didn't want to make the rest of the afternoon together awkward. I'd been pretending I was fine since August, so one more day couldn't hurt.

"I'm just not used to seeing you talk like this about girls. It's…different," I admitted. At least I wasn't lying.

"Yeah, sorry," he smiled awkwardly. "So, how have you been? Do you have any ideas for the Sociology project?"

"I've been fine. And no, I actually have no clue what I'll be doing. Up until today I had completely forgotten about it! What about you?"

"I think I'm gonna participate in one of the track practices and go to one of the track meets." He looked at me amusingly, like he wanted to say something else but wasn't sure if he should.

"You look like you've got something more to say," I prodded, returning the amused look.

He sat back in his chair and shook his head, and then finally smiled and said, "So…what's up with you and Daniel? That's new, right?"

"Oh right! Daniel's really cool, I've been talking to him a lot recently. Melanie thinks we've been talking a little *too* much, actually."

"Is that what was going on between you two today?" he asked.

"Yup."

"Well, I can tell he likes you. Which is weird because Daniel is probably one of the biggest players on the basketball team, and I'm not talking about basketball," he explained. I honestly couldn't tell if that was a good thing or a bad thing. *Hey, my friend is a player, but not with you!* What exactly was I supposed to do with that?

"Oh, really? Player as in, he cheats a lot, or player as in, he never commits?" I asked. I could deal with a guy who didn't commit, but I couldn't afford to lose sleep over a cheater. I already struggled with confidence sometimes; I didn't want the added pressure of wondering if he was cheating on me because he'd done it with other girls.

"He never commits. He loses interest fast and never really gives anyone a chance."

"*Or* he gets what he wants and moves on... I'll be sure to watch my back," I added. I was a little bummed because I knew Ryan was nothing like that, but how fair would it be to hold Daniel to the standard of being someone he's not?

"You don't have to watch your back; I've got that handled. He knows I'll kick his ass if he tries anything with you." He got so serious for a second. I was honestly caught by surprise.

"That means a lot, Ryan; you have no idea," I smiled. He smiled back and took the finishing bite of his burger.

No, seriously. You don't, I thought.

Ryan sounded like one of those fantasy guy friends you saw in movies and read about in books but never saw in real life (I mean, hello, you're reading about him right now). He was protective, a sweetheart, athletic—but what were his flaws? What made him *real*? Unfortunately, since you're getting this from my perspective, you're getting the biased, perfect version of Ryan. I'm sure there were some not-so-perfect things about him that I've chosen to ignore.

I think that sometimes we get so blinded by desire that we only see the things that make us want something. Truthfully, I didn't want to pay attention to anything that might pop my bubble. I didn't want anything to ruin the hypothetical happiness I'd have if Ryan were mine, but what if there were things about him that would make me *unhappy*?—things about him that were engraved in his character that I wouldn't be able to change? Sitting there, looking at him, I wondered what I'd blinded myself to.

CHAPTER 9

As Ryan pulled up next to my car in the school parking lot, I looked at him and couldn't help but wonder out loud, "Is there anything wrong about you?"

"Hmm?" He looked confused.

"I've never noticed anything bad about you—any flaws," I explained. He furrowed his brows, which was the opposite of what I was expecting.

"We literally argued about me not communicating with you like…last month, and now you can't think of anything bad about me?" he scoffed.

"Okay, yes, we did, but you handled it really well, and we haven't had that issue since!" I started. "Other than that, you've always been so kind and smart. You're athletic, loyal, a gentleman…" Ryan looked forward, seemingly unimpressed by my compliments. "Why do you seem so bothered by the fact that I notice all the good things about you? I mean, I'm sure everything I listed is the reason why Indya's with you, right?" I smiled, nudging him. I hoped that bringing Indya up would make him light up the way he had at the burger place.

"No. Indya's with me because she sees my flaws and my problems and likes me despite them," Ryan objected. "I kinda hoped that as my best friend you'd see the same, because I certainly see *your* flaws, and I like you despite them."

My heart skipped at those words. *Like me? Ryan liked me?*

"My flaws?" I asked, avoiding the question I really wanted to ask.

"You overthink things. You hold things inside and let them fester until you can't hold them in anymore, and then you blow up. You're prideful. You don't like to admit when you're wrong."

I looked down at my hands and fidgeted with my fingers as he spoke.

"I've noticed those things because you're one of the closest people I have in my life. And even knowing all of that, I can't picture my life without you around me. That's how you know it's real, Gabby. When someone can see you for *all* of you, and still choose to stick around," he explained, looking at me with disappointment on his face. There was a short silence before he spoke again, but at this point my heart had stopped and *short* felt like forever.

"Now I can't help but wonder if you've stuck around this long for all of me, or just the parts of me that are good enough to be put on a pedestal," he finished, staring straight ahead. This time, the lack of eye contact hurt me because I knew I'd hurt *him*, and all I'd done was compliment him. How had the afternoon gone so wrong so fast?

"Ryan, I'm sorry if I hurt you by saying that. I just—"

"It's okay, Gab. I'll see you tomorrow," he said. He sat there instead of getting out to open my door, and for the first time I was able to see Ryan in a new light.

I got into my car, locked the doors out of habit, and watched him drive off without so much as a glance in my direction. I sat there, baffled and scared. What had just happened? What had I done wrong? One second, things were fine, and the next, they just…weren't. Suddenly, I was consumed with anxiety. I could feel my heart race as I tortured myself with irrational what-ifs. *What if he never talks to me again? What if I lost him forever? What if—*

Just then, Daniel knocked on my window, startling me half to death. Why did he always seem to show up in the middle of my mental breakdowns? He scared me so badly that I actually got angry for a second.

"Why are you still here?" he asked once I'd rolled down my window.

"I could ask you the same thing. Stop sneaking up on me!" I snapped.

"I was just in the gym shooting around since there's no practice." He paused. "Are you alright?"

The minute those words left his lips I felt a surge of remorse. He clearly meant no harm, and I was taking my emotions out on him. "I—I'm sorry, Daniel. I just have a lot on my mind, and you scared the shit out of me," I explained. I looked around the parking lot to see if there were any other cars, but it was just mine—just us.

"How are you getting home?" I asked.

"I was just gonna walk and clear my head," he explained.

"No, no, get in. I'll take you home. My treat for being an asshole."

As he walked around to get in, I realized how messy my car was. There were jackets, fast-food receipts, unfinished water bottles, you name it. I frantically cleared my passenger's seat before unlocking the door. He stood outside, waiting and laughing to himself.

"This was on the floor," he said, handing me the Bible study flyer that I had found on my car months before at the grocery store and had completely forgotten about until that moment. I grabbed it and set it in one of the cup holders between us.

The drive to his house started off quiet, which was weird considering how much we talked via text message. I thought back to what Ryan had told me earlier. Had Daniel lost interest in me already? Why wasn't he being all cute and flirty, now?

"You okay?" I asked.

"I'm fine. Both of my parents are home, now, but it still feels like we're apart even when we're together, so when they're home I try to find ways to get home late every now and then," he admitted.

"Maybe it's because your house has different zip codes. I'd feel lonely in there, too!" I joked, trying to make him smile. The corners of his mouth turned up half-heartedly in return, but he continued to look out of the passenger window.

"So, what was up with you back there?" he asked me. "You looked like you found out someone died."

I looked like I killed my friendship, I thought. I definitely wasn't about to talk to him about Ryan and me. I didn't want him to be suspicious about my liking Ryan since they were teammates. The last thing I wanted was to cause tension between those two on top of everything else.

"I…was just stressing about this final project I have for Sociology," I lied. I probably *should* have been stressing about it, but come on, this is me we're talking about.

"I did that when I was in his class last year. He does the same final project every year," Daniel explained as I pulled into his driveway. "Did you think of a group, yet?"

"Yeah…um." I looked around as if an idea would magically present itself. And then it did, in the form of the flyer in the cup holder. "I'm gonna go to a Christian Bible study," I said, picking up the flyer and showing it to him. He took it and read it with amusement.

"'*Get lit by the light of Jesus Christ*,'" he scoffed. "Good luck with that." He shook his head.

"Are you not religious?" I asked. I wasn't very religious myself—I mean, I believed in God, but I didn't go to church or anything. Daniel seemed so put off by it, though.

"No, but my dad is, and I hate it. That's why we bump heads so much. He's like your cookie-cutter Bible thumper: always quoting scripture and telling me what God thinks."

"He just loves you, Dan."

"No, that's not love. Those people claim they love everyone, but all they do is throw their rules at you and judge you for not being the kind of person their Bible says you should be. All the while, half of them act like you and me Monday through Saturday." He shook his head. I understood what he was saying—up until the *"you and me"* part.

"What's *that* supposed to mean?" I asked, eyebrows raised. He was lucky we were already at his house, otherwise he may have gotten dropped off a couple blocks early.

"I just mean that you and I aren't very religious, you know? You can't look at one of us and say *'they must be a Christian'* based on how we act. Outside of church, you can't tell half of them are Christians, either. But let them meet someone less religious than they are, and suddenly their shit smells like Chanel No. 5." He sat up in the midst of his rant, clearly triggered.

I agreed with everything he'd said, but hearing him say it with so much disgust made me a little uncomfortable. I thought a lot of religious people were fake and hypocritical, but I didn't hate any of them. I was pretty apathetic, to be honest. That was between them and God.

"Well, it's just a project, right?" I said, hoping to end the conversation.

"Yeah," he sighed. "Thanks for the ride. I'm sorry I'm not my usual self," he said as he undid his seatbelt.

"I hope you feel better…and I'm sorry again for snapping at you."

"I hope you feel better, too, beautiful," he said as he got out. It was a bit of a moment, but I was still way too hung up on Ryan being mad at me to melt over Daniel calling me beautiful.

After Daniel closed the passenger door, I checked my phone, hoping to see a message from Ryan. Nothing. It was like everything I said that afternoon triggered the guys around me. I mentioned Ryan's greatness, and he didn't want to be great. I mentioned religion to Daniel, and he nearly cursed all Christians to Hell. This was *menstruation* at its finest. (I don't care what you think, men get periods, too.)

By the time I got home, my mom was already there, which is how I knew it'd been a long day. I was always home before her, and when she got home, I was usually somewhere in the house lounging, ignoring my responsibilities, and side-eyeing my homework. Tonight, though, the roles were reversed. I let out a deep sigh as I entered the kitchen, placing my keys and the Bible study flyer on the counter. My mom was rummaging through the refrigerator, and if she dared ask me to go get her some more fruit I was gonna scream.

She peaked over the fridge door at me. "You alright? Usually I'm the one who lets out a deep sigh and throws my keys on the counter."

"Long day," I said. I took a seat at the kitchen bar counter. She closed the fridge and then stood across the bar counter from me. "I don't really wanna get into it."

She nodded in understanding. "What's this?" she asked, reaching for the flyer. Instead of telling her, I decided to let her read it since she already was, anyway. I watched her crack a smile as she scanned it. "Are you gonna go?" she asked, looking up at me.

"Yeah, for a Sociology assignment," I explained. My mom was into religious stuff, but she didn't over-do it. She prayed before her meals and before she went to sleep, and every now and then I'd find her reading her Bible, but she never forced any of it on me. She had taught me the basics about Jesus, but that was it. She wasn't anything like how Daniel had described his dad.

"Mom, why don't we go to church?" I said suddenly.

When I asked this, she immediately straightened up, like I'd caught her attention.

"We used to before your dad passed, but you were too little to remember," she began, "and uh… after that I—" She paused, as if she wanted to choose her words wisely.

"You don't have to answer that if you don't want to," I said. Talking about my dad wasn't always a touchy subject, it just depended on the day. But the last thing I wanted to do was hit yet another soft spot in someone that day. I was already two for two.

"No, it's okay. I've been hoping to have this conversation with you one day." She walked around the counter and took a seat next to me. "When your dad passed, I fell into a deep sadness, and going to church didn't feel the same. I'd lost half of me and everyone knew it, and I didn't want to go back and deal with the pity. I didn't want any of it; I just wanted my husband back.

"After the sadness, I began to feel angry. How could God take him from me? After I had been so faithful? After *he* had been so faithful? I couldn't stand the thought of going back to church after that. I didn't want to worship a God who took away someone who was so good to me."

"Why do you still pray then? You still believe, don't you?" I couldn't help but ask.

She fell silent for so long that I assumed I'd offended her and apologized.

"No, you're fine. It's just that…no one's ever asked me that…" she murmured. "I still believe. It's just… I guess after a while, my faith became a routine," she explained.

"It wasn't always that way, though. When I first gave my life to God, it was because I felt an unusual sense of love and comfort. All I wanted to do was learn more about Him and be around other people who loved God, too. It was like a new obsession, really."

I know the feeling, I thought. That's how I felt with Daniel; all I wanted to do was talk to him, learn about him, and be around him.

"To answer your question, though," she began again, "I want you to fall in love with God the way I did—on your own. I grew up going to church because I had to, but it wasn't until I started going because I *wanted* to that I was able to grasp the love God has for me. Following God is a choice you have to make for yourself."

Maybe that's why Daniel was so repulsed by his dad's faith. He didn't want it for himself.

"If I ever do decide to go to church, will you come with me?" I asked. She looked at me with admiration, like she'd desperately hoped I'd ask.

"Of course, Gabby."

CHAPTER 10

March 16th. I found myself standing in front of my mirror, wondering if I was dressed appropriately for a Bible study. What exactly did people wear to these kinds of things? Did they dress fancy? Casual? How casual was *too* casual? If I wore shorts, would they be considered *too* short? If I wore jeans, would the rips and holes be taboo? I settled for a school t-shirt and ripped jeans. A little knee-action never hurt anyone, right? However, with my luck, I'd be labeled a knee-slut and banished for all eternity.

My stomach was in knots as I walked into the "holy lit-uation." I felt so small—so invisible. I looked around the church foyer for any indication of a Bible study. There were a few people scattered around talking, but I was too scared to interrupt a conversation to ask where the f—where the heck I was going.

"Hi, is this your first time here?" I heard a voice say from my periphery. I turned to find another girl looking right at me. She had beautiful, brown skin and long box braids that gave me second-hand neck cramps. I briefly scanned her outfit and saw that she, too, was wearing ripped jeans. Knee-sluts for the win.

"Uh, yes. I'm here for the Bible study," I explained.

"Awesome, I'm on my way there, too," she told me. "I'm Grace." She stuck her hand out and smiled warmly when I shook it.

"I'm Gabrielle," I smiled awkwardly.

She led me to a room not far from where we were; there were chairs and couches arranged in a circle and about fifteen people sitting and talking. When we walked in, everyone's face lit up in excitement. "Yo, Graaaace! What's up, girl? You ready for the study?"

Several people flocked to Grace, bombarding her with hugs and dapping her up with intricate handshakes. I awkwardly made my way to a seat and sat quietly. One of the questions for my Sociology project was about the social interaction between the group members; it was clear to me that these people were like family—the vast majority of them, at least. I could see a few other people sitting around awkwardly like myself; my guess was that they were also first-timers.

Grace spun around in the center of her welcoming committee, clearly looking for something—until her eyes landed on me.

"There you are," she said, making her way toward me. She sat down in an empty seat next to me and then looked at her watch. "Alright, guys, are you ready to start?" she asked. People whooped and hollered in excitement, and suddenly I felt like the least happy person in the room. Were these people on Jesus or crack?

"Well, for starters, I want to welcome our visitors to Agape Church! My name is Grace, and I'm leading tonight's Bible study! It's my first time leading one of these, so please bear with me. I'm a little nervous," she admitted. That explained all the love from her friends. They were hyping her up! How freaking sweet? My conversation with Daniel still lingered in my thoughts, but I didn't get any vibes of judgement or self-righteousness at all from these people. Then again, the study hadn't even started yet. For all I knew, this was just a show.

"If you guys could bow your heads and pray with me…" she invited. My heart immediately began to race. Pray? I mean, I knew how to pray, but it had been a long time since I'd done it. Without skipping a beat, though, everyone began to grab hands, so I quickly wiped my sweaty palms off on my jeans and joined them.

"Lord, thank you for bringing us here safely tonight to learn about your word. I pray that you speak through me and help us to lean not on our own understanding but on the guidance of your Holy Spirit. In Jesus' name we pray, amen."

"Amen," I said to myself with the rest of the group. I hadn't been to church in a while, but at least I'd remembered when to say amen! I could feel my pride inflate. I wasn't as much of a heathen as I thought I was!

"Who wants to guess what tonight's study is about?" Grace asked. Another girl raised her hand eagerly. She looked like she was born smiling with a full set of teeth instead of crying; that's how much happiness she exuded. It was uncomfortably abnormal to witness.

"Hope," Grace laughed, calling on the girl with her hand raised. Her name was *Hope*? First Grace, now Hope. Who was next? *World Peace?*

"Forgiveness?" Hope guessed. I looked around to see if anyone named *Forgiveness* was about to answer, or if that was genuinely Hope's guess.

"Not quite," Grace smiled. As she scanned the room for more hands, I pulled my notebook from my backpack and began to flip to a clean page so I could jot down notes for my project.

"Today's study is about love!" Grace beamed.

Great, I thought. As if I hadn't already been trying to run away from my feelings long enough.

"How many of you knew that Agape Church was actually named after the Greek term for love, *agape*?" Grace asked. A few people raised their hands, but they were mostly the people I had assumed attended this church regularly.

"Not gonna lie, I googled it to figure out what it meant, but that's it," one of the guys admitted.

"*Agape* is one of the four words the Ancient Greeks used to describe four types of love. Why do you think they made so many words for love instead of just one?" Grace paused, waiting for any answers. I felt bad that no one was responding, so I half-heartedly began to speak.

"Um… I guess we all love in different ways, so it's hard to use just one word to describe it?"

"Yes!" she exclaimed. "The other three words are *storge*, which is a love related to friends and family; *eros*, which is a love related to passion and eroticism; and *phileo*, which is a word related to brotherly love. *Agape* love, on the other hand, is an unconditional, selfless love—it is a love that isn't based on feelings—a love put into action again and again no matter the person or circumstance—a love that seeks nothing in return. So, as you could imagine, *agape* is the word used to describe God's love in the New Testament of the Bible!"

The room was silent. I couldn't tell if everyone was as confused as I was or if there was some silent prayer happening that I didn't know about.

Of course, it *was* a lot of information to take in. How could there be a love that isn't based on feelings? Isn't that what love is? A feeling? I wasn't sure how involved to get since I was just there to observe, so I waited to see if anyone else was thinking what I was thinking. Maybe *they* would ask instead.

"How exactly can you love someone you don't feel anything for?" someone surprisingly asked. I glanced at the ceiling, where I assumed God was hiding out and playing with me.

"It's not necessarily the lack of feeling, but rather, the choice to love no matter the feeling," Grace explained. "Have you ever felt so strongly about someone, even though they didn't feel the same way? Or maybe they didn't treat you the way you deserved to be treated? Maybe they loved you back, but not as much as you loved them? Ever been there?"

Psh. No, I lied to myself. *Never been there.* I nervously crossed my legs and glanced around to see if anyone else could relate.

"That's the way God loves us," Grace continued. "God loves you even though, even when, and even if. Fill in the blanks with whatever, and I guarantee you God still loves you."

I thought about Daniel. Someone who seemed like he didn't even believe in God. Does God love those people too? How could she "guarantee" God's love for them?

"What about people who don't believe in God? I'm not that knowledgeable about this stuff but...don't they go to Hell?"

Grace sighed, not in frustration or annoyance, but in what seemed to be hesitance. I immediately regretted my question. "Yes, but unlike us, God separates who we are from the things we do. You can love someone and hate something that they do..." Grace trailed off and got quiet.

"I'm sorry if I made you uncomfortable I was just—"

"No, no," she insisted, "these conversations are so important, it's just—I don't have all the answers, and I don't want to speak too much without Biblical support."

"That makes two of us," I smiled awkwardly. "I don't know about anybody else, but all of this Bible stuff is so intimidating to me because I don't go to church. To be honest, I'm only here for a school project, but if I were here to develop a relationship with God or just to learn a little bit, I'd feel much better with just having an open conversation. Even if you didn't have all the answers." I noticed nearly everyone around me nodding to themselves, even the ones who were obviously regular church-goers at Agape.

"I guess what I was saying was, sometimes I hate the things I read in the Bible. To clarify, I hate the thought of people going to Hell because of a lack of belief, but there's things about God I'll probably never fully understand. What I think is fair and what God thinks is fair are two different things sometimes because, well, I'm human and He's God. The only perspective I have is my perspective as a human. All I know is that God created us, and for that simple fact alone He loves us—why else would He create us—create life?

"So, when it comes to people in Hell, I don't think it's because God hates the person. But anyway, I'm sorry I don't have Bible verses at the tip of my fingers to support what I'm saying… To be honest I don't know if there *is* a verse to support what I'm saying. I'm young and new to this Christian thing, too. I don't, and never will, have all the answers," Grace said.

I nodded. "I respect that."

Grace continued her lesson on the different forms of love, and I imagined the different forms in my own life. Melanie was definitely a *phileo* type of love. Daniel… Well, I wasn't sure about him, yet. But Ryan? As much as I wanted to claim it as *agape* love, my love for him was very much selfish—very much based on emotions. But it wasn't *eros* love, either. I didn't have the luxury of a physical connection to him—physical *attraction*, maybe, but it didn't matter, anyway. Ryan was an untouchable love.

When the study ended, I felt relief, but not in a bad way. I was glad that I hadn't walked into a shaming session—glad that I hadn't felt unwelcomed. Was I ready to walk around wearing a shirt that said "I heart Jesus" like I had taken a tour of Heaven and stopped by the giftshop on my way out? No. I wasn't there with this longing in my heart to get to know God, but I did leave wanting to have more conversations with Grace. It was a complete one-eighty from the conversation I'd had with Daniel, and I hoped that talking to Grace would help me find the right things to say to Daniel, or at least the right way to listen. Maybe that's what he wanted: to be heard.

"Hey, Gabby?" I heard someone call as I made my way out of the church. I turned to find Grace approaching me through the crowd of minglers. "Thank you for coming today. We've never really had a Bible study turn out like that," she said.

"Again, I'm sorry. I didn't mean to ruin the study, I just—"

"You didn't ruin it. I actually think you made it better. It felt really…raw and real, and it reminded me of why I started pursuing a relationship with God in the first place."

I didn't really know what to say. I was glad that I hadn't ruined her study, but I still felt so weird. It was all really new for me.

"Anyway, I wanted to invite you to our next Bible study on Wednesday night. We get together every Wednesday and Saturday, but Wednesdays are more relaxed. This Wednesday we're meeting at my house for game night, and I just wanted to make sure I invited you before you left," she said, scribbling on a napkin that I assumed she'd grabbed off the snack table in the church foyer. (I may or may not have taken a few extra napkins for my car, but that's not important.) "Hopefully this helps you get more info for your school project," she added as I took the napkin.

"Lord knows I need all the help I can get," I smiled.

CHAPTER 11

I went the entire weekend without hearing from Ryan. It obviously wasn't the first time, because he'd been so busy lately, but knowing that this time it was because he was upset with me made me a nervous wreck. That following Monday before lunch, I gave Melanie a rundown of what had happened, and she seemed to know something I didn't. We were in the bathroom, per our usual gossip routine.

"Why are you looking at me like that?" I asked.

"Like what?" she said, clearly trying to look normal. She really thought she could fool me. *Me.* HER BEST FRIEND. I stared at her with a self-explanatory *bitch, don't act like you don't know* face, and she hit me with the *I know why you're looking at me like that but I'm acting like I don't* face.

"Spill it," I demanded.

"So, I may or may not have talked to Ryan over the weekend, and he may or may not have already told me what happened, but I may or may not—"

"JUST SPIT IT OUT, MELANIE, DAMN."

"Ryan told me how he feels but he doesn't want me to tell you. I don't know if he's going to tell you himself or not, but once you know what he told me, you'll understand, trust me."

"Okay, great! So, what'd he say?" I asked, ignoring the "I can't tell you" part of her explanation.

"Nope. He needs to tell you himself," she asserted, walking toward the bathroom exit. I could tell she thought she was off the hook, but I had information I knew Ryan *hadn't* told her.

"He told me he likes me," I announced.

Melanie stopped in her tracks and looked like she nearly broke her neck turning to look back at me. "I'm sorry, what? Like—he *likes* you likes you?"

"I don't know, we were kinda in the middle of an argument so I didn't ask, but he compared liking me *'despite my flaws'* to how Indya likes him despite his. So? Maybe he meant he *likes me* likes me?"

"Ohhh, this is RICH!" Melanie sang in amusement. "Y'all on some *telenovela* shit!"

"Yeah, so are you going to play your role and tell me what he said, or WHAT?!" I pouted.

"Nope!" Melanie turned around and walked to the restroom door. "You know? You and Ryan are just alike; you both have things you need to say to each other, but neither of you has the *cojones* to have the conversation," she finished, swinging the door open and holding it for me to walk out. She may have won the battle, but this was war.

When we got to our lunch table, Indya was sitting there, but Ryan wasn't. I scanned the cafeteria for him and found him in the pizza line with some of his teammates. I looked back at Indya as I sat down with my food. She didn't seem upset or anything; she had already gotten her food and was eating when we got there. Usually they got their food together, which was why I was so suspicious. The real question, now, was: would he sit with us?

I was so caught up on Ryan that I had almost forgotten about Daniel. Almost. It wasn't until I saw Daniel and Ryan walking toward our table that I remembered that there was a guy who *was* man enough to talk to me. So, instead of stressing over the one who wouldn't, I was gonna focus on the one who would. Part of me hoped that seeing me place my energy elsewhere would make Ryan realize how ridiculous he was being, and then maybe he'd come around.

Besides, I didn't want to risk making him more upset by begging him to talk to me. He clearly had no problem talking about it—as long as it wasn't *me* he was talking to. The fact that he'd told Melanie what was wrong took me for surprise. Yes, they were good friends, but it's only because they had *me* as a mutual friend. Did Indya know what had happened? Was I the only one at our table in the dark?

I thought back to Daniel's party, to looking around, seeing all those people, and wondering what everyone was secretly feeling, going through, and suffering from. I thought there was nothing worse than suffering in silence and acting like you were okay. But right there in that moment, I realized that sometimes other people in the room know exactly what you're going through and they choose to not get involved out of their own loyalties, reservations, or issues. That might just be worse.

Now, I can admit, it would be dramatic to act like I was enduring so much pain and suffering and no one was helping me. It wouldn't be too far off if Indya knew and didn't help; she was his girlfriend, after all. And Melanie's way of helping me was by holding me accountable for my own feelings, which I understood, but I seriously hated that she chose to play Switzerland in this situation rather than tell me what he'd told her over the weekend.

Daniel and Ryan walked toward us and then *past* us to the basketball table. I saw a glimpse of Daniel's confusion when Ryan didn't part ways with him once he got to our table like he usually did. Unbelievable. If Ryan wanted me to see the bad in him, I was certainly seeing it now. My biased view of Ryan was fading with every moment I spent facing the wrath of his pettiness.

"So, does Ryan act like a child when he's mad at you, too?" I asked Indya in a sarcastically happy tone.

"Not really, I'm usually the one with a problem, honestly," she said sympathetically, getting up to go join him.

"Is that seat taken?" Daniel asked, suddenly standing behind Melanie and me. We both jumped in unison.

"*Dios mio*, boy! You can't be poppin' up on people like that!" Melanie half-yelled. I *knew* I wasn't crazy. The boy had some crazy superpower where he could appear out of thin air, no matter how good your peripheral vision was.

"No, the seat's not taken," I said, checking the heart rate monitor on my smartwatch.

As Daniel walked around to Ryan's seat, I got a closer look at his attire for the day. He had on a plain black shirt that accentuated his shoulders beautifully—and it wasn't even tight fitting! It just made him look so…*good*. The gold chain around his neck caught the light ever so slightly whenever he moved, and from the looks of his perfectly straight hairline, he had a fresh haircut. Seeing how good he looked made me quickly realize how crusty *I* looked. My hair had been thrown into a fluffy, frizzy bun because of the failed twist-out I'd attempted the night before, and I had absolutely no makeup on. Usually, at the very least, I'd fill in my brows and throw on a little mascara, but it was too much of a bother that morning after fighting with my hair.

"What's up with you and Ryan?" Daniel asked. What gave him the impression that *I* was the reason behind him not sitting with us?

"Why did you automatically assume that I did something?" I rebutted.

"I didn't assume that *you* did anything; I just asked what's up between you two," he said calmly. He had a point. I guess I was just defensive because deep down I felt like I *did* do something—though I had no idea what.

"If I knew what his issue was, I'd tell you," I explained.

"So, it's *him* who's not talking to *you*?" he inquired. *Finally,* someone who was just as clueless as I was! "His loss," he said, looking at me before taking a bite of his pizza. Up until then, I'd felt like I was the only one losing, but maybe Daniel had a point.

After lunch, Daniel walked me to my last few classes of the day, and the stares I got in the hallway reminded me of when I was the new kid being escorted to class by Ryan. Of course, they were mainly from girls. Go figure. I thought back to what Ryan had said about how Daniel moves from one girl to the next, and it made me wonder how many of those girls—the one's staring me down—Daniel had once made feel as special as I did in that moment.

I was a little annoyed that some of them were side-eyeing me like I was some sort of downgrade, but part of me felt for them. I knew exactly how it felt to be on their side of the gaze. The interesting thing was, there was nothing extra about us walking together. Nothing that warranted all the stares, at least. We weren't holding hands (thank GOD, because my hands were a sweaty, nervous mess), and he didn't have his arm around me or anything like that. It was the simple fact that this had never happened before—him and I walking together. I was the new "girl" this time, not the "new" girl. Even still, there was no denying how good it felt to get his undivided attention. The entire time we walked together, all I could think about was how I looked.

Is he looking at my hair?

I look terrible today. I knew I should've put on some mascara.

Get yourself together, Gabby. You don't even look that bad.

Who am I kidding? I'm a hot mess.

The ball of anxiety in my stomach was ever-growing. My smartwatch even had the audacity to ask if I was exercising because my heart rate was so high.

We slowed down as we got to my Sociology class, and I was prepared to give him the same friendly side-hug that I'd given him before the last class, but he lingered behind me as I approached the doorway.

"Gabby," Daniel said, grabbing my hand. "Wait a sec," he added as I turned to face him. The way he looked down at me was always so alluring. It made me want to bury my face in his chest and wrap my arms around him just to get that feeling of being held by someone bigger than me. We were standing right in the middle of the doorway to my class, perfectly visible to the people inside. "What are you doing later tonight?"

"Uh…nothing, I guess?" I said, confused. It was a Monday, so as usual, I had nothing planned except procrastinating.

"Wanna grab something to eat with me? I'll pick you up and everything," he smiled.

"Yeah, that'd be great," I agreed.

"Cool, I'll see you around eight." He stepped closer to me, leaned down, and kissed me gently on the forehead. I stood in the doorway, surprised, frozen, watching him walk away.

"Cool," I said softly. I turned to walk into class, only to find Melanie and Ryan staring at me with the same surprised expression I'm sure was mirrored on my face. Ryan quickly looked down at his phone and proceeded to scroll like nothing had happened, but there was no use in his pretending he hadn't seen anything.

You see me, now. Don't you, Ryan?

CHAPTER 12

Food was the last thing on my mind that night. My stomach no longer existed; there were butterflies in its place. Have you ever been so nervous that you felt like you had to poop? No? Just me? Okay.

At 7:55, I stood in front of my mirror yet again wondering if it was too late to do another outfit change. I had on black ripped jeans and an acid-washed graphic t-shirt from God knows where; it might have been Melanie's shirt, to be honest. I was comfortable, though, and I liked the outfit. But for some reason, that night felt like it was supposed to be special—I mean, I'd practically agreed to a date, right? Looking in the mirror, though, I didn't see *special*. I saw *dollar menu*. On the other hand, my hair was freshly washed and actually behaving, and my eyebrows looked flawless, so those two rarities gave me some hope for the night.

"You look cute," my mom said from my doorway.

"You're supposed to think that; you made me," I replied, analyzing my reflection.

"True, and I made one cute kid," she smiled. "What time is he supposed to be here?"

I looked at my watch: 8 P.M. "Actually, he should be here by n—" I was cut off by the sound of my doorbell. *Good save, Daniel. Good save.* My mom would not be impressed if he was late. I followed her down the stairs and stopped at the last step to watch their encounter when she opened the door.

I couldn't see him because my mom hadn't opened the door that wide, but the sound of his voice alone had my heart racing.

"Good evening, Mrs. Perkins, I'm here to take Gabby out to eat."

Tell her your name, Daniel, I thought.

"I'm Daniel," he added.

"Nice to meet you, Daniel," my mom said, reaching out to shake his hand. I couldn't quite gauge my mom's impression of him since I couldn't see her face, but she sounded normal. So far, so good.

"Love you, Mom, bye," I said, kissing her cheek as I squeezed past her to get outside. I thought my walking out would be an obvious cue for us to start heading toward Daniel's car, but instead, he pulled me to his side and threw his arm around my shoulder. It took every ounce of me to hide the internal panic I was enduring in front of my mom. I'd never shown any type of PDA around her, like, *ever*! (I'd also never had a boyfriend, but that's besides the point.)

For some reason, Daniel wasn't letting go; he was just standing there in front of my mom, finishing up whatever small talk they had started before I walked out. He held me so close to his body that my left cheek was squished against the side of his chest as we stood there. I could feel my heart race as I waited for some sign of my mom's disproval, but the smile on her face gave me the impression that she was amused to see her daughter practically glued to the side of a large teenaged boy.

Daniel's heartbeat was smooth and consistent—the complete opposite of mine. The muffled sound of his voice in my left ear was strong and confident. He was clearly a pro at this; I sensed no sign of nervousness whatsoever. *How many times has he done this? And why on a Monday of all nights?* I thought suddenly. Was someone else reserved for the weekend? My intrusive thoughts were cut short at the sound of my mom finally finishing their conversation.

"Okay, well, I'll let you guys get going. Have her home by 11 P.M., please, Daniel. And don't bring her back with anything she ain't leave this house with," she said, looking at me for the last part. She was acting cool right now, but she'd kill us both if I came home with the faintest smell of sex on me. If I came home pregnant, she'd kill us, bring us back to life, and then kill us again. And don't get me started on STDs.

"Yes, ma'am. Nice meeting you," Daniel chortled, releasing me from his embrace. Now that my face wasn't smashed against his body, I could get a good look at him. He was still fine as hell, nothing new. He smelled amazing, like he'd actually taken a shower before coming to get me instead of just bathing in cologne after his basketball practice. He had on a dark blue jacket, a white t-shirt, and jeans—simple, but he made it look so good. I could see his chain peeking out from underneath his shirt at the collar. Somehow, it still managed to shine in the nighttime.

When we approached his car, I was surprised to see that he didn't drive anything luxurious. I'd thought for sure with a house like his, he'd be rolling around in something I couldn't pronounce on the first try. Granted, it was definitely not a base model—he had what appeared to be a custom, two-tone paint job: it looked black from a distance, but when I saw it under the porchlight in my driveway, there was a glimmer of dark red. His windows were cracked open, allowing me to see the red stitching in his black, leather interior.

"Let me get that for you," he said, opening the passenger-side door for me.

"Thank you," I smiled. In my mind, Daniel didn't really seem like the chivalrous type. Honestly speaking, I expected player tendencies from him—the nonchalant, *I'm not gonna chase you* act you see in movies. Ryan had painted him that way, but I had yet to see it.

"So," I began as Daniel got in the driver's seat, "where are we off to?"

"It's a surprise," he smirked, putting the car in reverse. He slowly let off the brake and then stopped suddenly. I looked at him in confusion.

"Safety first," he said, motioning for me to put my seatbelt on.

"Right." I rolled my eyes playfully. "For all I know, you drive like a maniac. How reckless of me," I teased.

We drove for a bit before pulling up to a drive-thru at a fairly insignificant-looking burger place I'd never seen before. Maybe it's my fault for watching unrealistic rom coms all the time, but this was far less romantic and cute than what I'd anticipated. Was he planning on eating in his car and then trying to swindle me into the backseat like he'd probably done with other girls?

"Order for Daniel," he said as he pulled up to the window. Apparently, he'd already ordered us our food for the night. "The surprise is coming, I promise," he said as he handed me the large paper bag they'd passed him through the window. I'm sure it was all over my face that I was less than enthused, but his affirmation rid me of any skeptical attitude I was carrying.

Give him a chance, Gabby, geez, I thought. The night had barely started, and I was already letting my expectations control my perspective instead of enjoying the moments for what they were.

"You seemed really comfortable talking to my mom," I said as we pulled off. I hoped that some small talk would help me relax.

"What makes you say that?" he asked. The look on his face seemed amused.

"You were just so…calm. Your heartbeat was normal, and you spoke so well. I would've been a nervous wreck talking to one of your parents for the first time."

"Why do you think I pulled you so close to me?" he asked, glancing at me briefly before looking back at the road.

"I…really don't know, honestly. You took me by surprise—*literally*. This is the most you've touched me, let alone in one day."

"I did it to calm my nerves. Having you to hold onto made me feel…strong, in a sense. I didn't feel so out in the open and—"

"Vulnerable," I finished.

"Yeah," he admitted. How sweet was that? Hugging me made him feel secure. Maybe he hadn't done this as many times as I'd thought.

"Although…girls usually hug me back when I hug them," he teased. I laughed at the thought of how ridiculous I must've looked with my face pressed against Daniel's chest and my arms dangling at my sides.

"I'm sorry. I just—I panicked because we were in front of my mom," I started. "I wanted to hug you back, though, I promise." I laughed. "I would've never guessed you were nervous."

"I know I have a track record with girls, but it's never been like *this*. You weren't *trying* to catch my attention, you just…did. When I started talking to you, you didn't try to play hard to get or try too hard to be interesting. So, here we are on a Monday night—which I've never done, by the way," he explained.

"Soooo, you like a girl that doesn't try at all. Got it," I joked. He chuckled to himself and shook his head.

"Not even that; it's the fact that you didn't just see me as some *'cute basketball player.'* You didn't see me at all, really, but it made me feel like I could get to know you without you seeing what you wanted to see in me. I felt like I had a clean slate with you."

Suddenly, things with Ryan made sense. But I must've looked like I'd found the cure for cancer, because my expression caught Daniel off guard.

"What's wrong? Why are you looking like that?" he asked, glancing back and forth between me and the road.

"I think I know why Ryan is upset, now. He's so used to being seen as one of the star basketball players that he felt like no one really saw him as *Ryan*. He must've thought I was like any other groupie who made him into what I wanted him to be," I explained.

"Why would he think that?" I could hear the agitation in his voice; I couldn't tell if it was because I'd brought Ryan up, or because he was confused.

"Remember that day you scared me in the parking lot? Right before that, I was with Ryan, and I asked him if there was anything wrong about him. I guess it triggered him that I only saw good things about him."

"Sounds like he had an expectation that you didn't know about and then got upset when you didn't meet it. That's not fair."

Had Daniel always been so insightful? Even though he was talking about Ryan, it applied to me, too. Moments ago, I was fighting an attitude in the drive-thru because of what I thought the night was going to be like.

"You're right; it isn't fair. I had to check myself a few minutes ago for letting my expectations get to me, too."

"What were you expecting?" he asked.

"Some silly, romantic comedy shit, I guess. I've also been hoping you won't live up to the *'player'* reputation I've been warned about."

"Well, maybe one of those expectations is actually true. We're here," he said, putting the car in park. We were at some sort of playground, but it sat at the top of a hill that overlooked the city. There was a picnic table, some swings, and a seesaw.

"I know it's kind of cliché, but I like coming up here every now and then when my dad and I get into it. It's a good place to clear your head."

"I love this!" The little kid in me wanted to race to the swing set, but we still hadn't eaten.

Daniel opened my door for me and then grabbed a folded sheet from his backseat. The food smelled nothing like burgers, but it did smell amazing. He took the sheet and spread it across the picnic table before we sat down.

"What's in here?" I asked, handing him the bag so he could sort everything out.

"That burger place we were at has a secret menu. I got us their Cajun chicken wings and Cajun fries. I don't want to brag early, but…let's just say I'm about to change your life."

I wish I could say he lied, but they were by far the best wings I'd ever had. Daniel sat across from me, waiting to hear my opinion, as if my face didn't say it all while I was eating. "Good, huh?" he smiled.

"*Good* isn't even the word. I'm in love," I gushed, picking up another wing.

"Hold on, I gotta get this moment on camera." He took out his phone and then began recording. "Just showed Gabby the best wings in the world," he narrated. I smiled shyly and shielded my eyes from the flash on his phone.

"Do you mind if I post this?" He turned his phone toward me so I could see what he'd captured. He'd recorded me on his Instagram story, and put heart-eye emojis in his caption.

"I don't mind, but only because you got my good side. Oh, and…don't tag my account in it. I don't want random girls stalking my profile because of this."

"Trust me, they'll find a way. They're like little piranhas trying to find the next girl to devour."

Oh, I know, I thought. Because I was one of them. I'd spent most of that afternoon looking through his social media. Did he have any pictures with girls? Which girls were commenting on his posts a lot?

Was he commenting back? Did he like their pictures? Were they flirt-buddies? And so on. Truthfully, I liked being posted; it felt like he wasn't ashamed to be with me. Even though we were just hanging out as friends, it meant something…right? I felt like I was being shown off—claimed even. The evil part of me liked the fact that some girl's hopes of getting with him may have been shattered. *Fall in line, sweetheart. It's my turn.*

"Wanna go to the swings?" he asked once we were done eating.

My heart jumped a little. "I thought you'd never ask!"

I sat on one of the swings and let Daniel push me. I was in my very own romance movie at the moment. This was typically one of those scenes where something cute but corny happened, like the guy pulling his love interest toward him by the chains of the swing so they can have their long-awaited first kiss together. If my night went the same, it would be my first ever.

"You know, one of the reasons why I wanted to take you out tonight was to get your mind off of this thing with Ryan," he admitted.

"And what were the other reasons?" I asked. My grip tightened around the swing chains as I prepared for whatever answer he gave me.

"I wanted to show you the way you deserve to be treated," I heard him say as I gently swayed back to him.

"What do you mean?" I stopped the swinging with my feet and readjusted myself so that I was facing him.

"Is what *might* be going through Ryan's head worth him treating you the way he's treating you?" he asked.

From my own, selfish standpoint, it wasn't worth it, but from a standpoint that considered Ryan's emotions, I was willing to respect his process. Who was I to force someone to speak to me? I didn't think this situation was worth losing him as a friend completely, and if that meant waiting for him to be ready to have that conversation, then so be it.

"At first I was really upset, but the more I think about it, the more I know that I don't want to force him to speak to me," I sighed.

"Gabby," Daniel said, squatting so that he was just below face-level to me. "I know it doesn't involve me, but the way he walked past you today shocked me, and I could see that it bothered you. It's one thing to need space, it's another thing to not even tell you that he needs space."

We were quiet for a moment while I digested that, and then he grabbed my hand and placed it on his chest. "Feel," he said. His heart was pounding. "This is how I felt from the moment I rang your doorbell up until the moment I held you. I think you're amazing, and for Ryan to treat you like you're not blows my mind.

"Watch this." He stood up, pulling me up with him. He wrapped his arms around me in a bear hug, and I did the same. I laid my head against the center of his chest, and after only a few seconds, the frantic, pounding heartbeat he'd shown me moments before became steady and more relaxed.

"Wow," I said softly. "But why me?" I took a step back to look at him. "How is it that I can make your heart pound like you're terrified and then return to normal like nothing ever happened?"

"I don't know. I just know that I've never met anyone like you, Gabby. I feel crazy even talking about this, but…" He shook his head and looked at me for a moment.

"But what?" I asked, my voice barely above a whisper.

"I see you, Gabby, and I won't ever treat you like I don't. I know Ryan's your best friend—shit, he's probably mine, too—but…I can't just sit around and watch him treat you like you don't exist."

Daniel stepped closer to me, placed his hand under my chin, and gently tilted my head up toward his. He leaned down and brought his face dangerously close to mine. I could barely breathe. I was frozen. This was really happening.

"May I?" he asked softly. I nodded, and he finally ended the anticipation with a kiss. His lips blended softly into mine, like puzzle pieces that fit smoothly into the empty spaces of one another.

He was detail oriented, exploring my bottom lip, and then the top, and then both of them again. His hand under my chin kept me in perfect sync with his direction; when he needed me low, I was lower, high, I was higher. His other hand rested firmly on my waist, pressing me against him tightly. I rested my arms atop his shoulders, interlocking my hands behind his neck. He was very good at his craft, if I did say so myself—not sloppy, not too aggressive, yet passionate. First kiss or not, I knew it was exactly how every girl wanted a kiss to feel.

When he pulled away from me, he kept my chin in his hand. "I want to be the guy who never lets you forget how special you are," he asserted. I bit my lip in an attempt to conceal the fact that I was flattered, but I'm sure my enjoyment was peeking through.

"Okay," I smiled, burying my face shyly into his chest. This was better than any movie scene I'd pictured.

CHAPTER 13

Tuesday crept up on me faster than I'd anticipated. I was nervous for how the day would go now that Daniel and I were a thing. I hadn't even told Melanie, yet, and I wasn't sure how she'd react.

I pulled into my usual parking spot between Ryan and Melanie, and to my surprise, Daniel was there, too. He had parked his car in the spot in front of mine and was leaning against the hood of his car talking to Ryan when I pulled up. Melanie was sitting in her car, finishing up her makeup, as usual. Ryan and Daniel watched as I pulled into my spot with smiles on their faces, and I immediately felt my face heat up. My embarrassment was immediately interrupted with confusion; had Ryan magically forgotten about being upset with me? What had they been talking about before I got there?

Daniel walked up to my door and opened it for me.

"Thank you." I smiled coyly as I got out. He kissed me on my forehead and pulled me into a giant hug. My left cheek was pressed against his chest again, and I was able to catch Melanie look at me funny as she got out of her car.

"Good morning," Daniel said warmly. I could feel the vibration of his voice through his chest.

"You smell really good," I smiled, pulling out of our hug and grabbing my backpack. "Where's Indya?" I said to Ryan, who was looking at me with the same, funny look Melanie was giving me now that Daniel and I were holding hands. Melanie walked over and stood next to Ryan; they leaned against the side of his car, and Daniel and I leaned against the side of mine. We stood there, facing each other awkwardly as I waited for Ryan to answer my question.

"What's going on?" Melanie asked.

"Well, I asked Ryan a question, and now we're all standing here looking at each other like we're stupid. Does that about cover it?" I said to Daniel sarcastically.

"Yeah. That's pretty accurate," Daniel agreed.

"No, not that. *That*," she said, referencing Daniel and I holding hands.

"It's exactly what it looks like," Daniel laughed.

"No way?!" Melanie asked enthusiastically. I nodded my head, happy that she was excited and not upset. "We're *definitely* talking in health class," she smiled. She was smiling a lot harder than I would have expected, especially since we had just argued about Daniel a couple weeks ago.

"Indya's at home sick," Ryan finally answered, straightening up and adjusting his bag on his shoulder. "Congrats, bro," he said to Daniel, dapping him up.

We had barely made it across the parking lot to the main building before I noticed the stares again. It would continue throughout the day until it somehow felt normal. Even when Daniel and I weren't with each other, I still got stares. That's high school, for you. News travels fast.

One thing I appreciated about Daniel was that he wasn't corny. He didn't insist on carrying my books everywhere and didn't race across campus to walk me to every class. The times we were around each other were simple; there was no excessive touching, kissing, or whatever else. It was chill, yet I still felt special.

Since I hadn't really known Daniel until that semester, I wasn't aware of any past relationships he had been in—that is, until my second class of the day. That's when I learned that there was only one other girl at our school who he'd been in a relationship with.

I learned this when I overheard some girls behind me whispering about her (and me) in class. Her name was Tanya, and I'd always known we had that class together, I just never knew her name or that she was Daniel's ex. Apparently, this was the day that she'd also learned my name, because I caught her staring at me multiple times throughout class. Unfortunately, her staring at me gave me the chance to realize how beautiful she was.

Her skin was about the same as mine: rich and chocolate in all its splendor. She had curls with a looser curl pattern than mine, and she had her hair in a high puff that made mine look like I had just rolled out of bed. I liked my hair sometimes, but I didn't love it. I'd always envied the looser curl patterns and how they seemed to be more willing to cooperate. When the bell rang, I got to examine her figure as she stood up to leave and… Let's just say I've insulted myself enough in this paragraph, so I won't compare myself to her any further. We never exchanged words, but the look she gave me said it all: she was bothered.

I never really talk about my other classes, just Advanced Health, lunch (my favorite class), and Sociology, because that's where all the important stuff happens, but every class that day felt significantly different. People I had never talked to before felt the need to say hello to me. Some didn't even bother saying hello and skipped right into asking me if Daniel and I were together. I answered every person assertively, without hesitation, until it was Melanie who asked during Advanced Health.

"Sooooo, Daniel made you his girlfriend?! How'd he ask?" she whispered during our health class. (We were watching a documentary on substance abuse, but naturally, Melanie and I weren't paying much attention.) I glanced over at Daniel across the classroom and pondered her question. He'd never really said, *"Hey, Gabby, will you be my girlfriend?"* so I wasn't quite sure how to answer.

"What do you mean?" I asked. I knew what she meant, but I needed to buy some time to think about my response.

"Well, remember when Marcus asked me? We were at a pizza place, and he got the cooks to make my pizza in the shape of a heart. When they brought our plates out, he asked me! It was really cute," she gushed, like I hadn't heard this story a million times.

"Wait a minute, why are you so excited all of a sudden? Weren't you telling me not to get too invested in Daniel not too long ago?" I said, remembering how weird it was that Melanie was actually happy about this.

"Yes, but I talked to my mom about it, and she said sometimes the best way to get over someone is to just move on. Plus, I see how happy you are when you talk to Daniel, so the least I can do is be happy that you're happy."

Move on. I had considered moving on when I first started talking to Daniel, but only because I was desperate to avoid telling Ryan how I felt. Now that I was actually taking steps to move forward and not obsess over Ryan, though, I started to wonder: could I truly move on from him? I almost felt like I'd be betraying him if I did. Was that weird?

"Wow, thanks, Mel. I'm not gonna lie, I was hella nervous to tell you," I said as we packed our things to go to lunch.

"So back to my question! How'd he ask?!" she repeated. She clearly wasn't gonna forget about this question.

"Actually, he—"

"Forget about me already?" Daniel said, catching Melanie and me at the door. I turned around and smiled.

"Sorry! Force of habit," I laughed, grabbing his hand.

"Hey, Dan. Can I call you Dan? Yeah, so, a lot has happened in the past twenty-four hours, and my best friend was *just* about to catch me up on everything. So, could you give us some girl time while she fills me in?" Melanie said, grabbing my other hand and swinging our arms playfully.

"Fine. As long as you promise to give her back," he said, winking at me as he walked ahead to catch up to some of his friends.

♥ ♥ ♥

Since Indya was out sick and Ryan was still being weird, Melanie and I had our end of our lunch table to ourselves and I sat across from her instead of next to her; it made talking easier, but I could also look at Daniel at one of the tables behind her for my own personal enjoyment.

"So—"

"Yes, yes, *'back to your question,'* I know! He didn't really *ask me*, ask me. It was sort of implied," I explained—more so as a question than a statement.

"Well, how did he *'imply'* that he wanted you to be his girlfriend?" Melanie asked with air quotes.

"He took me to this playground with an amazing view, and we ate some *really* good wings from some secret menu at this burger place. And after that, he pushed me on the swi—"

"Okay, usually I'm all for the details, but, please, just fast forward to the point!" Melanie interrupted.

"I'M GETTING THERE. So, I'm on the swing set and he brings up Ryan. He asks me if I feel like I deserve to be ignored by Ryan, and then proceeds to tell me how special I am and how he wants to be the one to treat me the way I should be treated. It was way more romantic than that, but since you want the movie review version instead of the movie premiere version, that's how it happened. And he's an amazing kisser, by the way."

"And you're *sure* he meant that he wanted you to be his girlfriend? I'm not trying to kill the mood, I just don't want you to get played. Boys love to treat you like you're the only one and then out of nowhere they're talking to someone else and they hit you with the *'we were never official'* line," she explained.

She had a point, but I didn't want to look stupid and be that girl who asks "what are we?" to the guy she's into. It seemed like such a pitiful thing to do, and I barely had enough dignity as it was. I mean, look at how pathetic I was over Ryan!

"I think so," I muttered. I glanced over at Daniel's table, only to find his seat empty. I scanned the cafeteria and found him near the trash bins talking to Tanya. They seemed to be arguing about something.

"Look over there," I said to Melanie, gesturing toward them with a head bob. "Do you know anything about Tanya?"

"No, I've never even heard of her, why?"

"That's his ex."

Melanie nearly choked on her French fry and snapped her head back toward me. "No way? Why are they talking?"

"Your guess is as good as mine. Should I go over there?"

"No. Going over there makes you look threatened—like you have to mark your territory. Just watch and see how it plays out," she said, turning back around to watch them.

Their exchange didn't last long; it looked like she was still trying to argue when he walked away from her. He glanced in our direction as he headed back to his table and Melanie and I quickly averted our eyes and tried to act like we weren't just watching them intently.

"Have you and Ryan talked yet?" she asked. "I was just thinking about what Daniel asked you, and even though I totally understand where Ryan is coming from, I kind of agree with Daniel. Do you think you deserve to be treated the way Ryan's treating you?"

"Not for this long, no. I think I'm just going to walk up to him today after school and ask him straight up why he's upset with me."

I felt confident when I told Melanie that, but my heart was nearly beating out of my chest as the school day wound down. Confronting him in my head was much easier than doing it in person. What was I even going to say? How was I going to ask? Was I going to demand that he talk to me, or be easygoing and nice?

When our Sociology class ended, Melanie was giving me a *"what are you waiting for"* look as we packed our things, but I chickened out.

Daniel was waiting for me outside of class, and unfortunately smiling wasn't my immediate reaction. I'd started this day out with such a different energy, but now my head was a mess of emotions. Was I his girlfriend? What was wrong with Ryan? And why the hell had Tanya been talking to Daniel at lunch?!

"What's wrong?" Daniel asked, frowning when he didn't get my usual smile.

We started making our way to the gym since he had basketball practice, and I came right out with it, "What was Tanya talking to you about at lunch?"

"Ah, so you saw that," he started. "She's still upset about our breakup. She thinks I was talking to you while she and I were together and that *you're* the reason I broke up with her before winter break."

"I didn't even know you existed before winter break," I laughed.

"Exactly. It drove me crazy how insecure she was. It felt like she never trusted me."

I wondered if I would come off as insecure if I asked him to clarify whether I was really his girlfriend or not. "Maybe she was just scared to lose you to someone else," I said, speaking on behalf of myself more than her.

"She had no reason to feel that way. Yes, I get a lot of attention, and yes, I can be a flirt, but when I decide to commit to someone, it's because I truly want them and only them," he explained. I loved seeing how serious he got about his emotions. He didn't blow them off, he actually talked about them. It was kind of cute.

I thought back to what Ryan had told me: *"He never commits."* Was I actually a commitment to him? Everything in me was telling me I was. It didn't feel like something that had to be explicitly declared, but Melanie had made a *damn* good point at lunch that day. I just couldn't bring myself to ask him, though. Especially not after his saying Tanya's insecurity drove him crazy.

We'd been hanging around outside the gym for a few minutes when Ryan approached us. "Do you mind if I talk to Gab, real quick?" he asked Daniel.

Daniel took a moment before responding, looking between Ryan and me like he was debating whether or not to share me. We all looked at each other awkwardly before Daniel finally answered, "Go ahead, bro. She's been in high demand all day." He smirked at me and then gave me a hug before heading into the gym.

"Hey," Ryan said on a long, drawn-out breath. His hands were tucked behind his back, and his gaze met the tiled floor between us, like there was weight on his shoulders keeping him from holding his head high.

"'Sup, stranger?" I said.

"I'm sorry I haven't spoken to you lately. I've just been, uh…dealing with stuff," he started.

"Look, Ryan, I don't know what I said wrong, but I didn't mean to hurt you, and I'm really sorry that I did."

"You don't have to be sorry. I know you meant well. There's just something I've never told you and I don't know how to open up about it…" he murmured. Oh my god. Was he going to confess his love for me now that I was in a relationship (maybe) with Daniel? Oh my god.

He sighed and then continued, "When you asked if there was anything wrong with me, it wasn't that you saw so much good in me that made me upset, it was that that's *all* you could see. It felt like you only had room in your life for the 'perfect' Ryan. Just like my dad." He paused.

Your dad? I thought, furrowing my brows in confusion, but he looked troubled, so I decided to stay quiet and let him finish.

"I take basketball pretty seriously. I mean, you know this already because we always talk less during basketball season, but a big part of that is because of my dad. When I lose games or I don't do as well as he wants, he gets so angry and…and abusive—verbally, physically, you name it. It's like he only recognizes me as his son when I'm the Ryan who everyone puts on a pedestal—the all-star, the perfect gentleman, the guy all the girls want.

"There have been so many days that I've come to school after fighting with my dad the night before, and no one seemed to notice that I wasn't okay, not even you. Last summer when I was talking to Indya, she noticed it one day and asked me what was wrong—after only a couple months of talking to me, she noticed. She was the first person I really opened up to about it, and I never imagined I'd be telling her and not you.

"And sometimes I would get so angry with you…because not *once* have you ever noticed that pain in my eyes and said something about it. You're my best friend, and I wanted so badly to confide in you without having to just blurt out *'by the way, I have an abusive father.'* I wanted you to notice and speak up because I didn't have the strength to admit it by myself. There were some times when you would look like you had something to tell me and I would desperately hope that you were finally going to ask me what was going on, but it never happened. I needed you to be my reason to let it out.

"But sometimes people don't know things unless we speak up, so it wasn't fair for me to hold that over your head, and I really am sorry. I mean, how *could* you notice what I was going through when I distance myself from everyone during basketball season? You would've never known from the times you were around my dad because he's really good at saving face when he's with other people, and now that I think about it, so am I. And really, the only reason Indya could tell something was wrong was because she stopped by my place unannounced one day, right after a fight I'd had with my dad. So, once again, I'm sorry, Gabby. I really am."

Oh. My. God. I could see the weight evaporate from his shoulders as he spoke, but there was now a cloud over me raining all of it onto mine.

"Ryan, I—I'm so sorry, I really had no idea. I feel terrible." I shook my head. At Daniel's party I was wondering what *strangers* were secretly going through, not knowing that my own best friend had a secret battle of his own.

He gave me a hug and reassured me that he wasn't mad at me anymore, but *I* was mad at me. How terrible was it that I had such deep feelings for him but couldn't even notice when he was hurting? What kind of friend was I?

CHAPTER 14

My heart was in my stomach as I left the school parking lot. How do you go back to normal after learning something like that? I headed straight to Melanie's house—unannounced and most certainly unexpected. How was she able to keep something so dark to herself but not seem troubled by it? Did she even know what Ryan told me, or did he give her a watered-down synopsis? If she *did* know what Ryan had told me, then I completely understood why she had chosen not to fill me in.

I didn't know what to do with this new information; it almost felt like a burden, because what could I do? How could I help? After he'd told me what was going on, I'd demanded we speak to someone about it, but he was adamant that we didn't.

"I'll handle it on my own, Gabby, really," he insisted.

All I could do now was knowingly see Ryan suffer through something and offer an ear to talk to, or a shoulder to lean on. I wished that I could make it stop, but how exactly would I do that? Did I walk up to Ryan's doorstep and tell his dad *"hey, you need to stop abusing your son!"* and risk him hurting Ryan even more for telling me? What if his mother knew nothing about it, and I tore apart a family by confronting them?

When I pulled up to Melanie's house, she was still sitting in her car in her driveway with the engine running. She rolled the window down as I walked up to her. "Hey, what are you doing here?" she asked.

"I need to talk to you," I said, choking on my pride as I fought the urge to cry. When I got closer, she noticed my expression and unlocked her car door.

"Get in! What's wrong? What happened? We were together not even forty minutes ago!"

"Did you know?" I said as I got into her passenger's seat.

"Know what? Here, mama," she asked, handing me a napkin. I was now in full-blown tears.

"Ryan!" I huffed. Her face immediately showed understanding.

"He finally told you."

"So, you knew?" I said, melting into her seat. "Did you find out when he told you why he was mad at me?"

"Yeah, and it shocked the hell out of me, too, but it really wasn't my business to tell. He just kind of exploded during a random conversation we were having about a class assignment. I don't even think he meant for me to know."

"I feel like such a shitty friend. How could I not notice? As much energy as I spent on him—as much attention I gave him, and I didn't even notice. But guess who did?" I cried.

"Okay, but you know what, Gabby? You have a place in Ryan's life that is special in its own way, and honestly, this moment isn't even about making comparisons between yourself and Indya— really, it never has been. What matters now is that you *do* know, G. And all you can do is what *you* can do, and that's to be Gabby, Ryan's friend."

"I just hate that what I *can* do can't make it stop," I sniffled.

"I feel the same way. But you can't put that weight on yourself. You feel bad for not noticing, and now you want to overcompensate by making everything okay again. The best thing you can do for him is be a better friend now that you know what you know. Maybe simply being there for him will give him the strength to deal with it when he's ready."

Melanie was my therapist; she just didn't know it yet. She was so right, so absolutely 100% right. Sometimes it surprised me how wise this girl was when it came to helping me. Deep down, I knew if she told herself half of what she said to me, she would worry way less about losing Marcus.

We sat there for a while, until I was okay.

"Thank you for the talk," I sighed, finally coming down from my emotions.

"Anytime. Text me when you make it home, mama," she said, reaching out to hug me before I got out.

The next day at lunch was like seeing things through a new set of glasses. I scrutinized every emotion on Ryan's face, trying to sense whether he was alright or not to see if there were any mannerisms I had missed before. Things were normal, though. He was back at our table, but Daniel was sitting across from me now. Ryan was sitting across from Melanie, and Indya was still at home sick.

"So…are you two good now?" Daniel asked. We were all recovering from laughing at a meme Melanie had shown us on her phone.

"Yeah," I confirmed, briefly looking at Ryan and then at Daniel. Now that Ryan and I were back on good terms, this Daniel situation was really smacking me in the face. I was sitting across from one guy I really liked and another guy I had an unspoken love for. Yikes. I thought about what Melanie had told me, though: "…*be Gabby, Ryan's friend.*" It would be a lot easier said than done.

As I casually spoke with Daniel, I noticed Tanya glaring at me from the table right behind him. Had she really sat at that table this entire semester and I hadn't noticed, or was she sitting there now to get a better view of Daniel and me? Whichever the case, her staring problem was starting to piss me off.

"Your ex is staring at me," I said, cutting him off. He began to turn his head, but I kicked him under the table.

"DON'T look! She'll know we're talking about her," I explained.

"Never look unless instructed, D, everybody knows that," Melanie said. "So…who are we not looking at?" she asked.

"Tanya. She's staring at me and Daniel." Since Melanie was sitting right next to me, all she had to do was glance between Daniel and Ryan to see her, so it was less obvious that she was looking.

"Don't worry about her," he said. "She's jealous."

"Yeah, well, I'm tired of her staring at me, so I'm gonna see what her problem is," I said, abruptly leaving my seat and walking to Tanya's table. There was an empty seat right next to her, so I uninvitedly took it.

"May I help you?" she asked with an attitude that matched the facial expressions she'd been giving me.

"Yes, actually. You can help me understand why you keep staring at me. I'm intrigued," I retorted.

"Well, now that you're up close and personal, I no longer have a reason to stare. I was just trying to see if you were important enough for Daniel to give you a necklace when he asked you out," she explained, fiddling with a diamond necklace she had around her neck, as if to imply that he'd given it to her.

"And what would that prove exactly?"

"That you're actually his girlfriend, but judging by your neck, you're just another clueless girl who'll think she's special for the next month or so," she smirked. "How *did* he ask you out, by the way? With a chicken wing?" she laughed with her friends. Apparently, she'd seen his Instagram story from when we hung out that Monday.

"You know, I was wondering why Daniel was no longer with someone as gorgeous as you, but now that we've had a chance to chat, it makes perfect sense," I replied, getting up from the table. "Oh, and stop staring, it's creepy."

"Well, now that I know there's not much to look at, that won't be a problem," she smiled sarcastically.

That bitch.

The bell rang, and instead of walking back to my table, I walked out of the cafeteria. I started to make my way to the girls' restroom but realized that Tanya could easily follow me there and see how bothered she'd made me. Somehow, she'd managed to hit the one soft spot I had with Daniel: not knowing for certain whether I was his girlfriend.

I felt someone grab my arm from behind as I tried to evade public attention. "Hey. *Hey!* Where are you going?" It was Daniel.

"I just needed some air," I explained, turning to face him.

"Are you okay? What did she say to you?"

"She showed me her necklace," I said, looking away from him at the people passing by. I didn't want him to see that I was bothered because I wasn't prepared to ask him if I was actually his girlfriend. I was so scared that Tanya would actually be right—that maybe I wasn't as special as I thought I was.

"Her necklace…" Daniel said to himself, clearly trying to figure out what I was talking about.

"You gave her a necklace when you asked her out," I explained to jog his memory.

"I didn't give her a necklace," he said, confused.

"That's what she said—well, she never really said it." I paused, recalling our conversation. "She said she was trying to see if I had a necklace as a sign that you had asked me out. She made it seem like the necklace around her neck was from you," I finished, realizing as I spoke that I'd gotten played and that my reaction to what she'd said made it clear that I was insecure about my relationship—or whatever I was in—with Daniel.

Daniel sighed, then seemed to realize something. "That necklace is from my mom. She was cleaning out her jewelry collection one day while Tanya and I were at my house, and she gave it to her," Daniel explained. "I never gave that to her to make us official, and she knows that. She's trying to make you feel like you're not special to me because that's how she feels about herself," he finished, wiping a tear from my cheek that had managed to escape from the utter embarrassment I felt.

We were only a couple classrooms away from the cafeteria because I hadn't made it far before Daniel caught up to me. I was facing the cafeteria with my shoulder against some lockers, so I could see the crowd beginning to thicken around us as students left the lunch room. It wasn't long until I spotted Tanya walking in our direction with her friends.

"Why don't we show Tanya how stupid her little game was?" I asked.

"And how do you suggest we do that?" he prodded.

"Surprise me," I said, staring Tanya down.

Without warning, he pulled me closer to him by my waist and kissed me just like he had the very first time. It wasn't exactly what I'd had in mind, but I had no complaints.

"How was that?" he said softly as he pulled away.

"Perfect," I replied. I'd been so enchanted by his kiss that I had nearly forgotten that it was to get back at Tanya for her mind games. He followed it up with a forehead kiss and then held me in a hug.

I turned my head back in Tanya's direction and saw a look of sadness on her face as she passed us, but instead of satisfaction, I felt empathy. I saw myself in her eyes. I saw the feeling of watching someone you care about be with someone else, and knowing there's nothing you can do about it. And the worst part was, no matter how good his kisses were, it still didn't satisfy the fact that I simply needed to hear—directly out of his mouth—that I was his girlfriend.

And I still hadn't. I'd let this become a bigger deal than it should've been, just like I had with my feelings for Ryan. All I had to do was open my mouth and communicate, but fear had a hold on me that was tighter than Daniel's grip around my waist.

CHAPTER 15

That evening was the Wednesday Bible-thing at Grace's house, and to tell you the truth, I wasn't sure about going to a stranger's house after only meeting them once. I probably shouldn't have, just to be safe, but it was something to distract me from everything I had on my mind.

Plus, if she actually did end up being a serial killer, she would kill me and cut me into a million pieces so I could finally, as they say, *"rest in peace,"* or, in my case, pieces. (Was that too dark? Yes? Okay. Only a thousand pieces, then.)

I could hear people inside when I rang Grace's doorbell, and it eased my nerves a little to know this wasn't a ploy to get me alone and "Jesus" me to death. I had hoped that there would be newbies like myself there, so I wouldn't feel like the only clueless one as she discussed the seemingly mystical concepts of the Bible. As I waited at the door, I suddenly became conscious of what I was wearing (yet again). Did I have on anything that they might see as too short or too revealing? Nope. I was in the clear, not even ripped jeans. No knee-sluttery this time.

"Gabby, hi! I'm glad you made it!" Grace smiled as she opened her door. "Feel free to grab some snacks in the kitchen, we'll be meeting in the living room."

Her kitchen was set up with cute stations with everything from vegetables to fruit, meat kabobs, and even sweets. There were about eight of us so far from what I could see—mostly girls, but there were a few guys in the mix. Grace went around and introduced me to everyone, but I forgot their names just as soon as I'd learned them. The only one I remembered was Hope, the girl who seemed like she was happy every minute of every day.

I was determined to take better notes for my Sociology project this time around since all I had so far was the phrase "strangely happy." I'm quite sure I wrote that because of Hope.

That night, I had to look for things such as their demographics, social structure, and social interactions. Unfortunately, the only way I'd be able to get this information was by *actually* socializing. I couldn't get away with being a fly on the wall like I wanted to. I had to talk and mingle and get shit done. Oh boy.

Grace had left my side after all the introductions to tend to other guests and answer the door, so I gravitated to the brownies on her kitchen island. Chocolate was my comfort food.

Maybe that's why I gravitated to Daniel during my Ryan crisis, with all of his chocolate-skinned beauty—but now, I needed *real* chocolate to cope with my human-chocolate stress. Hope was also lingering in the kitchen, looking around at everyone else. For someone who was so radiant, I'd expected her to be more social.

"Hi, Hope," I said meekly as I walked over to her. She was by the baby carrots, for some reason. Who eats carrots when there's brownies?

"Hi, Gabby!" she beamed. "How are you?"

Part of me wanted to lie and passively tell her that I was "good," but another part of me liked the idea of being transparent with a stranger. A stranger doesn't know you—they have no context about you to judge you by, so if I told her my Ryan and Daniel issues, she wouldn't know that this would be my millionth time whining about it instead of facing my problems head-on.

"I'm a little stressed," I admitted.

"What's wrong?" she frowned. It was the first, and probably last, time that I would see a frown on her face.

"Boys," I said.

She chuckled. "I've already heard all I need to hear, but what happened?"

"There's some important conversations I need to have with two guys in my life, but I'm scared," I explained.

"Scared of what they'll say?"

"Yes," I confirmed.

"Well, think of it this way, what's the worst they can say? And if they say it, then what? Will your life be over, or will it just hurt for bit before you're okay again?"

"Hmph," I let out, drifting into thought.

What's the worst they can say...and then what? I'd never thought about it like that. I'd never thought about life after the conversations I needed to have. All I focused on was my fear of being hurt—that alone made me forget that there was life after pain.

It's like being a little kid and having to get a vaccine; you cry and cry because you're convinced it's going to hurt, and then when it's all over you awkwardly calm down and jump back into life like it never happened. At some point, the process of getting a shot no longer evokes the same response out of you because you know the discomfort only lasts for a moment—with maybe a little soreness after. Just like a kid getting a vaccine, I had convinced myself it would hurt to talk to Ryan and Daniel—but what if it wouldn't? And if it did, *"then what?"*

"Alright, guys, we're gonna start our game!" Grace excitedly announced from the living room. I followed Hope to one of the couches and plopped down. Before I got too comfortable, I remembered to take out my notebook so I could actually write down important information for my project.

There were thirteen of us, now: six boys and seven girls. There was one other Black girl, making three between her, Grace, and I. One girl looked to be Hispanic, and the other girls were White. There were two Black guys and two Hispanic, and the other two were White. (I would figure out the percentages later, math wasn't my thing.) This wasn't a bad mix. Most of my family members attended churches that were predominantly Black, but I was glad to see multiethnic churches were also a thing. Demographics? Check. Well…sort of, I still had to figure out our age range without being weird and going "hey, how old are you?" to everyone in the room.

"Okay, so to start the night off, we're playing Forehead!" Grace declared, and nearly everyone seemed like they knew what she was talking about. Everyone except me.

"For those who don't know, it's a game where you have a word placed on your forehead, and you have to guess what it is based on the people on your team, who will try to act out or describe the word. You have sixty seconds to try to guess as many words correctly as possible. The team that gets the most words right wins!" Grace explained.

At first, I thought it would be a pretty stupid game—I mean, it was another version of charades, after all, and charades is only fun if the people playing *really* get into it. However, after one round of everyone guessing I was warmed up and actually enjoying myself. By the last round, we decided to make it boys versus girls, and I must say, I was utterly and pleasantly surprised by this group! I wasn't expecting that much fire from them since they were, as I would typically say, "churchy" people, but they got just as rowdy, just as slick with the banter, and just as competitive as I would have with my own friends. (Well, minus the cussing, of course.)

"Braylon, you're up!" Grace announced, holding out the deck of cards for him to choose from. He was the last person to go. When it was your turn, you had to put on a headband with a clear pocket on it that held the card. He picked the word "giraffe." One of the rules we established was that you couldn't tell the guesser what category described the word; for example, since Braylon had the word "giraffe," the guys couldn't tell Braylon that his word was an animal.

"Really tall!" Jesse shouted.

"LeBron James!" Braylon answered. I was holding back laughter already.

"No. It has a long neck like Veronica!" Victor joked. All the boys got hysterical, and I badly wanted to join them. Her neck *was* pretty long, to be honest, but she was also 5'11", so it fit her frame.

"At least I can see over the shopping racks at the mall, Mr. Tippy Toes!" Veronica retorted, followed by a unanimous chorus of "ohhhhhhh" from everyone else.

"TWENTY SECONDS LEFT!" Grace shouted.

"What?! That's not fair! They only gave me two clues so far!" Braylon complained.

"Blame it on the Mexican Kevin Hart over there," Veronica smirked.

The boys quickly scrambled together into the form of what I'm assuming was supposed to be a giraffe. One guy got on all fours, while Victor stood by his head to act as the neck and head. Another guy stood up straight with his arms above his head like a ballerina to form a tree.

"Mmmm, I'm loving these leaves from this really tall tree on an African safari!" Victor said in a cartoonish voice.

"Five, four, three—"

"A GIRAFFE!" Braylon yelled.

"YEAH!!!" the boys cheered.

"Congratulations on your ONE word, boys. That makes," Grace stopped to do math in the air sarcastically, "ONE POINT," she finished.

"Yeah, whatever! What's the *total* score, though?" Victor asked.

"The boys have seventeen points," she confirmed.

"And the girls?" Veronica asked smugly. She already knew how many points we had, but I'm 100% sure she'd asked solely to rub it in Victor's face.

"The girls ha—"

"No, wait! Let Victor tally up our points," she said, handing him the notebook. Victor snatched the notebook and began to count the tally marks in the girls' column.

"The girls have twenty-three points." Victor rolled his eyes, giving the notebook back to Veronica. We smiled amongst ourselves and gave each other high fives.

Grace moved toward the center of the room for her next announcement. "For the last half of our fellowship night, we're going to break into groups of two or three and talk about the importance of relationships—friendships, romance, the whole nine. Try to use the game we just played as guidance as you reflect."

Relationships?! Of all the things we could've talked about, it had to be RELATIONSHIPS? That was the *last* thing I wanted to focus on—the whole reason I was there was to NOT focus on my relationship—or whatever the heck it was!

We all scattered to various places around the kitchen, dining, and living areas. I reluctantly sat with Grace on her couch, where Hope joined us. I didn't care how much they tried to get me to participate; I wasn't going to say a word.

CHAPTER 16

"…but he never actually asked me to be his girlfriend. I'm afraid that I feel more special than I actually am, but I also don't want to ask him and risk my fears coming true, so now I'm just stuck," I gushed. (I know, I said I wasn't going to say a word. I say a lot of things. Mind your business.)

"You're not stuck, you're scared. 'Stuck' doesn't have options, and you definitely have options," Grace advised.

"Remember what I said earlier?" Hope began. "You tell them what you need to, and then what? Let's say you get your heart broken. You lose a friend, a boyfriend, or whatever else. You don't have to go through that alone. Relationships aren't just about who you're in love with. Your friends, your family—those are relationships, too," Hope said.

"Right. I know we're still kind of strangers, but you see how we all worked together in teams to help one person during Forehead? It's the same in everyday life. God encourages us to have relationships where we can look out for one another. He even calls us to look out for strangers," Grace explained.

"I think you know what you need to do, but you find comfort in your conflict," Hope suggested.

"What do you mean?" I asked.

"Your conflict is within yourself, so you still have hope that things could turn out the way you want them to. Since your conflict isn't with anyone else, there's nothing pushing you to solve things. There's no tension that you want to resolve with another person; it's just a matter of the torment you have in your head because of a simple *'what if'* that you have yourself stressed over. But you find comfort in not facing your problem because that means you don't get hurt by the thing you're afraid of," Hope surmised. Yep, she'd read me like a book, yet all I could wonder aloud was—

"How old are you?" I blurted out.

"Huh?" Hope and Grace said in unison.

"I'm sorry, you're just so weirdly wise, so I was wondering how old you were," I explained.

"I'm eighteen," Hope laughed.

"I'm also eighteen," Grace smiled. "This is our high school ministry. I guess I should've explained that sooner, huh?" They were the same age as me. Interesting. Did I miss an extra step in puberty that erased the dumb-teenager syndrome I clearly had? I was ready to be smart like them!

"I only seem wise because I've been exactly where you are, and I've gotten my fair share of advice," Hope explained.

"Well, once again, this discussion didn't go exactly the way I'd planned, but I'm glad it went the way it did," Grace said. "We're having another Bible study on Saturday if you want to come again. I know you're here for your school project, but you're always invited to hang out."

"If you need anything, we're here for you, Gabby," Hope assured me.

"Thank you," I said warmly. "I guess I know what I need to do."

♥ ♥ ♥

The next night was the first game of the playoff season for our basketball team, and I was both excited and a nervous wreck. The entire day I avoided having the conversation I was supposed to have with Daniel because I wanted his head clear during the game.

I sat with Melanie in the fourth row of bleachers, across the gym from the home-team bench, so I could see Daniel's and Ryan's faces. I considered sitting *behind* the home bench instead, but that's where all the groupies were, and I didn't need anything else threatening my security with Daniel or fueling my jealousy over Ryan.

Though of course, I spotted the one and only Tanya sitting directly behind Daniel's chair near the coach. I don't know why she even bothered. He was one of the starters, so he was rarely on the bench except to rest—same for Ryan. I'd been to enough games over the years to know that vying for any of the players' attention was futile at best when they were in the heat of a game. Especially during playoffs.

I spotted Indya walk in with Ryan's parents, and my heart jumped at the sight of his father. "Indya! Up here!" I waved, encouraging her to come sit with us. If she was anything like me, she'd rather sit with Melanie and I than be around her boyfriend's worst nightmare. From my periphery, I could see Melanie whip her neck to look at me.

"What?! Are you feeling okay? You know who you just invited up here, right?" Melanie asked as Indya made her way up the bleachers after pointing me out to Ryan's parents. They smiled and waved at me, and I waved back, hoping they wouldn't follow Indya to sit with us.

"Yes, I know," I said. "But would you want to sit with Ryan's parents knowing what we know? Plus, I don't see her friends here, so I'm just trying to be nice," I explained.

"I never thought I'd see this day," Melanie said, fake-sniffling and wiping at imaginary tears.

Me either, I thought. Indya smiled awkwardly as she sat next to me. "Thank you," she said in a low voice, watching the players warm up in front of us.

"Don't mention it," I mumbled.

Daniel and Ryan made quite the duo on the court. I'd seen Ryan play plenty of times, but this was the first time I'd paid attention to Daniel. By halftime, it became apparent to me how much more popular Daniel was with the crowd than Ryan, and I could see why. Daniel was authoritative on the court; he made things happen, and the people around him did great because of him, including Ryan.

This was not how I remembered it, though; I had always seen Ryan as the star, and so did other people. What if that's what triggered Ryan's dad?—knowing his kid wasn't the center of attention anymore. He seemed calm and collected from what I saw; only yelling here and there when the game got intense. He looked like any normal parent in the public eye. Maybe that's why I hadn't suspected anything all this time.

During halftime, I stood in the concessions line with Indya, making small talk here and there. For a moment, my nerves had calmed down and I was finally starting to relax—that is, until I overheard Tanya's voice ring out from behind us.

"Mr. and Mrs. Ross! It's so good to see you again. It's been so long!" she sang.

My heart nearly stopped. *Daniel's parents are here?* I thought. I had yet to meet them, and for some reason, it hadn't even occurred to me that they'd be there for their son's first playoff game of the season. I inconspicuously turned to get a glimpse of them.

Daniel's mother was gorgeous; if I hadn't known she was a linguist I would've assumed she was a model because of her tall, slender frame. Her hair was pulled into a sleek, low ponytail that complimented her cheekbones beautifully. Mr. Ross was just as tall; his glasses definitely gave me preacher vibes, but his suave business attire had real estate agent written all over it. It was evident that Daniel had inherited his rich brown skin tone from both of them.

"Oh, hi, Tanya! How are you, sweetheart? I see you're still wearing the necklace I gave you," Mrs. Ross replied. Suddenly, Tanya didn't feel the need to speak as loud, and I couldn't hear them very well after that.

"What was it like meeting Ryan's parents for the first time?" I asked Indya.

"What? You mean you've never met his parents? I thought you did?" she asked, confused.

"No, I have! I just mean, you know, as his girlfriend?" I clarified.

"Oh, right. Well, he had mentioned me before we met, thankfully, so it wasn't a surprise to them when he introduced me. They were very kind and welcoming, and it wasn't as nerve-racking as I thought it would be. They didn't force us to all eat dinner together or anything corny like that. We just sat in the living room and talked a little with the TV on in the background. It was very chill," she depicted. "Why?"

"I haven't met Daniel's parent's, yet, and they're here. I honestly don't even know if I'm his girlfriend for real or if I'm just his *thing* for the time being," I confessed.

"I definitely think you're his girlfriend. A couple of my friends had a *thing* with Daniel in the past, and he was *nothing* like how he is with you. But the parent thing... I understand how nervous you must be. Especially if he hasn't told them about you yet," she explained.

"I should probably hang low and wait for him to introduce me, huh?"

"Definitely," she advised.

It didn't matter how much assurance I got from other people, the only thing that would help me feel better was to rip the Band-Aid off and ask him. Thankfully, we won the game, so he would likely be in a good mood when he got out of the locker room. There was just one issue: I was waiting for him, and so were his parents.

There was an excited crowd of students and parents mingling in the gym lobby, so I would have to make myself known to him if I wanted him to see me. To be honest, my best bet was to wait by his car in the parking lot, but I didn't want him to feel like I wasn't right there waiting to congratulate him—especially because Tanya the leech was still too comfortable around his parents. She was legit waiting there with them, casually talking, as if Daniel would be happy to see her when he approached them.

"Gabby! Come here, *hermosa*! It's been so long!" I heard Ryan's mom call out. It *had* been so long, but still, they looked just the same as the years before. His mom was about 5'8", with the same golden complexion as Ryan. Her dark, curly hair fell gorgeously down her back, and her smile was quite infectious. Ryan's face was almost a direct copy of hers. His dad was maybe 6'5"—undoubtedly the reason Ryan was so tall. He kept his hair short, and though his complexion was slightly lighter, everything else about his athletic build had been passed down to Ryan.

"Hi, Mrs. Alvarez!" I smiled, giving her a hug. Pausing for a moment, I hugged his dad awkwardly. "Hi, Mr. Alvarez."

Their hugs were just as warm as I remembered, and sadly, the anger I felt toward his dad melted in that hug. It was as if I was reminded of his humanity with one simple embrace, and I felt sad for him as well. Hurt people hurt people.

"What have you been up to?" she asked.

"Oh, same old, same old. Keeping Ryan on track in his classes; you know me," I joked. They laughed heartily because they knew it was quite the opposite. Over the years, Ryan and I would always joke with his parents about my attention span and how he practically did most of my schoolwork for me.

"I'm glad you guys are still good friends," his dad commented. "Hopefully that continues in college?" he inquired, like he was hoping to hear I had some sort of plan for after graduation.

"Of course!" I half-lied. I planned to go to college, but not some big university like what Ryan was destined for. I was content with doing community college for my first two years and then transitioning later, and honestly, I had no idea what that would do to our friendship.

"Excellent," his mom chimed. "Come by the house soon, missy! You're always welcome."

"Okay! It was great seeing you," I smiled, parting ways with them in the crowd as we went to search for our players. I couldn't help but wonder if his mom knew about what was happening between her husband and her son. Talking to them wasn't as bad as I'd anticipated, but still, I felt so…uncomfortable.

I turned back toward where Daniel's parents were and saw them talking with him. Tanya was gone, though. *Dangit,* I thought. *I really wanted to see what happened when he got there.* They all looked pretty happy, which surprised me because of what I knew about their relationship not being the warmest.

Okay, Gabby, breathe. Everything is okay. Do I walk up to them? Do I lay low? I should lay low. Just wait for him by his car, I concluded. Melanie knew I needed to speak to Daniel by myself, so she'd decided to stick around with Indya by Ryan's parents. I waved them goodbye as I made my way through the exit and out toward the parking lot.

"Leaving already?" I heard Daniel ask right as I began my descent down the steps outside. I spun around and found him standing in his warm-up suit. There was a slight draft flowing from the doors behind him, and I could smell the same amazing smell from him as when he'd met my mom. He had definitely taken a shower before leaving the locker room.

"I—I saw you with your parents, and I wasn't sure if you'd told them about me, so I didn't want to intrude," I said shyly. "I promise I wasn't leaving; I was going to wait by your car until you came out," I finished.

Daniel smiled and held out his hand for me. "Come on, I want you to meet them," he said warmly. "They surprised me. I had no idea they would be here, but when I saw them during the game, I knew I had to introduce you all tonight," he told me, holding the door as I walked inside.

I looked back toward where Melanie and Indya were, and we made eye contact as I squeezed through the crowd. They gave me a *"what's going on?"* face and I mouthed "Daniel's parents!" Their eyes widened in shock, and I knew I now had an audience waiting to see how this show would turn out. I followed Daniel through the crowd, gripping his hand tightly. I had a feeling that the sweatiness between our palms was from my hand and not his, since he seemed so chill.

When we emerged from the crowd, I immediately made eye contact with his mother, who grinned as soon as she saw me. His dad was definitely an intimidating figure, with his tall stature and serious demeanor. It wasn't until his face relaxed into a smile that I finally felt like I could breathe again.

"Mom, Dad, this is Gabby," Daniel introduced. *That was it? Just "Gabby?" No "my girlfriend" tagline?*

"I was beginning to question my son's taste in women; we thought you'd left him! I'm Paul," his dad joked, reaching out for a handshake. I smiled nervously and shook it.

Well, after dealing with Tanya, I'm quite sure you were nervous to meet me, huh, Mr. Ross? "Nice to meet you," I said.

"Don't mind him, he's not as funny as he thinks he is, Gabby. I'm Jennifer. It's so good to meet you!" his mom said, reaching out for a hug instead of a handshake. I immediately realized where

Daniel had learned the art of good hugs. She hugged me like she'd known me forever—like I was a child of her own. I liked her a lot already.

We all stood there awkwardly after that, looking at each other, before I broke the ice. "Knowing Daniel, I'm sure you were quite surprised when he mentioned me, huh?" I said jokingly.

"Well, not really. We're well aware of how popular Daniel is with the girls at this school," his mom started, "I was more surprised that he was finally telling me about one instead of my finding another girl hanging out at my house like she pays the mortgage," she said. Daniel rolled his eyes and smiled.

"Gabby's not a random girl," he said, grabbing my hand.

I smiled to myself, feeling slightly more confident for a moment.

"You know, I thought you looked familiar! You were at Agape Church over the weekend, weren't you, young lady?" his dad asked randomly. He had been studying me like he couldn't figure something out, and I had been ignoring it so that I wouldn't ruin the first impression.

"Yes, sir," I confirmed shyly.

"Well then, I am so happy my son has finally listened to something I've been telling him and found himself a church girl!" he enthused. "I minister in my free time at Agape, and we attend services there. Well, not Daniel so much anymore, but maybe you can convince him to go with *you!*"

"She's not a 'church girl,' Dad; she was just there for a school assignment," Daniel argued. I could hear the irritation in his voice, which meant we needed to wrap this up before his mood was ruined.

"Hey, I don't mind what she was there for. God finds people who weren't looking for Him all the time!" he preached, smiling at me. I could sort of see why Daniel got so frustrated with him, but my heart was starting to warm up to his dad's weird way of showing love.

"We're gonna head out, now. I'll see you at home," Daniel concluded, quickly hugging his dad, and kissing his mom.

"It was nice to meet you, Mr. and Mrs. Ross," I reiterated.

"You too, Gabby! We'd love to have you over soon," his mom assured me.

"This is Gabby," I replayed as we walked away. *"Gabby's not a random girl."*

There were certainly signs of my being more than just a fling to Daniel, yet still, I went back and forth with myself about it. I thought maybe when he introduced me, he would clarify that I was his girlfriend and I could avoid this conversation, but I could see it wasn't going down like that. Gabrielle Perkins had to suck it up and do the hard thing. I didn't even look to see if Melanie and Indya were still there on my way out. If they were, my lack of eye contact probably made them feel like something was wrong. I guess that was technically true, anyway. Ryan was right. I was an overthinker.

The crowd was starting to clear up, but there was still the typical groupie or two (or seven) lingering outside, trying to be seen. Daniel said his "thank-yous" here and there as they congratulated him, but he didn't sound phased or even excited when he spoke. It seemed like he was bothered, and that was about to make this conversation ten times harder.

Daniel's car was parked in front of mine again, and Ryan and Melanie's cars were there, still, as well. When we got to them, I sat against the hood of my car, and he sat against his.

"I'm sorry," he said.

That took me completely by surprise.

"For what?" My heart began to race. Did something happen that I wasn't aware of? Was he about to confess that he'd been messing around this entire time and introducing me to his parents had helped him realize that this—whatever *this* was—wasn't what he thought he'd wanted?

"My dad. He has a special way of ruining my mood with his unsolicited church remarks," he chuckled sarcastically, fidgeting with his fingers, "but I can tell you one thing, he really likes you. My mom is easygoing; my dad's the tough one," he remarked, looking up at me.

"Am I your girlfriend?" I asked him frankly.

"What?" he said, his face was confused—offended even.

"I feel like I am, but you never really asked me to be. And even back there, you didn't introduce me as your girlfriend, you just said 'Gabby,'" I elaborated.

"Are you serious?" he asked, standing up. "I sit with you at lunch, I walk you to class, I park in front of you every day, now. I just introduced you to my *parents*, and you don't know that you're my girlfriend? Tell me, what do I need to do next? Huh? Do a backflip off the roof of the school? Juggle flaming basketballs? Or better yet, do you need me to go to church with you? Would that be enough for you, Gabby?" he erupted, the irritation in his voice became more apparent the longer he spoke.

"That's not what I'm saying," I said shakily, fighting back tears.

"Then WHAT do you want, Gabby? Hmm? Tell me what you need from me, then," he pleaded, standing in front of me. I wasn't scared of his emotion; he didn't give me the impression that he was angry with me, but I could feel the hurt emanating from him. The last thing I'd expected was to be the one hurting *him*, especially not with this question.

"I just need you to say it," I cried. "I know they say actions speak louder than words, but this is something I need to hear you say. I love that you walk me to class and—and park next to me and all that other stuff, but I have voices all around me who think I'm not good enough for you—who think you deserve someone more attractive and more fun and more popular than me—and one of those voices is my own. I just need to know I'm not crazy because I really like you, Daniel.

I've never been with someone before, and it's all really new to me. I just need to hear you say it. I need that security," I breathed pathetically.

I couldn't look at him, I felt so stupid and weak. He probably thought I was just as insecure as Tanya.

"Look at me," he said, pulling on my hand until I was standing right in front of him. I couldn't bring myself to look at him, though. I probably had mascara all over my face by now.

"Hey," he said again softly. "Gabby." I finally looked at him, and saw that all the irritable emotion he'd had before was gone.

"Gabrielle Middle Name Perkins," he said, making me laugh at the fact that he really said "Middle Name." "You are 100% my girlfriend. And if I didn't make that clear before, I'm sorry. If anyone has a question about it, you tell them to come see me. Including you. Okay?" he asserted.

"Okay," I smiled, burying my face into his chest.

He wrapped his arms around me and chuckled.

"What?" I asked.

"My girlfriend's a wittle crybaby," he said in a baby voice.

"Shut up!" I laughed. "And my middle name is Linette," I added.

CHAPTER 17

What better way to start spring break than with the new confidence that you, indeed, were Daniel Ross' girlfriend? It was too hot for a letterman, but Daniel thought it would be cute to let me wear his warm-up jacket to school the next day to let anyone who was wondering know that I, Gabrielle Perkins, was in fact, that girl—*his* girl.

"What do you say we all grab lunch together?" Daniel asked, placing his arm around my shoulder as we left Advanced Health. It was an early release day to kick off the break, so we were heading to the parking lot.

"Speaking of eat," I said, pulling him to the side while Melanie, Ryan, and Indya continued, "I want you to come eat dinner at my place tonight at eight. It'll be super chill—I just want you and my mom to get to know each other."

"I'm down," Daniel agreed as we resumed walking to the parking lot. "I feel like your mom likes me; we really hit it off on Monday, if I do say so myself," he bragged.

"Oh, is that right?" I chuckled. I thought again about how it really had only been four days that we'd been dating—not even that. It felt like Monday was so long ago because the week had been so stressful for me mentally—you know, with all my overthinking.

"Where are we gonna eat?" Daniel asked as we approached Melanie and Ryan at our cars.

"I was actually gonna go get something to eat with Indya—just the two of us. We haven't had time alone in a while." He scratched his head awkwardly.

"And I sure as hell am not third-wheeling with you and Daniel, so I'm going home to take a nap before I meet up with Marcus," Melanie added.

"Fair enough." I turned to Daniel. "I guess I'll just see you tonight, then? Knowing my mom, she'll probably want the entire house cleaned before you come. I might as well do it before she gets home," I threw in.

"Alright. See you later," Daniel concurred, kissing me on my forehead.

♥ ♥ ♥

Being in my house alone was never a big deal to me—most of the time, being by myself was when I thrived. As an only child, I'd cultivated my loneliness into a gift for entertaining myself. Imaginary friends, movies, toys, you name it, I'd probably done it to keep myself occupied.

That day, I made my way through the living room, dusting surfaces and picture frames, and stopped when I got to the ledge above our fireplace. There were photos of my mom and dad on their wedding day, photos of my mom and I, but this one photo—it was one I hadn't seen before. It was in a new frame, and from what I could see, there was no dust to clean off. It was a photo of my dad holding a baby—it couldn't have been more than a few months old—in fact, the baby was me.

"That was a few months before he passed," my mom said from behind me, giving me the scare of a lifetime.

"JESUS! WHEN DID YOU EVEN GET HOME?!" I screamed, nearly dropping the picture frame.

"I just got here." She walked toward the kitchen. "You left the door to the garage cracked open," she added, placing her purse and keys on the kitchen counter.

"But still, isn't it early?" I asked, checking the invisible watch on my wrist. As a creative director, my mom could pretty much make her own schedule, but even so, she *rarely* took off early.

"Yes, I figured I'd come home and get the house ready for tonight, but clearly we had the same idea," she chuckled, walking to the kitchen.

"How come I haven't seen this photo before?" I found it strange how nonchalant she seemed about it.

"I found it last night!" she said excitedly. "I was going through the boxes in my closet and *voila*—there it was at the bottom. Do you want it?"

"Absolutely!" My eyes lit up. My mom had a photo album from the nineties of when she and my father were dating and when they first got married. I'd gone through it with her a million times and even had a few of the photos posted around my room. Anytime I got the chance to add a new photo to my collection, I jumped. I had very little memory of my dad, so having the photos made him real—not some imaginary character that used to be in my life.

"What are we having tonight?" I walked over to the kitchen to better observe my mom pull out pots and pans.

"Chicken fettuccine Alfredo." She winked.

"My favorite," I smiled.

"Yeah, yeah, *'favorite'* the living room floor and go vacuum, please." Why did Black parents always feel the need to turn random words into verbs when they were giving orders?

I walked over to our sound system and turned on the radio to set the cleaning vibes.

"Oooh, ain't this the song y'all be doing that dance to online?" my mom asked, mimicking the viral dance that had been trending at the time. I covered my mouth in utter shock and embarrassment. Thank *God* we weren't in public.

"Ew, mom, NO!" I laughed, setting down the sound system remote. "It's like this." I showed her the proper way to do the dance from the living room, and she mirrored me in the kitchen.

"Yeah! Like that!" I exclaimed, surprised. She was actually getting the hang of it, to the point where I immediately pulled out my phone to record. "Come on, I wanna post this on my Insta story!" I waved her over as I set up my phone on the kitchen bar counter.

We stood comically in front of my camera waiting for the chorus to play again, and then performed two 8-counts of the dance for my socials. I laughed at the playback as I edited a caption for my story while she observed from over my shoulder. We looked damn good, and I just knew my friends were going to go crazy.

"I trained her well." I typed.

"HA!" my mom let out, making her way back to the kitchen. "Need I remind you who you got it from?" She was right; she was a dancer when she was in high school, after all.

I loved the relationship I had with my mom. We were open with each other, and she gave me space to be a teenager while still setting boundaries as my parent. This was our first time preparing for a dinner with a boyfriend because, well, it was my first boyfriend.

And before you ask, *no,* I hadn't told her how I felt about Ryan, but I wouldn't have been surprised if she already knew. Ryan and Melanie had been at my house countless times throughout high school, and *nothing* gets past my mom. Even though she encouraged me to be open with her, she also wasn't one to pry, which I appreciated. I think her way of seeing if I was ready or willing to talk to her about Ryan was her occasional, *"By the way, how's Ryan?"* To which I'd respond, *"Ryan's Ryan."* with a nonchalant smile.

♥ ♥ ♥

Picking an outfit for the evening was my usual battle of *this or that?* My hair was a surprisingly easy (but long) task of washing and styling; I went for a wet hair look, gelling strand by strand until it all lay perfectly in a beautifully defined array of kinks and curls that stopped right at my shoulders. My makeup was simple as well, a little tweeze-and-fill for the brows, some mascara for the eyes, and my lip choice would be decided on after my last and final task: getting dressed. I was at odds with myself over whether I should choose something dressy or casual. Rather than continue arguing with myself in my closet, I asked my mom for help.

"Is this too much?" I announced from the doorway of my mom's room. In my hand was a sleek, black, spaghetti-strap dress that had a satin finish and stopped just below the knee—very classy and simple. Her face lit up when she saw me; she was sitting on her bed with a photo album open on her lap, and I quickly recognized it as the album with photos of her and my dad.

"Come sit." She patted a place beside her.

"Look—" she pointed to a picture of her and my dad all dressed up. She was wearing a dress exactly like the one in my hand. "We took this right before going out for a date."

I looked up at her. "How'd the date go?"

"We went out to some super fancy restaurant and hated it," she laughed. "The food was terrible and overpriced and the waiting staff were *rude* and stuck up, so we ended up going back to his apartment and ordering Chinese. Even though our dinner plans for that night were a fail, it was probably my favorite of all our dates."

"Well, fail or no fail, you looked beautiful, Mom!" I returned my focus to the photo, marveling at how much of me came from her. "So, the dress is too much, huh?" I smiled.

"For tonight, yes. Keep it casual! Save the dress for a fancy outing gone wrong," she joked.

"Okay," I agreed.

I settled for a simple floral romper—something cute but casual.

Once again, Daniel was right on time. I was convinced that he sat in his car outside my house and waited until it was time to ring the doorbell so that he could have perfect timing. I was moving the decorative glassware off the table when my mom opened the door, and I nearly dropped them when I saw him walk in. He was just so…*damn* beautiful. He was wearing a striped polo shirt with the first couple buttons unbuttoned, giving a sneak peak of his finely chiseled chest.

"Thank you for having me over, Mrs. Perkins," he said as he walked through the door, giving my mom a hug.

"Thank you for coming! I don't know if Gabby texted you and told you, but we're having chicken fettuccine Alfredo," she shared.

"Gabby's favorite," he remarked, tossing a smile my way. "I don't know if Gabby told *you*, yet, but she's my girlfriend." A smug smirk crept up on his face. I rolled my eyes playfully as I finished preparing the table.

My mom laughed and nodded. "Yes, she told me."

During our dinner, I sat across from Daniel, and my mom sat at the head of the table, all in close proximity since we obviously didn't need the entire length of the table. I was amazed yet again at how well Daniel spoke to my mother. It was as if they were friends; the conversation just flowed so nicely.

"How long have you gone to school with Gabby, Daniel?" my mom asked, gracefully twirling pasta around her fork.

"About two years, but if you ask Gabby, she'll say three months," Daniel joked.

I let out a chortle mid-bite, and quickly sucked the pasta through my lips.

"Gabby Linette! You know better!" My mom had taught me proper pasta-eating etiquette at an early age, and slurping pasta noodles through my lips certainly wasn't a part of the curriculum.

"I'm sorry! He made me laugh!" I covered my mouth as I explained myself, suppressing the giggles I still had left.

"I'm sorry; that's my fault." Daniel tried to conceal his laugh behind his fist. "I tease her all the time about how she never noticed me until this semester."

"Yeah, that sounds like Gabby." My mom shook her head fondly before indulging in the perfectly wrapped pasta on her fork. Daniel and I laughed silently at each other as we waited for my mom to finish chewing, twirling our forks simultaneously in what became a race to see who could do it the fastest.

"So, how did you get her to notice you?" my mom finally spoke again.

"Well, a couple months ago, I saw her at the grocery store after one of my games. She was standing in the produce section and she seemed lost so I recommended the—"

"Tangerines!" my mom interrupted excitedly. "I remember her bringing those home and being so impressed that she'd chosen something that didn't have the word 'berry' in it," my mom cackled, realizing the truth of the situation.

"Yeah, you have Daniel to thank for that…because everything after that was my choice, and I'm quite sure it all had 'berry' in it," I shamelessly admitted.

"Well, congrats on being discovered, Daniel. The hardest part is over." She held up her glass of water playfully before taking a sip.

"Thank you." He nodded in agreement, drinking from his glass along with her. I could see in their faces that they were enjoying the night so far, and so was I.

With the ice broken, they ventured into more serious discussions. He told my mom about himself like he was an open book, and she soaked it all up. There was no question that she liked him—she tended to wear her emotions on her sleeve, and there were a slew of faces I would've seen her make had she not. When her turn came around, she told him about us and had his undivided attention.

"I'm sure Gabby already told you about her dad," my mom assumed. She had just finished explaining her job as a creative director and how it was the reason we were able to buy the house we were living in.

"She told me that he's not around," Daniel confirmed. Up until that moment I had forgotten that I'd never explained to him that my dad had passed when I was a baby. It wasn't exactly something I led with when I was getting to know people. *"Nice to meet you! By the way, my dad's dead."* didn't have a nice ring to it.

My mom glanced at me and then took the finishing bite of her fettuccine.

"Actually, Daniel," I set my fork down, "there's more to it than that." I looked at my mom, who was chewing calmly and glancing back and forth between me and Daniel. He seemed confused, waiting for either of us to say something. I decided to let my mom do the talking since she could recall it better than I.

"My husband passed away when Gabby was a baby, Daniel." My mom placed her hand on top of his as she spoke. Daniel sat up straighter, and his face washed over with sympathy.

"I—"

"I'm sorry I didn't tell you," I spoke, cutting Daniel off.

"You don't have to apologize, Gab. It's not an easy thing to tell someone. I may not relate, but I definitely understand," he assured me.

"Thank you." I pressed my lips into a small smile. I was relieved that he had handled the news so well. I didn't want him to be upset that I hadn't told him.

"I hope you don't mind me asking," Daniel set down his fork on what was now an empty plate, "but how did he pass away?" My mom and I glanced at each other awkwardly, as if we were giving each other the green light to say something. "I'm sorry. I shouldn't have." Daniel quickly retracted.

"Oh no, honey, you're fine, really. Gabby and I have had almost eighteen years' worth of healing, now. It's a natural question to have," she assured him. I took that moment to get up and take our dishes to the kitchen since we'd all finished eating. As I rinsed the plates and placed them in the dishwasher, my mom began the story.

"Christian—that was his name—passed away in his sleep. The doctors couldn't figure out why, of course, and that haunted me for years. I remember waking up before him that morning and taking a shower before work. Gabby was almost a year old, and she was still in her crib sleeping—everything was normal. Usually he'd wake up before me, but I was having trouble sleeping that night, so I figured I'd just get up.

"When I finished my shower, I could hear his alarm going off through the bathroom door, and after a few seconds I checked to see why he hadn't turned it off yet. He was just lying there. I shook him, I called his name, but he wouldn't respond. He had no pulse, and he wasn't breathing. I did CPR while the ambulance was on the way, but he was gone. For years all I could wonder was: when did it happen? Was I awake and I didn't even notice the love of my life had stopped breathing? Did it happen while I was in the shower? What if

I hadn't gotten up before him? Would I have noticed sooner? Would I have been able to help him?"

I returned to my seat across from Daniel, but he didn't seem to notice, his eyes were locked on my mom.

"He was actually a lot like you, Daniel. Funny. Tall. Smart. Even the way you grabbed Gabby into that hug when you first came to our house the other night—that's how her dad was with me when we were dating."

"Well, I'm honored at such a comparison, Mrs. Perkins. Thank you for sharing that part of your lives with me. I'm sorry for your loss—both of you."

"No, thank *you*, Daniel, for being such a wonderful guest. I know you'll be good to Gabby." My mom sat back in her chair with a satisfied expression. "So, what do you two have planned for the remainder of the night?" She got up from her seat and made her way to the kitchen.

We both looked at her in complete shock. "I—uh…" I glanced at Daniel, who returned my same, off-guard look. "We didn't have anything planned besides the dinner," I explained, standing up from my seat. Daniel followed suit, eventually coming to stand at my side.

"Well, you guys are all dressed up, you might as well make the most of it! I know I am." She opened the wine fridge and pulled out her favorite bottle of rosé.

"Wanna go for a drive?" he asked gently in my ear.

"Sure," I agreed, looking up at him.

"We'd like to go for a drive if that's okay with you, Mrs. Perkins." Daniel placed his arm around my shoulder, and I instinctively threw mine around his waist.

"Of course. Have her back by midnight." She gleamed as she poured herself a glass, and I looked at her in disbelief, checking my invisible watch.

"*MIDNIGHT?!* I mean, I'm not complaining, but where is this coming from? It's only…nine o'clock right now!" I chimed, looking at Daniel's watch instead.

"It's spring break, isn't it?" She looked up from her glass. "Now go, before I change my mind. And don't come back—"

"With anything I ain't leave the house with! Yes! I know. Love you!" I finished, hurriedly opening and then closing the front door behind me.

CHAPTER 18

Daniel drove us to the spot where, in some ways, it all started—the playground on the hill. We walked to the picnic table, and I smiled to myself at the thought that this was becoming our "spot."

We sat on top of the table and let our feet rest on the seats. Our proximity was comfortable: close enough to feel a pull toward one another, but not touching, which made his presence next to me all the more alluring. He was staring ahead at the view of the city, and he was so focused that I don't think he noticed I was staring at him.

"Can I ask you something?" he said, breaking the silence.

"Yeah, go ahead," I agreed.

"When we were first getting to know one another, why didn't you mention your dad died?"

I sat and thought about what to say. The reality was, I missed my dad, but not in a way that someone who knew their dad would. I missed the idea of him. "I don't really bring up my dad's death because I don't have the same grief attached to losing him that my mom does. I don't remember him at all. I just have a longing for him, you know? So when it comes to telling people he's dead, it feels weird because…"

"You don't really feel like you lost him," Daniel finished.

"Exactly. But people hear that one of your parents died and they make it this big thing and…it makes me feel awkward because, to me, it's not a big thing—at least not emotionally. But I can't say that to people or they'll think I'm a sociopath who doesn't care about her dead dad. I do care. I absolutely wish I knew him and had him in my life."

"I feel you." Daniel nodded. "I can't lie, I kind of feel like a jackass."

"What? Why?"

"Because here I was complaining to you about my own dad, and you don't even have yours around anymore. I'm so sorry, Gabby," he said earnestly, shaking his head.

"Hey, it's fine! I didn't tell you, so you couldn't have known. How are things at home, anyway? You seemed cool with your parents at the game last night, but we were in public, so I'm not sure if it was a show or not," I asked.

"Last night was genuine. They have their good moments. Things have actually been pretty good at home, too. I just hope it lasts." He turned to look at me as he spoke, never breaking eye contact with me. Half of me was listening, and the other half of me felt like I was being hypnotized by some sort of mystical fairy that was whispering *"kiss hiiimmm"* into my ear. After the night we'd had, Daniel learning about my dad and being so supportive and understanding, he was beginning to feel like a safe space, and all I wanted was to melt into him.

When Daniel finished speaking, he was still looking at me, and I was so enticed by his gaze that I couldn't process a reply. Judging by his stare, there was a fairy telling him to kiss me, too. I felt a tension between us, like a rubber band that was stretched to its maximum capacity and was either going to break or retract back to its original shape at full force.

"I—that's good." I cleared my throat. "I hope things go well with you all during the break." I broke eye contact and looked down at the table so I could form a coherent sentence. Our hands were millimeters from touching, and I immediately thought of all those movie scenes where the love interests' hands touch accidentally and they make it this big dramatic moment, as if touching hands were a sign that they were meant to be.

"What's wrong?" he asked. I didn't want to admit how strange I was feeling. What if everything felt normal to him, and it was just me who felt this way?

"I don't really know," I laughed quietly. I looked straight ahead. I feared that if I looked at him, I'd become that rubber band—either I'd break, or I'd smash into him full force, and I didn't know what either outcome would look like.

"You look like there's something on your mind." I could tell his eyes were still on me, which made not looking at him even harder. I didn't want to seem rude.

"I just have this…strange urge to kiss you," I explained.

"Oh yeah, kissing your boyfriend is *so* strange," he teased.

"That's not what I mean," I laughed, "I just… I don't know. It's like, when you were talking a minute ago, I just felt this—"

"Tension?" he finished.

"Exactly. I don't know if it's because we're sitting so close, or what, but this time it doesn't feel like every other time I've wanted to kiss you," I explained, glancing at him again.

"Is that a good or a bad thing?"

"I don't know. I think that's what's scaring me," I admitted.

"Okay," Daniel said, scooting farther away from me.

"'*Okay?*' That's it? Just '*okay?*'" I asked. He took me by surprise. I could feel the tension getting stronger as we spoke, and with one swift move, he dismantled it completely.

"Yeah," he chuckled. "Isn't that what you wanted? To not feel so *'strange'* anymore?"

"I—I don't really know what I want. I was hoping you would make that choice for me. I've never felt like this before," I confessed.

"I don't want you to do anything you're unsure of. It wouldn't feel right to me—I'd feel like I was taking advantage of you," he explained.

A guy with consensual awareness? I couldn't tell if this was some sort of reverse psychology ploy, but in that moment, he had stretched the rubber band to full capacity again, and I was ready to bounce back.

I slid toward him and met him in a kiss that I could tell he had been wanting as well. His lips were authoritative, but sweet, and even though I initiated it, I was following his lead. I felt like no matter how deep the kiss got, my appetite for him was insatiable. I was pulling him closer to me by his shirt, leaning farther and farther backward. He held me firmly by the waist as we descended, as if not to drop something precious to him.

"Gabby, wait," he breathed, pulling away from me. "Are you a virgin?"

The four words caught me completely by surprise; I hadn't planned on having a conversation about sex. I was so caught up in the moment that I would have let things go whichever way the moment took us without a second thought.

"Yeah, why? What's wrong?" I asked, sitting up.

"Nothing's wrong, I just…don't think we should go there tonight. Not like this," he explained.

"What do you mean 'not like this'? I thought things were going good just now?" I was frustrated that he'd interrupted what I felt like was the best part of our night so far.

"Well, for starters, I don't want to have sex outside on a picnic table," he laughed. "I also wasn't planning on having sex with you tonight, so I didn't bring any condoms. Besides, your first time should be special." He took my hand, interrupting my finger fidgeting.

"Good point," I chortled, looking down. My senses were coming back to me. "I'm guessing you're not a virgin?"

He shook his head. "Lost mine the summer before junior year."

"Was it special?"

"I mean, if you consider sneaking into someone's house and three minutes of trying to be quiet so we don't get caught special, then yeah!" We laughed.

In that moment, I was glad Daniel had stopped us. Who knows, I may have been satisfied with the outcome if he hadn't, but looking back, I'd probably wish I'd done things differently.

To be honest, I hadn't planned on having sex, either, but when the moment came, I couldn't fight it—I didn't want to. I certainly wasn't expecting Daniel, with his reputation, to have any regard for the moment being special. What even qualified sex as "special," anyway? Was it the place you did it? Was it the person it was with? Did there have to be rose petals scattered around the room like some sort of romantic ritual? Whatever it was, I wouldn't be finding out that night.

"If I wasn't a virgin, would you still care about it being *'special'*?" I asked.

"Absolutely. Even if it wasn't your first time, it'd be our first time with each other. Plus, I want the moment to be special for the *both* of us. It may not be my first time, but it's my first time with *you*, and that means something to me. And honestly, I don't care if it's our first time or the second or third, it should be special every time for the simple fact that you deserve it." Daniel spoke with so much conviction that his grip on my hand got tighter as he talked, and I don't think he even realized it.

"I feel like this conversation was supposed to talk me *out* of having sex with you on a picnic table, but honestly, you're making me want you even more," I confessed, hopping off the table, and moving to stand in front of him, hoping that a change in position would help dispel the sexual tension I was feeling.

"I guess we should head out then, huh?" He grinned at me, clearly amused by my honesty.

I nodded, holding out my hand to help him down.

"Are you okay?" he asked when we got in the car. I was ruminating on what had just transpired—and what hadn't.

"I just feel really stupid." I shook my head. "A picnic table?" I laughed.

"Don't," he chuckled. "I still really enjoyed tonight. I learned a lot about you."

We sat there for a moment, and I slowly started to wonder why we hadn't taken off yet.

"What are you waiting for?" I asked him.

"Safety first," he intoned, referring to my seatbelt.

"Right." I playfully rolled my eyes as I fastened my seatbelt. Playing it safe seemed to be our thing, now.

CHAPTER 19

I must say, going from trying to lose my virginity on top of a picnic table to attending a Bible study was quite the overnight transformation, but school projects didn't finish themselves.

As I entered the church foyer, I wondered if there was some sort of x-ray system built into the doorway of the church that told them who had just sinned and who was squeaky clean. Did attempted fornication count for anything? Would they take me to a special room and throw holy water on me, screaming *"Repent!"* over and over?

No, is the answer to all of those questions. Instead, I walked into the room we were in the week before and saw everyone sitting in a circle, including Grace.

"Are you not leading today?" I asked her, taking the empty seat beside her. She didn't have her notecards out like the last time.

"No, my mom is," she answered, fidgeting with her thumbs. She tried to smile, but she seemed more on edge than anything.

"Is that a bad thing?" I asked.

"Well, our studies haven't exactly been going as planned, so my mom is taking over today," she explained. I instantly felt bad; I was without a doubt the reason why their studies kept derailing. I hadn't yet met Grace's mom. She wasn't at the game-night thing Grace had had at her house.

"Hey, everyone!" The sound of someone's voice rang from the entrance.

I turned to see one of the most beautiful women I'd ever seen in my life, and that was saying a lot considering all the seemingly perfect women I saw on social media every day. Her skin was every Black girl's dream: radiant and glowing from within. Though we were similar in complexion, it didn't much matter how dark or how light her skin was; it was how she wore it that inspired me—that gave me fulfillment. Her hair was the biggest array of kinks and curls that I had ever witnessed in real life. Everything about her was my picture definition of "goals."

"I see a couple new faces, so I'll quickly introduce myself," she started, taking her seat, "I'm Éva Thomas, Grace's mom. I'm the lead youth pastor here at Agape Church. Today we're doing part two of our relationship discussion! Who can remind me of what we've gone over so far, just in case we have any visitors?"

Hope raised her hand in her typical cheery fashion.

"Yes, Hope!" Mrs. Thomas said warmly.

"We've talked about love and the importance of community so far."

"Have you?" she questioned. We looked around nervously. What did she mean with that *"have you?"*

"From what I've heard, our last couple studies haven't exactly gone as planned," she confirmed. Technically she was right, but that didn't mean we hadn't still talked about love and community.

"That's my fault," I admitted, raising my hand. "I really don't know much about God, or what the Bible says about Him, so I had a lot of questions. Grace has been so patient with me and I've been really grateful. I hope I didn't get her in trouble."

On the outside, I was playing the timid newbie who didn't know the ropes, but on the inside, I was testing Mrs. Thomas to see what her response would be in front of all of those teenagers. Surely she wouldn't have an issue with someone asking questions about her beloved God even though it didn't correlate with their Bible study plans, right? And there's *no* way she could be upset at her patient, compassionate daughter for taking the time to have real, honest discussions with me. I may have been there for a Sociology assignment, but I was the queen of reverse psychology.

"No, not at all, Gabby. In fact, our lead pastors were really excited to hear that the Bible study was becoming more interactive, so today we're taking a completely new approach to our study!" Mrs. Thomas announced. She dug into her purse, found what she was looking for, and then handed papers to none other than Victor and Veronica, the two who had been roasting each other when we played Forehead earlier in the week.

"Uh, what is this?" Victor asked.

"A script! Today we're doing a play," Mrs. Thomas smiled mischievously. "Victor and Veronica are going to act like a couple and read some scenarios from the script. After each scenario, everyone else is going to vote on whether Victor or Veronica should *dump* or *date* the other person!"

"Can I choose for them?" Veronica asked. A few people snickered in the room, me included. This was going to be pure gold.

Mrs. Thomas chuckled and shook her head. "I chose you two on purpose after hearing about how *competitive* y'all were in the Forehead game this week. I want you two to channel your inner actors and make us believe it's real," she encouraged.

While Victor and Veronica took time to familiarize themselves with the script, we rearranged the room so the chairs were facing the stage near the front of the room. The stage was set up with a couch and a small coffee table. Mrs. Thomas was really going all out, and I was thoroughly excited to see Victor and Veronica pull this off.

When everything was set up and the actors were ready, Mrs. Thomas announced theatrically, "Ladies and gentlemen: Scene 1."

"WHERE HAVE YOU BEEN?" Veronica yelled, storming across the stage as Victor made his entrance. I was already sold. There's no way she was acting.

"I've just been hanging out. Calm down," Victor replied, sitting on the couch. He pulled out his phone and started scrolling.

"*'Hanging out?'* I haven't heard from you in days! I've been texting you and calling you, and you haven't responded!"

"It's no big deal, babe, chill." Victor was entirely too good at this. He had yet to look up from his phone. Veronica snatched the phone from his hand, and it was clear by the look on his face that that was *not* part of the script.

"What was the point of asking me to be your girlfriend if you aren't going to spend time with me or communicate? Do you know how that makes me feel?"

Victor stood up and grabbed Veronica's hands, finally looking her in the eye. "I know I'm not the best at showing it, but I love you, Veronica. I didn't mean to hurt you. I'll do better, I promise."

"You say this every time, and then you do it again. I'm tired of this; all I want is to know *for sure* that you love me and for you to act like it," Veronica said, taking her hands away from Victor. As she turned and started walking away, Victor dropped to his knees.

"Babe, please. Give me another chance," he begged.

"And scene!" Mrs. Thomas announced.

We all clapped and cheered, and I thought it was pretty obvious what we would choose. "So, by show of hands, how many people think Veronica should still *date* Victor?"

No one raised their hands, but Mrs. Thomas continued. "How many people think she should *dump* Victor?" Of course, everyone's hands shot up.

"Veronica, what about you? Will you date or dump Victor?" she asked.

"Definitely dump," she scoffed.

"Why?" Mrs. Thomas asked.

"What kind of relationship lasts when one person doesn't talk to the other for days? I could understand if my character never reached out, because communication works both ways, but I was texting and calling him, and he wasn't answering. And then to add salt to the wound, his only reason was that he was *'hanging out,'*" she explained.

"So, we can all agree that communication is major in a relationship, right?"

We all nodded.

"I have another question for you, then, and you don't have to answer out loud," Mrs. Thomas continued. "When was the last time you spoke to God? If you were Victor, and God was Veronica, would you still want God to dump you?"

I could see that everyone's mind was blown—including mine, especially since I didn't have much of a relationship with God to begin with.

"Is there a specific way to talk to God?" I asked.

"Yeah—or spend time with Him? How do you spend time with someone who's not there physically?" another guy added.

"Those are excellent questions!" Mrs. Thomas encouraged. "First, I want to know, how do you *think* you're supposed to talk to Him? This question is for anyone, not just Gabby."

"Growing up, my family always made me pray on my knees with my hands folded before bed," Shaniece answered. She was the other Black girl I'd noticed at Grace's house on Wednesday.

"Was it a rehearsed prayer or different every time?" Mrs. Thomas asked.

"It was rehearsed. The typical, *'now I lay me down to sleep'* prayer," she admitted.

"Do you still pray that way?"

"No. I rarely pray at all, to be honest. I might pray before I eat, if I remember. It just got old—or maybe I got lazy. I kinda grew to hate it—doing the same thing over and over. I feel guilty about not praying sometimes, though. It makes me feel like I'm not a good Christian," Shaniece elaborated.

Even though I didn't grow up in a household where prayers were instilled in me, my visits with family members over the years had allowed me to understand exactly where she was coming from. I would always hear my cousins rhythmically recite the same prayer before eating, yet when the adults prayed over the food as a group, there was nothing rehearsed about it.

At what point were we supposed to graduate from the nursery-rhyme prayers into mature, intentional praying like the adults do? Why didn't they show us how to pray like that? If I, Gabby Perkins, at eighteen, wanted to develop a prayer life, where would I start? Would a *"God is great; God is good..."* prayer be frowned upon past a certain age? Does God even like those prayers?

"My experience growing up was extremely similar, Shaniece. When I prayed, I did it because I was told to, and I would just go through the motions—like any kid would. In fact, I didn't truly understand why I prayed until I stopped doing it for my parents. They stopped chaperoning my prayers around third grade, and that's exactly when I stopped praying. If they weren't there to make sure I said them, there was no point, you know? They would still make me go to church every Sunday, but it wasn't until I went to college that I started to wander into a relationship with God on my own terms.

"Praying to God can be as casual as the conversation you and I are having right now. I learned that praying on your knees is about the posture of how you come before God. It's a display of honor—of deep respect and devotion, but, above all else, God cares about the posture of your heart.

"Whether or not you kneel when you pray isn't something to stress about. Sometimes I pray while I'm driving; sometimes I pray in the shower, but my heart seeks the companionship of God, nonetheless. Sometimes I yell when I talk to God because I'm angry. Sometimes I cry. Sometimes I ask Him for more than I thank Him for. My prayers aren't rehearsed, either. I come to Him knowing what I'm going to talk about, but I don't come to Him with a monotone, robotic prayer that I've memorized for the sake of having something to pray.

"When I learned about the character of God, I realized that I don't have to have it all together to talk to Him. I talk to Him because I trust Him, and I trust His will for my life. Don't get caught up on doing things just to be a *good Christian.* Keep your focus on God, and maintain your relationship with Him through things like prayer," Mrs. Thomas explained.

"Does the Bible say anything about how to pray?" Shaniece asked.

"Yes, actually. In Matthew 6 of the New International Version, Jesus teaches the crowd how to pray. I'll read it:

> *"And when you pray, do not be like the hypocrites, for they love to pray standing in the synagogues and on the street corners to be seen by others. Truly I tell you, they have received their reward in full. But when you pray, go into your room, close the door and pray to your Father, who is unseen. Then your Father, who sees what is done in secret, will*

reward you. And when you pray, do not keep
on babbling like pagans, for they think they
will be heard because of their many words. Do
not be like them, for your Father knows what
you need before you ask him.
"This, then, is how you should pray:
" 'Our Father in heaven,
Hallowed be your name,
your kingdom come,
your will be done,
on earth as it is in heaven.
Give us today our daily bread.
And forgive us our debts,
as we also have forgiven our debtors.
And lead us not into temptation,
but deliver us from the evil one.' "

I frowned in confusion as Mrs. Thomas read. I thought we'd *just* talked about how we don't have to recite a memorized prayer, but here He was, teaching them the words to say! As she read, Grace was handing out a study guide for what we were talking about so we could follow along with the scriptures and the notes.

"What's up, Gabby? I see something's bothering you," Mrs. Thomas asked when she was done reading.

"Well, it's… You just told us about how you don't pray a memorized prayer like you used to when you were little, but in the passage you read, Jesus starts teaching them what to say. I'm confused," I admitted.

Mrs. Thomas smiled at me, nodding with understanding. "That was my exact reaction when I first read this passage! But I learned that Jesus was giving them a template to follow. It's not so much about memorizing the prayer as it is about the *elements* of this prayer.

"The first thing I want to point out is that Jesus tells the people to call God 'Father.' Now, I don't know about y'all, but I don't call just anyone 'Dad.'"

I don't, either, I thought. *Because I don't have one.* How was I supposed to treat God like a father when I didn't know what it was like to have one?

"Fathers are people who have personal relationships to us, and that's exactly what Jesus is showing us about God in this prayer. Your relationship with God is personal, so your prayers can be, too. I have the elements of this prayer outlined in your study guides, but just to quickly review, the basic elements Jesus tells us to incorporate in our prayers are: praise, God's will, our daily needs, forgiveness, and the things we struggle with.

"Do I always have all of these elements in my prayer? No, but this is a good guide to follow as you develop your relationship with God. Since we all have different needs, struggles, and things to praise Him for, our prayers should be personalized. Not to mention how our lives change from day to day. Something we need today may be different from something we need tomorrow. And if you pray for the same things over and over again, don't be ashamed. Your persistence doesn't go unnoticed."

I nodded to myself quietly, taking it all in. It made sense *logically*, but I couldn't imagine what a relationship with a father was like outside of TV shows and movies. Talking to God like He was a father figure still kinda felt out of reach for me.

"Any questions before we move on?" Mrs. Thomas asked, surveying the room for hands. When there were none, she instructed, "Okay, now for the last scene! Take your places."

Victor sat back on the couch, and Veronica exited the stage.

"And, action!"

"Yeah, that was so fun," said Veronica, entering the stage. She was on the phone. "Hey, I made it home, so I'll talk to you later, girl.

Okay, bye," she said, hanging up and sitting next to Victor on the couch.

"Hey, babe." She leaned over to kiss him and he moved his head away from her. "What's wrong?" she asked.

"Have you been smoking again? I can smell it all over you," he said.

"Yeah, but I told you, it's no big deal—"

"No big deal? Veronica, we talked about this, I don't like it when you smoke. I can't stand the smell, and it's not good for you!" Victor said, standing up.

"It's not hurting anyone, though! I have the right to do what I want, you know!" Veronica stood up, too.

"It hurts *me*. You may think it's harmless, but the sheer fact that you don't value my terms for this relationship hurts me. And yes, you can do what you want, but you're in a relationship, it's not all about you! We had a talk about things we did and didn't feel comfortable with and made an agreement. It's not like I'm trying to keep you from doing what you want!"

Dang, this one was hard. On one hand, I could see where Veronica was coming from, but the relationship expert in me also understood Victor. (Yes, I said expert. Being a *girlfriend* and all, I could already get the implication that Victor's role represented God's commands for us, and Veronica probably represented sinning or something.)

"So, what? Are you breaking up with me, then?"

"That's the last thing I want to do, but you can't expect me to be happy in this relationship if you're not willing to honor the agreements we made when we got together. I want to be with you, but I'm not going to lower my standards just to let you do what you want." Veronica swayed slightly, not saying anything for a moment.

"I guess I need some time to think, then," she said, turning and walking off stage.

"And, scene!" Mrs. Thomas declared, applauding them. We all stood up and joined her. The chemistry they had on stage had me suspecting that there might actually be something going on between them.

"Okay! What do you think? Should Victor *date* or *dump* Veronica? And should Veronica *date* or *dump* Victor?"

Hope raised her hand and began to speak. "I say Victor should dump Veronica. If someone can't choose between you and smoking right away, they clearly don't value you as much as they should," she declared.

"But what if it's not about smoking, though?" Jesse countered. "What if she's taking time to think about whether or not she wants to feel restricted in her relationship? I say, she should dump *him*. It's clear that she's uncomfortable with his so-called standards, so she should just be honest with herself *and* him and leave," he argued.

While people were talking amongst themselves about what Victor and Veronica should do, I was thinking about the idea of discussing the terms of a relationship before it actually started. They'd really (hypothetically) sat down and made an agreement for their relationship? That felt so…weird. So artificial. Why not just go with the flow and be with one another because you like each other? I felt like outlining terms and conditions ruined the romance.

"These are great perspectives I'm hearing! There's a decent split between dating and dumping. I want you guys to think about how you form friendships and relationships, and how that compares to a relationship with God," she said, handing out pens so we could write our thoughts down in the second portion of the packet she had given us.

How was I supposed to know? I had friends, sure. But, God? I didn't have much to say about some guy in the sky I never really talked to. I sat there silently while everyone around me wrote. I glanced at them without turning my head, trying to think of something Sociology-related that I could write down to appear productive. At some point I accidentally made eye contact with Mrs. Thomas, and immediately I knew I'd opened the door to conversation.

"Gabby, are you alright?" she asked.

"Yeah. I just…can't make the comparison…" I shrugged. She shook her head in understanding.

"Well, what are your thoughts on what happened in the second skit?" I could tell she was trying to help me feel included.

I inhaled, thinking about how exactly I would articulate my thoughts without coming off as hypercritical. "I think it's weird to have…rules, I guess, when forming a relationship. With my friendships, they all kinda formed because I had classes with the other person and we got along or shared interests. We never really said *'hey, I don't like this or that.'* We just went with the flow of things," I explained.

"Yeah, the rules kinda just come as we go," Grace added, which surprised me. I looked around to see people nodding to themselves.

"What do you mean, *'they come as you go'*?" Mrs. Thomas inquired.

"Uh—well, Girl Code, for example," I started, "it's not necessarily something we lay down at the beginning of the friendship. It's usually circumstantial; something comes up, we talk and come to an agreement, and then the rule kinda stands the test of time from there on out," I elaborated.

"So then…I guess it's not necessarily rules that bothers you, then, because you just gave an example of rules in a relationship. Is it more so the idea of establishing rules before the relationship progresses? Because it sounds like you let feelings start the car, and then you learn how to drive as you go," she challenged.

Grace and I looked at each other. She had a point.

"Did anyone make a comparison between our relationships with friends and partners versus our relationships with God?" she asked.

"I wrote down that our relationships with friends is kind of a go-with-the-flow thing, like Gabby and Grace said, whereas God's relationship with us is intentional from the beginning—like…a promise…or an agreement," Hope shared.

"I like that," Mrs. Thomas smiled. "Throughout the Bible you hear about the different covenants God made with His people. A covenant is exactly the way you described it, Hope. It's an agreement, and within that agreement, God makes promises to His people. For example, in Jeremiah 29:11, God assures His people that He has plans to prosper them and not to harm them—even though they were experiencing exile from their homeland.

"Now, let me ask you this: do you think making an agreement when forming a relationship leaves out the *love* aspect of a relationship?"

"Yes," I answered almost instinctively.

"How so?"

"It just feels very mechanical. Like clocking into a job with no attachment—checking tasks off a to-do list and then going home," I told her.

"Feels," she repeated. "I think it's safe to say we all lean on feelings when we think about our relationships. It's hard to disconnect the two—not to say it should ever be disconnected, but rather, we should shift their importance when it comes to why we do the things we do.

"Last Saturday, Grace talked to you guys about *agape* love. Do you remember what it is?" She glanced around the room for a hand.

"I do," Victor announced from the stage behind her. "It's the word used to describe God's love for us. It's a selfless love that isn't based on feelings—it's unconditional."

"Exactly, Victor. This is something I hope that each of you will realize as you continue your walk with God, that it's not due to a lack of love that God forms agreements with His people; rather, it's *because* of His love that He does it," Mrs. Thomas confirmed.

This confused me further.

"But wait, Mrs. Thomas," I broke in. "If *agape* love is unconditional, then why does God form agreements with people? Isn't that actually very conditional? Like—follow these rules or I won't love you?"

"When we describe God's love as unconditional, we do so from an understanding that God Himself is love—the Bible says so in 1 John 4:8. So then, because God is love, everything He does comes from love—everything He produces comes from love. So, it's not following rules or honoring agreements that makes God love us, He does that, anyway," she told me.

This confused me *further*.

"Well then, if He loves us anyway, and His love is unconditional, then why bother making agreements in the first place?" I rebutted.

"Because even though His love for us is unconditional, spending eternity with Him is not. Like a smoker and an asthmatic, there are things that shouldn't be around each other. It's the same idea with God and sin. The terms He gives us for a relationship with Him are designed to keep us from falling into sin, because He knows we can't be around Him if we do. We would literally die. Now, tell me, could you stand to *not* be with someone you loved?" She paused. I immediately thought of my anguish over not being with Ryan, despite my love for him. (I mean, I'm writing a whole book complaining about it, after all.)

"It's because of God's desire to be with us that He lays out His terms before us. But we can either accept the terms, or not, because God has no desire for *'mechanical'* relationships."

Hmph. Everything she was saying made sense, now, but it was as if I could just barely wrap my head around it. The concept was still slightly beyond me.

"Today's Bible study was intended to be a challenge for any of you who are already saved, and a conversation starter for any of you who aren't. We're out of time, but before you go, I want to leave you with these thoughts: why are you friends with your friends, or dating who you're dating? What happens when making rules as you go turns into your relationship being on the line? What happens when you enter an agreement you can't uphold?" She smiled warmly.

I sighed as I packed my things along with everyone else. Maybe I should've hung out with the chess team or something. This was turning into more than just a Sociology project.

CHAPTER 20

Typically, I'd sleep in when the menacing sound of my alarm wasn't urging me to get up for school, but this particular Monday was different. Even though it was spring break, I couldn't sleep in no matter how hard I tried.

I was going to Daniel's house later that day, and my nerves were getting the best of me. I hadn't seen him since the night I'd tried to lose my innocence with him on a picnic table at the park. The more I replayed that night in my head, the stupider I felt. It was so cringe-worthy and completely unlike me. Or was it? What if this was a part of me that had lain dormant all these years? Was I a reckless, horny teenager like in those coming-of-age movies where everyone has perfect skin and they all look way too old to be in high school? Of course not…hopefully.

♥ ♥ ♥

Gabby,
I'll see you when I get home. There are leftovers in the fridge.
Be safe,
Mom

My mom had left a note on the fridge before heading to work, which I would've missed had I not gotten thirsty from all the reflecting I was doing. I didn't have much of an appetite; I was too anxious. Must have been one of those fight-or-flight things Ms. Redlich was telling us about in Advanced Health, but don't quote me on that—we all know I wasn't really paying attention.

Since I was up earlier than I'd planned, I decided I would fill my time by preparing for the day ahead. My hair was still in twists from the day before, so all I had to do on that front was unravel them. Today was dedicated to body care: facial, shaving, nails, the whole nine. I mean, why not? I never treated myself. To be honest, I'd never felt the need to.

That morning, I hopped in the shower and stared blankly at my four-blade razor. Shaving my legs and under-arms was a given, but…what about *down there*? The most I usually shaved was my bikini line, and I would trim the rest, but would Daniel find that disgusting? Wait. Was Daniel even going to see it? What if he'd seen it on Friday? I wondered how that would've gone. Did it even matter what he thought, though?

After a five-minute existential crisis, I settled for my usual bikini line maintenance, figuring that I'd rather be comfortable than walk around feeling like a porcupine until it all grew back.

I put on a facemask and turned on some music while I painted my toes. I debated between red or white for minute, and then went with my usual white. There was something classic about white polish that I never got tired of. As it dried, I scrolled mindlessly through Instagram until I came across a fresh selfie of Daniel. I rolled my eyes at all the girls who, despite him being off the market, felt the need to let him know how attractive he was with a flood of flirtatious emojis and comments.

Should I be petty? I thought. I wanted to comment something snarky to remind them that *I* was the chosen one.

Can't wait to see you. I typed with single, simple heart emoji. I didn't have to be petty when I could flex on them instead. Comments are cute, but I had him in real life, too.

Hurry up, he replied with the heart-eyes emoji. I smiled at my phone like a little kid and hopped up to find something to wear. We were just planning to have a chill day at his house, so I was looking for something that said: *I'm chillin', but I'm still cute.* But in an *I'm not trying* way, you know? I also had to keep in mind that his parents would be home…I think. Regardless, I wanted to make a good second impression to seal the deal. The last thing I wanted was to look like another girl prying for their son's attention with my body.

♥ ♥ ♥

My stomach was a jungle of butterflies as I pulled into his driveway. This was only the second time I'd been inside his house, and I was curious to see Daniel in his own habitat with no one but me around. His party was one thing, but when guests are gone, the home is a sacred place—there are things about us that no one sees or knows about. I had no reason to feel like Daniel was holding back from me, but now that I knew about Ryan's private life, I was more aware of the possibility that there may have been things I didn't know about the people closest to me.

Daniel's doorbell was strong and assertive. It said *"I'm here,"* rather than the timid *"Is anybody home?"* that I was feeling. Daniel swung the door open with a charismatic grin and pulled me into his signature bear hug, rocking me side to side as he walked backward. I collapsed into his arms, trying not to trip over his feet as he pulled me through the doorway. I laughed at his playfulness and steadied myself in his arms.

"Took you long enough," he said, I could feel the vibration of his voice through his chest. He smelled like…dare I say, sex? Not that I knew what sex smelled like, but his cologne made you want to cut to the chase, if you know what I mean. Oh *God*. Maybe I *was* a horny teenager from an unrealistic high school movie! Did that mean that they were actually…realistic, then?

"I'm thirty minutes early, thank you very much," I smiled, looking up at him.

"You hungry?" he asked, releasing me. I nodded, following him through his foyer and into one of the prettiest kitchens I'd ever seen. Despite all the wandering around I'd done at his party, I'd never quite saw the kitchen in full—after all, there were teenagers all over the place and the lights were dim—but I was astonished now that I got to see it for the first time in the light of day. The neutral tones of their granite counter tops and their backsplash complimented one another perfectly, the island was huge, not to mention the appliances. You could feed his entire basketball team out of his refrigerator and still have leftovers. I looked around for a private chef—that's just about all that was missing.

"Ryan's mom hooked me up yesterday with some empanadas, rice, and beans. I made sure I got enough for you," he explained, placing food for me in the microwave. He must've been eating when I arrived, because he already had a plate prepared for himself at the kitchen bar. I'd forgotten how good Ryan's mom's food was, and I'd definitely forgotten how generous Ryan's mom was when it came to sharing her cooking with his friends.

I sat nervously beside him. I'd eaten with him plenty of times, but this time I was in his *house*. It just felt like such a big deal.

"You guys hung out yesterday?" I asked. He nodded as he finished the bite of rice he'd taken.

"Yeah, we got some shots off in his backyard and went over a few plays, why?"

"Nothing, I just didn't realize you guys hung out outside of school. I didn't even know you two were friends until you told me, to be honest," I admitted.

"Coming from the same person who didn't even know I existed until the last five months of senior year," he laughed.

"*Touché*," I smiled. "So, you guys have grown pretty close because of basketball then, huh?"

"You can say that. It's been a little weird lately with this being our last season of high school ball. I think he's just under a lot of pressure," he added.

My first bite of Mrs. Alvarez's rice was euphoric. Memories of hanging out with Ryan throughout high school flooded back as I ate. Even though I was there talking to Daniel, the vibe screamed *"Ryan."* It was dangerously eerie. I even had to stop myself from calling him "Ry" multiple times during our conversation.

"Ah, I thought I heard someone down here! Hello, Gabby!" Mrs. Ross sang as she floated into the kitchen, looking like she was about to head out somewhere. I could smell her perfume as she rummaged through the fridge a few feet away from me. I didn't even have to ask what scent she was wearing to know it was expensive—it had a beautiful undertone that the stores at our local mall couldn't pull off.

"Hello, Mrs. Ross," I smiled.

"Gabby! Nice to see you again," his father said cheerily as he came around the corner, adjusting his watch. "You'll have to come back for dinner, soon, okay?"

"That sounds great," I confirmed.

"We'll be back later on, Dan. Call me if you need anything," Mr. Ross said, patting him on the shoulder as he headed toward the front door.

"Be safe," Mrs. Ross smiled as she kissed him on the forehead. She came around and hugged me before following Mr. Ross out.

Be safe. I wondered what she meant by that, even though part of me felt like I knew. I know I was ready to give it up on a picnic table a few days ago, but I hated the idea of Daniel's mom thinking I was another girl Daniel was messing around with haphazardly.

"Be safe," I repeated once his parents were gone. He looked up at me from his plate and gave me an amused face. "What kind of girl do they think I am?"

"The kind of girl who likes picnic tables," he retorted.

I felt all the blood drain from my face. "Did you tell them?!"

"No, no. I didn't," he reassured. "My mom knows I've been sexually active in the past, so that's just something she tells me, it's no big deal, I promise."

Sexually active in the past. He'd told me he wasn't a virgin, but suddenly I was curious as to how many people he'd been "active" with. Was Tanya one of them? Matter of fact—was Tanya the only one? Did I even want to know? Or would knowing make me feel insecure?

"You finished eating?" he asked, pulling me from my thoughts.

"Yeah." I handed him my plate so he could place it in the sink.

Once he was done tidying up, he walked over to the stairs and motioned with his head for me to follow. Even though I'd been there before, there was considerably better lighting this time around, and the experience felt new all over again. He led me to his room, which was surprisingly normal—large, yes, but something you'd expect of an eighteen-year-old athlete.

Daniel lay on his bed and looked at me, amused, as I visually toured his room. I hadn't realized that he was staring at me until my eyes met his.

"What?" I laughed, embarrassed.

"I just hate that I waited so long to make myself known to you," he admitted, sitting up. I crawled onto his bed and lay my head in his lap, and he gently started to wrap the coils of my hair around his finger.

"How long have you known that *I* exist?" I asked, skeptical that he'd noticed me any sooner than I'd noticed him.

"Junior year, right around homecoming," he started. "You and Melanie were walking up the bleachers at one of the football games, looking for Ryan. He and I had been talking about the upcoming basketball tryouts while he waited on you two. He waved at you guys to get your attention, and I got up to go sit with Tanya," he explained.

"My biggest fan," I said sarcastically, rolling my eyes.

"Yeah," he chuckled, "Tanya and I had just started dating, so I was with her a lot of the time, but I still remember thinking to myself, *'who's that?'* when I saw you."

"How long have you known Ryan?" I asked. "I still can't believe I never noticed you with you and Ryan being such close friends."

"I met him the summer before junior year. We played against each other at an AAU basketball tournament and chopped it up after one of our games. I found out he was attending the high school I was about to transfer to, and we kept in touch."

"Wow, so you were a new kid, also?!" I said, sitting up in excitement. "So was I! Ryan was my first friend, here, too," I smiled.

"I wasn't just *a* new kid. I was *the* new kid," he joked, pulling me toward him for a kiss much like the one we'd shared on the picnic table.

"Where'd your parents go?" I asked before things got carried away. The last thing I wanted was to prove his mom right if they mysteriously popped up out of nowhere like Daniel had a habit of doing.

"They went to some *thing* for church, I forgot what he said," Daniel told me.

"Oh my gosh! Speaking of church," I said, pulling away abruptly, "I was pleasantly surprised last week."

"Really, now?" Daniel asked, propping himself up on his elbow. I could tell he wasn't exactly excited to talk about it, but I wasn't sure if it was because I'd cut our make-out session short or because I was about to talk to him about church. Maybe it was both.

"Last Wednesday, we played this game called Forehead, and it got really intense. I thought the people in the group would be really prude and proper, but they got just as rowdy and competitive as like…Melanie, Ryan, and I would've! And then on Saturday, they had this thing where they made two people act out scenes—like a mini play, and we talked about how it related to relationships in our everyday lives. They brought up some stuff that really got me thinking. I'm really surprised by them, honestly," I gushed. Daniel nodded at me like he was trying to act interested in what I was saying.

"Really? You're not gonna say anything?" I whined.

"I just don't know what you expect me to say, Gabby. I told you, you can't tell us apart!"

"Yeah, but you say it like you *hate* them! You'd see that they're really nice people if you gave them a chance," I encouraged him, hoping to show him the bright side. But I was doing the exact opposite. I could see the shift in his body language as he sat fully upright and leaned his head back against the wall.

"I don't hate them. I'm just not interested, and I don't wanna be forced into giving *them* or *church* a chance," he said sharply.

"That's fine, Daniel. I just don't understand why your whole attitude changes when someone mentions religion. To not be interested is one thing, but it clearly bothers you and I'm trying to figure out why."

He let out a deep sigh and looked at me. "Because my dad has been shoving it down my throat since I could walk, that's why. I don't even think he truly sees me for who I am, just who he wants me to be. I feel like I'll never be good enough for him unless I succumb to his squeaky clean standards. I just wanna live my life without the pressure of being good enough for him with every move I make," he vented.

"Have you ever told him any of this?" I asked. He looked at me with an expression that made it clear that he had.

"That man hears what he wants to hear. And you know what's worse? He's always gone. How can you always be gone working, and then come home and try to change the son you barely even know? At least give me the respect of getting to know me before you decide I'm not good enough. I'm tired of jumping through imaginary hoops. I'm tired of failing tests I didn't know I was taking. I'm tired of being looked at as just his son—his fucking property. I'm an individual. I'm me."

Suddenly, it all made sense—his response to me the night of his basketball game. All I'd done was ask him if we were official and he seemed to mistake it for me telling him that what he was doing wasn't enough. It was clear, now, that this thing with his dad was something he constantly carried on his shoulders, and it was affecting the way he perceived the people around him—their intentions and what they thought about him.

What would life be like without standards, though? Without pressure or goals we wanted to attain? Wouldn't you feel lost aimlessly making your way through life? Even if we freed ourselves of the standards of other people, we at least had standards for ourselves, right? What would life be like without either?

"Who do you want to be?" I asked.

"I really don't know. I've been too busy avoiding who my dad wants me to be. It's funny, because they ask you that question when you're a little kid—like in first grade or something—and to me, it's like, how the hell should I know? Can I be a kid? Can I discover who I *am* before I decide who I want to be?" he vented.

I sat up straight when he said that. I don't think he even realized how profound of a statement that was. *"Can I discover who I* am *before I decide who I want to be?"* I mean, wow. How can we figure out our destination when we don't even know our starting point—our current selves?

"Well, Daniel," I started, moving to cuddle him in hopes of getting him to relax again, "I want you to know that I wouldn't be with you if I didn't think you were good enough. I like who you are right now—whoever you think that is. I'm not here to make you jump through hoops and do magic tricks. I won't bring up the Bible studies if it makes you uncomfortable, but please know that I don't have some hidden agenda to transform you into the perfect guy. I just really wanted to share my experience, that's all."

He unclenched his jaw and turned his head toward me. "Okay," he sighed. "I'm sorry. Finish telling me about the Bible study—you were saying something about a play?" he finished.

"Are you sure? We really don't have to if it makes you uncomfortable," I conceded.

"No, you made some good points. I don't wanna treat you like you're my dad. Go ahead and finish what you were saying," he said, placing his hand on top of mine.

"Okay," I smiled, "well, there was this one skit they did, where one of them gets home super late—I think it was Veronica—and she had been out smoking. Her boyfriend, Victor, got upset, and they started arguing about the agreement they made regarding what they do and don't like before they got into the relationship. Part of me was like *'Boy, bye,'* but the other part of me was like, *'Dang, if you made the agreement the least you can do is honor it,'* you know?" I explained.

Daniel started chuckling at my side comments.

"What?" I smiled.

"I just appreciate you giving me your inner monologue—it really paints the full picture," he teased.

"Isn't that mind-blowing, though? I mean, I never really considered making rules for a relationship before getting into one. They usually just happen randomly," I explained.

"Yeah, Tanya did something like that. She tried to lay down some rules in the middle of our relationship," he told me.

"What were her rules?"

"She wanted me to stop liking pictures of other girls on IG." He rolled his eyes, but I wasn't completely opposed to the idea, and I think he could see that in my face. "What? Don't tell me you feel the same way?" he asked.

"It depends on what kind of pictures she was talking about! Were you liking thirst traps or just simple selfies here and there?" I inquired.

"There may have been a thirst trap here or there, but it was mainly selfies! BUT, at the end of the day, it's just a picture. It doesn't mean anything," he defended.

Just a picture, I thought. That was something I was willing to debate. "You guys are so simple-minded," I retorted. "Even if you don't mean any harm by liking a picture, it sends a message— *multiple* messages, actually."

"Yo, that's the same thing she said! I can't believe this! You really do agree with her!"

"I didn't say I agreed. I'm just saying it sends a message. For example, let's say one of your teammates posts a photo with his shirt off—and I mean his chest and abs are straight *glistening*—'cause it's spring break and he just got out the pool, right?"

"—You don't gotta be so graphic," he interrupted, clearly less than amused.

"I just thought I'd *'paint the full picture'* for you." I winked. "Anyway, let's say I like the picture. How would you feel?" I asked.

"I wouldn't trip," he said nonchalantly, but I could tell he was just standing his ground. "It's unrealistic to expect someone not to find other people attractive when you're in a relationship," he added. "Plus, you're *my* girl, not his. I'm still winnin'."

"And I completely agree, it's *not* realistic, BUT, just because you find someone else attractive doesn't mean you have to *act* on that attraction by liking the picture. How would you feel if, in person, I saw that same guy I just described—while we were together—and was like *'Damn, I like what I see!'*?"

"That's unnecessary."

"Exactly! And it's the same thing on the internet, except it's summarized in the form of a red heart. For me personally, it's the fact that now some girl is walking around school knowing *my* boyfriend is falling into *her* thirst traps that I don't like," I clarified.

"Okay, and I get you, I do. But Tanya was a whole different level of insecure. I couldn't like pictures of girls—*period.* It didn't matter if it was a selfie, a thirst trap, my cousin—she was just overboard with it. She assumed I wanted every girl I liked a picture of, and I couldn't stand it," he argued.

"Was she insecure in response to things you did, or insecure in general?" I asked.

"Both—and I never realized it before we started dating. Before I asked her to be my girlfriend, she demanded my attention *all* the time, and she always wanted to know my every move. I just thought she was the clingy type and wanted me to herself, but it turns out the girl was just—"

"Crazy," I finished. He laughed and nodded his head in agreement. "Well, I'm not like that. I know I'm a good catch. I just don't wanna feel like my place in your life is insecure."

"What do you mean?"

I thought for second about how I could break it down, and then it hit me. "Okay, check it. Let's say you and I get on a rollercoaster and there's double seats. I take the seat next to you, and we pull the seat-restraints over our shoulders for safety. Your seat does the little *clink-clink* sound and you know you're locked in, but my seat won't *clink-clink*, so now I'm stressing because I don't feel safe next to you.

Meanwhile, you're *kee-keeing* and giggling with the girls who are waiting in line for their turn while I'm trying to get help with my seat. I feel insecure about my place next to you. I don't feel like I'll make it through this ride with you. It's not that I'm insecure about myself—because I know I'm cute—*too* cute to be falling off this rollercoaster with you on the loop-the-loop. You feel me?"

"Wow. You girls think too much," he remarked.

"You *guys* don't think enough," I shot back.

"Okay, Ms. *'Clink-Clink,'*" he said, pulling me back into his chest.

"Can that be our thing?" I asked.

"Can what be our thing?"

"If one of us does something that makes the other person feel insecure in the relationship, the other person should say *'clink-clink.'* That way, we can negotiate a way for the person to feel safe."

"Okay. I like that," he agreed.

We lay back down against his pillows, and I fell into my usual place in his arms, relaxing to the rise and fall of his chest with each breath. I couldn't help but close my eyes in comfort, after which I heard the sound of a picture being taken.

"Why didn't you warn me? I would've shifted to my good side." I smiled, my eyes still closed.

"You on my chest *is* your good side," he told me.

I looked up at his phone to see that he was posting the picture on his actual Insta profile this time, rather than just his story. *Being safe,* he wrote in his caption, with a winking emoji, which I assumed was him poking fun at what his mom had told him before leaving the house. I took out my phone and commented: *#clinkclink.* He laughed and I closed my eyes again, smiling at the thought of us now having our very own agreement.

CHAPTER 21

I remember my first time at Ryan's house—the anxious feeling in my chest, my sweaty palms—and today felt like that first time all over again. Actually, *every* time felt like the first time all over again, but it had been so long since I'd been there that standing in front of his door on Tuesday felt very much like my freshman year.

I know what you're thinking: *you were just at your boyfriend's house yesterday, and now you're at Ryan's?* It only sounds bad when *you* say it. To me, it sounded like angels singing on Monday night when he texted me inviting me to hang out.

I was definitely surprised to hear from him, though, don't get me wrong. It's not like I had been plotting on how to get within proximity of him. I had honestly started to accept the dynamic between us being different than how it used to be.

It was his mom's birthday, however, and he wanted me to come over and help him decorate the house before his parents got home from work. He was planning on throwing her a surprise party with a few of her relatives who she hadn't seen in a while. Isn't he amazing? Uh—I mean, in a no feelings, solely platonic, strictly best friends type of way?

"Hey, G, what's up?" Ryan smiled, opening the door and stepping aside so I could walk in. He closed the door behind me and walked past me toward the living room. Immediately, I remembered what the friend zone felt like. When Daniel opened his door, I could barely get him off me, but Ryan opened his door like I was…well, *just a friend*, obviously.

"Hey, Ry," I said, looking around. Aside from the decorations Ryan had already put up, not much had changed in the few months that I hadn't been there. "So, what's the mission for the day?" I asked, following him to the living room.

"Honestly, I have mostly everything finished. All that's left is the dining room," he admitted, sitting on the couch. "I just wanted to hang out like old times," he finished, patting the seat next to him.

"You know, you could've just said that," I chuckled. Once again, I couldn't help but wonder where Indya was, and if she was okay with us hanging out alone. And before you flip the script on me, Daniel knew I'd be with Ryan and had no issue with it. I decided I wouldn't press the issue, though. Indya had proven herself to be a very understanding girl, and I respected her for it.

"I know. I just wasn't sure how to ask. This is our first time really talking since…" He trailed off. I immediately caught that he was referring to his confession about his dad.

"Right." I nodded, assuring him that I knew what he meant so that he wouldn't have to say it again.

"I just wasn't sure if you'd be comfortable coming here again knowing what you know, now," he confessed.

"I get it. But I'm here, and that's what matters," I reassured him. "So, how are things? Have you chosen a college, yet?"

"Things are better, for now. And I'm still debating on colleges; I don't want to commit too early just in case I get any other offers before playoffs end."

"*'Other?'* You've already been given offers?! Why haven't you told me!" I exclaimed, hitting him on the shoulder.

"I don't wanna reveal anything yet so that no one tries to persuade me on which one to choose. I want to make this decision on my own, so act like you don't know," he told me.

"But, Ryan, what if saying something gets your dad off your—"

"It won't. The last thing I need is for him to pick a fight with me because I didn't choose the school he wanted, okay? Just…trust me on this. I've already gone back and forth with myself, and this is the way I wanna go about it," he asserted.

"Okay. I get it. I'm sorry," I said, sinking into the cushion. I should've known better than to intrude. I'm lucky enough that he opened up to me about it in the first place.

"What about you, though? Still going through with the community college plan?" he asked, playfully nudging me on my shoulder. I could tell he was trying to re-lighten the mood after putting me in my place.

"Yeah." I shrugged half-heartedly. "I'm not really sure what I wanna do with my life, yet, so I figured I would do the basics at a community college so I can sort it out. I just wanna make it through senior year, honestly," I sighed. If there was one conversation I hated, it was the one about "the future."

Even though I was legally an adult, I still felt very much like a child who hadn't fully discovered herself, yet—if at all. When I looked at Ryan, though, I saw a man in the making. His jaw had already surpassed the sharpening phase, and he was starting to settle into it. He had always been muscular from basketball, but he had finally grown out of that scrawny-buff look and was more filled out now.

I studied him throughout our conversation, shuffling through memories of how he used to look and comparing them to the present. Everything I used to appreciate about him had only gotten better—I liked those things a few years ago, I loved them, now. I loved the way he held eye contact with me when he was passionate about what he was saying, and the way he always dropped his head whenever he laughed and then looked back up at me with his gorgeous smile, and the way he always had to spread his arm across the back of whatever chair he was sitting in. I even loved the way he waved his hand in my face when I wasn't paying attention—

"Helloooo? Anybody there?" He waved, bringing me back to reality.

"Uh—I'm sorry. What did you say?"

"I asked how your Sociology project is coming along?" he repeated.

"Oh! Right! I actually really like it. I thought it was going to be boring, but it's been very interesting," I admitted.

"How so?"

"Well, for starters, the Bible study group is full of pretty regular people—and I know that sounds weird to say, but…I don't know, I was expecting some uptight, squeaky clean group of teenagers that said 'Jesus' every three sentences. They're actually really funny and relatable, though, and even though I feel awkward sometimes because I'm not very religious, I never feel unwelcome when I'm there," I gushed. "I told Daniel about it yesterday, but I can tell he's not completely comfortable with it, yet. I'm glad he at least listened, though," I added.

"Did he tell you why?" Ryan asked.

"Yeah. He said his dad tries to force it on him a lot, and I understand how he feels. I just really wanted to be able to share my experience with him because I thought it would give him hope that not everyone is like his dad," I explained.

"Well, you can talk to me about it anytime. My daddy issues won't get in the way of that." He winked. It amazed me that he could find a way to make light out of his situation despite how terrible it was, but I liked that his father hadn't taken away his light. He was still Ryan, and my feelings were still very much there.

"Do you believe?" I asked.

"In God?" he replied.

I nodded.

"Yeah, I do. My family is mostly Catholic. I wouldn't call myself a devout Catholic or anything, though. I'm pretty much Catholic-by-association. Why?"

"I don't know. I was just wondering. It's not something we typically talk about, you know? I think we just kinda assume something until our friends clarify it for us on their own," I admitted.

"Do *you* believe?" he asked as his phone buzzed on the coffee table. He quickly checked it and then put it in his pocket.

"I do! I'm like you—I believe by association. It's been cool to kinda explore it for myself, though."

"Well, I'm looking forward to hearing more about it," he smiled, getting up from the couch. "Wanna set up the dining room, now?" he asked, reaching out to help me up.

I took his hand and rolled my eyes. "Of course. I mean, that's what you asked me to come over for in the first place, right?" I joked.

Once I'd stood up, I realized I was much closer to Ryan than I'd anticipated. Our bodies were nearly touching, and I had to turn my head to the side to avoid our gazes breaching the friend zone proximity. Like Daniel, he was also pretty tall compared to me, so it's not like it was hard to keep our faces away from each other, but the tension of being so close to one another was obvious.

There was a time when neither of us batted an eyelash at being so physically close, but our new relationships had brought a newfound awareness of what was comfortable, versus what was appropriate.

Ryan awkwardly adjusted his stance so that we weren't as close, and then gestured for me to lead the way.

I knew it had been a while since I'd been to Ryan's house, but I was pretty sure I remembered where his dining room was; I had passed it on the way to his living room. For some reason, though, as I turned toward the dining room, Ryan continued toward the front door. I paused in the foyer outside the entrance to the dining room, puzzled.

"Did the doorbell ring?" I asked.

"No, Indya texted me a couple of minutes ago letting me know they were outside," he explained, opening the door.

Lo and behold, there was Indya, smiling and ready for action. Maybe I *should* have asked him where she was so I wouldn't have looked and felt so stupid. As she walked inside, he pulled her in for a hug and kissed her on the forehead sweetly. I rolled my eyes and turned away. I was definitely in the friend zone compared to that. But what did he mean by *"they"*?

"What's up, bro?" I heard Ryan say seconds later. I turned back around and saw him dapping Daniel up as he walked inside. The smile on Daniel's face when we made eye contact let me know that he'd been planning on surprising me from the beginning. Maybe that's why he was okay with my being there with Ryan alone. Nevertheless, I couldn't help but blush as he approached me with his enormous smile and his "gotcha" attitude.

"Funny seeing you here." He teased, then put his arm around my shoulder as we walked into the dining room.

I was relieved, now, to know I wouldn't have to third wheel with Prince Charming and Cinderella. Admittedly, though, it felt a little weird adjusting from admiring Ryan to being held by Daniel. My feelings for both clashed in the pit of my chest, and I started to feel a little uneasy.

Suddenly, being affectionate with Daniel in front of Ryan and Indya felt like being affectionate in front of my mom. I was uncomfortable showing my affection for Daniel—I didn't want it to turn into a battle of who could be the cutest couple. I was embarrassed to have feelings for both of them, especially knowing they were stronger for one than they were for the other. It was much easier to let my feelings flow when we were at school or when it was just Daniel and I, but here, with just Ryan and Indya, it was harder to ignore the truth—my truth.

♥ ♥ ♥

"Thank you, guys, for helping me knock this out," Ryan said later as he placed the final picture on the photo-wall we'd created. "Are you sure you don't want to stay for the party?"

"No, it's okay! Give your mom an extra hug for me," I insisted. The last thing I wanted was to see the difference in how Ryan's family treated his girlfriend versus his friend. Daniel and I were heading toward the front door; Ryan and Indya followed.

"Save some food for me!" Daniel requested.

"I got you, bro," Ryan laughed, closing the door.

Daniel looked at me and immediately cut to the chase. "What's wrong?" he asked. "You seemed a little uncomfortable today."

"I just felt really awkward being doubled up in there," I told him truthfully. He put his arm around my shoulder as we walked to my car on the side of the street. Daniel was parked behind me.

"Yeah, that was kinda weird with them being all lovey dovey and shit," he chuckled. Apparently, Ryan was ten times more affectionate with Indya in the comfort of his home than he was at school. I was disgusted.

"Right? The last thing I wanted was for it to turn into a cutest couple competition," I scoffed, leaning against my car door.

"We all know who'd win that competition," he said, smiling down at me.

"You really think so?" I blushed.

"Of course, girl, do you see me?" he said, turning to look at his reflection in my car window. "You are with one fine man, if I do say so myself," he joked.

"I am, aren't I?" I said to myself more than him.

"More importantly, I have you," he said sweetly. He stood beside me and rested his arm on the top of my car. "I'm not sure why Ryan had you in his face for so long and never kept you for himself, but I'm glad he didn't. I know it can be tough seeing your best friend act like you don't exist when his girlfriend is around, and that's why I made it a point to come over when he told me Indya would be joining you two.

"And I know we've barely been dating, but I meant it when I told you that I see you, Gabby, and if for some reason I start acting like I don't, you know which words to say," he finished, pulling me into a hug with one hand and opening my car door with the other in one fluid sequence of motions.

I was so shocked at Daniel's thoughtfulness and how well he paid attention. It almost felt like he knew I had feelings for Ryan, but that was just my guilt talking. The fact that he'd put himself in the mix, as if to protect me from a pain that I hadn't told him I was feeling, well, that was beyond seeing me. It was damn near seeing *through* me, and if I didn't pull my head out of Ryan's ass, it wouldn't be me saying *"clink-clink,"* it would be Daniel.

CHAPTER 22

I looked forward to Wednesdays, now. Even though this wasn't a "relaxed" Bible study at someone's house, I didn't feel like a sore thumb sitting in that circle at Agape Church that particular Wednesday. Maybe it was the freedom of spring break, but I was actually smiling at people as they sat down, making small talk with Hope, and feeling genuinely excited for what the Bible study would be about this time around.

My notebook sat eagerly on my lap, open to a fresh page. What would they surprise me with today? Would I have another cool story to tell Daniel?

"Hey, everyone!" Grace chirped as she and her mother walked in.

"Hey, guys," Mrs. Thomas echoed, "who's ready for another play?"

Everyone's hands shot up.

"Awesome, I'll need about six volunteers," she declared. Five people stood up, and then we all looked around at each other continuously, as if someone else would randomly pop out of their seat like a game of whack-a-mole.

"I'll do it," I said, standing up. Hope and Grace smiled at me from their seats, which only made me more nervous. I'd gone there to be a fly on the wall, not a fly on the stage.

"Alright, you guys, hop up on stage," she instructed. We stood in front of the curtain, and watched as she pulled the rope, revealing six school desks set up facing the audience—two rows of three, with the desks in the back row placed in a checkerboard fashion between the desks in the front row.

It's supposed to be spring break, I thought, standing in a pool of instant regret.

"Today's play will be a mix of improv and scripted acting so we can capture the genuine reactions of our volunteers," Mrs. Thomas told the audience.

"Pick a seat," she told us actors. Instinctively, I sat in the back row, and though it didn't make much of a difference, I still felt comfort from not being in the front.

As we chose seats, I noticed Daniel's dad join us on stage with a stack of papers in his hands. I hadn't even noticed him walk in, and *nervous* was now an understatement. What if I turned out to be a horrible actress? Would he tell Daniel to find a girlfriend with more talent? What if I was too *great* of an actress? Would he tell Daniel I couldn't be trusted?!

"Are you ready?" Mrs. Thomas asked, taking her seat in the audience. All the volunteers looked around at each other to gain a consensus, but before we could answer, she yelled, "Action!"

"Good afternoon, class, today we will be taking an exam. You must get a 100% on this exam in order to proceed to your next grade level. If you get anything wrong, you do not move forward," Mr. Ross explained as he passed out the tests.

"What?!" Braylon (who I remembered from the game night) exclaimed. "What kind of test is that?!"

"You have two options, however," Mr. Ross continued, "you can take the exam yourself, or you can have one person take the exam for you. If that person passes the exam with a 100%, you can move forward as well," he finished.

I looked down at my *"exam"* and on the front page, it read: *You will not take one for the team, and you will decide to take your own exam.* This must've been the "scripted" aspect of the play; everyone else must've had their lines and instructions on their first pages as well.

"Only one person can take it for us?" someone asked.

"Only one," Mr. Ross confirmed.

"So, who's gonna take one for the team?" Shaniece asked. We looked around briefly until Jesse (who I also recognized from the game night) stood up.

"I'll do it," he said.

"Alright, then! Who's going to accept Jesse's score on their behalf?" Mr. Ross surveyed.

Shaniece, Braylon, and another girl who's name I didn't know raised their hands. Veronica and I did not. I scanned my front page again for any other lines, but there weren't any. I was basically an extra, and I was cool with it. Can't mess up if you don't say anything, am I right?

"Okay! With that being said, Jesse, Gabby, and Veronica, you may begin the exam. You have fifteen minutes."

How bad can this be? I thought, flipping the page. Apparently, very bad. It had everything from geometry problems to questions on U.S. history. They were things I knew at one point but had forgotten over time. I didn't even have to make it past the first page to know where this was headed for me. I debated looking over at Veronica, who was next to me. Would that still be considered cheating, even though this was just a play? I didn't want to see her answers, I just wanted to see whether or not I was the only idiot on stage. To pass time, I flipped through the test, answering what I could until I reached the last question—there were fifteen questions in total.

"Pencils down," Mr. Ross announced, "please pass your exams forward."

I sighed and looked over at Veronica to gauge her expression. I was minorly relieved to see that she looked just as hopeless as I did.

After a couple minutes of Mr. Ross enthusiastically marking answers wrong on what were undoubtedly mine and Veronica's exams, he stood up again.

"Congratulations, Jesse, you got a 100% on your exam! Shaniece, Alana, Braylon, this means you'll be progressing to your next grade level as well." They all celebrated with high fives and laughed amongst themselves while Veronica and I sat there in silence, waiting to hear about how we flunked whatever imaginary grade we were in.

"Veronica and Gabby, I'm sorry, but you did not pass your exams," he confirmed, giving us back our tests.

"Mr. Ross?" Jesse said, raising his hand. "Is it okay if we still offer them a chance to accept my exam on their behalf, even if they tried to do it themselves and failed?"

Aw, that's sweet of him, I thought.

"That sounds great, Jesse, but there's a consequence for failing. They knew that when they took the exam, so it wouldn't be fair to let them get off scot-free," he argued.

"Then I'll stay back in their place! I'll take the consequence for them. If my test score can cover multiple people, why not my punishment?"

Our mouths fell open. Being sweet was one thing, but was he stupid, too? We whipped our heads in Mr. Ross' direction to see his response.

"Well—"

"And I'd like my score and my punishment to apply for future students as well. Let's make this a one and done thing. Please, Mr. Ross? No more exams," Jesse insisted.

After a moment of contemplation, he gave in. "Okay, ladies, due to Jesse's generosity, I will still allow you to accept Jesse's score on your behalf if you'd like. He will take the consequence on your behalf, but if you deny his exam score, you'll be held back as well. What do you say?" Mr. Ross offered.

I was torn. It didn't feel right to let him be held back because of *my* failing score. I looked briefly at the back of my exam packet, where my last line was.

"Absolutely," I said, trying to sell it with some enthusiasm.

"I'll take it," Veronica confirmed. "Thank you, Jesse."

"And scene!" Mrs. Thomas announced. The room erupted in applause, with a couple cheers here and there. "Everybody, take a quick five-minute break, and then we'll come back and discuss!"

I couldn't make it off the stage fast enough. I walked to a table with concessions in the hallway and grabbed a cup of water. Everyone was scattered around, talking amongst themselves. Some went to use the bathroom, and some stepped outside for some fresh air. As I looked around at the different photos along the walls, I caught eyes with Grace and Hope and walked over to talk to them. They smiled as I approached them, and I could tell they were amused with my performance.

"How was the exam?" Grace giggled.

"It was so ridiculous! I haven't seen problems like that since I was a sophomore. I don't retain unnecessary information for longer than I need it," I complained, sending them into a hysterical bout of laughter.

"I wish…you could've seen your face," Hope gasped between words.

"You looked at the first question, and the face you made had us thinking your test was in a different language," Grace added, wiping away tears.

At least I didn't have to worry about being seen as the knee-slut for my ripped jeans. No. I had a new identity instead: Gabby, the dumbass. It had a nice ring to it. Still, I couldn't help but crack up with them because their amusement was so contagious. As we finished laughing at my pain, Mr. Ross entered the hallway.

"Hey, Mr. Ross!" Grace waved.

"What's up, Grace! Hope!" he started, "Gabby, I'm so happy to see you here again! Don't let these two get you into trouble," he joked, laughing with the girls before continuing down the hall.

"You know Mr. Ross?" Grace asked.

"He's my boyfriend's dad," I admitted nervously.

"Boyfriend?!" they said in unison. "Daniel's your boyfriend?!" Hope added.

"So, you finally had the conversation with those guys, huh?" Grace smirked, nudging me on the shoulder.

"Not exactly," I hedged. "I only had a conversation with Daniel, and now we're...*us*," I confessed. Before they could react, Mrs. Thomas called us back into the room. *Saved by the Bible,* I thought.

As we got back to our seats, we each found another study guide waiting for us on our chairs. There were a multitude of Bible passages and lined pages for us to take notes. Did I ever take the time to look through these when I got home? No. But I appreciated having them to guide me in the moment.

"At the last study, I asked you all, *'What happens when you accept an agreement you can't uphold?'* Did anyone reflect on that? I know it's spring break for a lot of you, so I understand if you forgot," Mrs. Thomas said forgivingly.

"I came up with something," Victor offered, "I wrote down that someone probably gets hurt when you make an agreement you can't honor."

"That's a good point, Victor. When it comes to God's agreement with His people, do you think it's God or His people who get hurt when the agreement isn't upheld?"

"I'm not sure if God gets hurt the way we do, but I do think it upsets Him?" Hope responded unsurely.

"Why?"

"Because He loves us," Hope answered.

"Why else?"

There was a pause while we thought—or pretended to think—for an answer.

"Remember when I said that God's love is unconditional but spending eternity with Him is not?" she nudged.

"Oh! So maybe God gets upset because when we dishonor His agreement with us, we prevent ourselves from being able to spend eternity with Him?" Veronica added.

"Bingo. God's standard for spending eternity with Him is to be sinless. Sin, simply put, is the act of disobeying the commands of God," Mrs. Thomas explained.

"Wait, wait, wait!" I exclaimed before I got dragged into a never-ending rabbit hole of confusion. "We've been talking about God's *'agreement'* with His people a lot, but I don't even know what the agreement is! Or was? Does the agreement even still exist?"

"Oh, I'm sorry, Gabby! If you look at the first page of your study guide, there's a quick recap of the agreement in Exodus chapter 19, verses 5 through 6. It reads:

" 'Now if you obey me fully and keep my covenant, then out of all nations you will be my treasured possession. Although the whole earth is mine, you will be for me a kingdom of priests and a holy nation.' These are the words you are to speak to the Israelites.

"Now, if you wanna see all the details of God's commands for the Israelites, pages two, three, and four of your study guide give you a summary of all the customs, laws, and regulations they needed to follow. It's a lot, so we broke it down into simple terms and put the scripture references in the footnotes," she explained.

"All of this is a part of the agreement they made with God?! How were they supposed to remember all of this, or even avoid mistakes?!" I asked, flipping through the study guide again. It was a lot more daunting now that I knew the context of all these scriptures.

"I agree, Gabby! I imagine you felt similarly when you took that exam during our play today?" she asked, immediately sending Hope and Grace into another round of hysterical laughter, only this time, they tried miserably to keep it to themselves.

"Yes, actually! It's not that I couldn't answer the problems, it's that I forgot the material. I haven't studied that stuff since I was a sophomore," I admitted, trying to dispel any possible suspicion that I was an idiot.

"But, luckily, Jesse got a 100% on your behalf!" Mrs. Thomas smiled.

"Yeah, it was nice of him to volunteer," I agreed.

"Mr. Ross was even nice enough to let his score benefit future students as well!"

Nice? I thought. *He also let Jesse take our consequence.*

"Do any of you think God would do something like this—let someone fulfill an agreement on behalf of everyone else?" she continued.

"Isn't that what Jesus did?" Victor asked.

"You tell me," Mrs. Thomas responded.

"Well, he lived a perfect life according to God's law, but he still took our punishment and died for our sins on our behalf. So, I would say yes."

"Prove it," she encouraged.

"2 Corinthians 5:21," Victor started, looking through his study guide, *"God made him who had no sin to be sin for us, so that in him we might become the righteousness of God,"* he finished.

"Wait," Jesse said as he rose his hand. "Isn't that circular reasoning? The Bible is the same book that tells us that Jesus died for us in the first place, and so when you say prove it and then point to the Bible again, it's like...how can we trust that the Bible isn't making stuff up?"

Ooo, good question, I thought. I looked at Mrs. Thomas to see how she would handle this one—we all did. Even I hadn't thought of that, and I asked more questions than anyone else.

"You're thinking critically, Jesse, I like it. Do you know why we believe the Bible?"

"Not really, no," he admitted.

"I want you to imagine you lived in the Middle East two thousand years ago along the eastern-most border of the Mediterranean Sea. All is normal in your daily routine, and then you meet this man named Jesus. He asks you to follow him, so you do. You witness Jesus teach the Jewish scriptures flawlessly, prophesy of things to come, heal the sick, restore the sight of the blind, rebuke demons— you name it. The authority of God is clearly within Him, and it's obvious that Jesus is no ordinary man. But then, He tells you something the perplexes you. He tells you that He and the Father are one—He is in the Father, and the Father is in Him—"

"What does that even mean!" Jesse interrupted, throwing his hands up. "I thought Yoda from Star Wars was bad."

"Well, the Jewish crowd that Jesus was speaking to understood Jesus' remarks to be claims of His being equal to God. So, then, when you fast forward to Jesus being publicly killed by the Romans, it would be natural to question how someone who is supposedly equal to God could die, right?"

"Yeah, that's like the biggest L of the millennium, honestly," Jesse agreed.

"That's what his disciples were thinking! In less modern terms, of course," Mrs. Thomas laughed. "Now, I wasn't there obviously, but I imagine some of their thoughts were, *'What do we do now? This man we've been following, who we thought for sure was the messiah, is DEAD. Was everything He said a lie?'*"

"That's embarrassing. I'd change my name and flee the country," Victor added, earning a few chuckles.

"YES! Exactly. I mean—they killed Jesus, so what do you think they had planned for His followers? After Jesus' death, His disciples were locked in a room together, scared for their lives, when suddenly Jesus appeared—alive and in the flesh. Not a ghost, but a man—with the wounds from His death visible on His hands and on His side—and in that moment they knew everything He had told them was true.

"So, Jesse," Mrs. Thomas looked at him, "Christians believe that Jesus is fully man and fully God, that He died for our sins, and that He resurrected on the third day not because the Bible says so, but because everything Jesus prophesied to His followers and everything that the prophets that came before Him foretold about Him was proven true the minute He returned from His death.

"If He told them He was going to die and come back and that turned out to be true, then surely everything else He said was also true. So then, we know that what we read in the Bible is the truth because it is comprised of the teachings of Jesus Himself and testimonies of His life that were pieced together by hundreds of eyewitness accounts.

"Now, tell me, if a hundred people give the same eyewitness account in a court of law, do we not regard it as trustworthy?"

"We do," Jesse confirmed, seemingly satisfied with Mrs. Thomas' explanation. The room was silent for a moment as we took in the plethora of words that had just spilled out of her mouth. I looked back and forth between Mrs. Thomas and Jesse and everybody else, trying to read the room. We were all silent, but there was no tension. It was as if we were all simply…speechless.

I took the opportunity to open my Sociology notebook and take down some notes about how everyone interacted. For the most part, everyone got along. Veronica and Victor were the hilarious exception, of course. Though Mrs. Thomas was clearly the leader of the Bible study, there was enough room for others to step into the conversation with questions, even if it caused a detour in the original direction of the study.

I didn't know everyone well enough yet to determine if the church had shaped any of them on an individual level, but I had seen a variety of personalities thus far. Victor was the comedic relief, Veronica was sassy, Hope was super cheerful, and Jesse seemed to be the critic.

Before the silence got awkward, Mrs. Thomas spoke again, though I was only half listening as I jotted down my Sociology notes. "Before we move on, it's only fitting that I take this moment to ask. Now that we've learned about what Jesus did for us, is there anyone here who hasn't accepted Jesus as their Lord and savior who would like to do so today? This is a judgement-free zone, so please do not feel pressured to raise your hand."

The significance of her question pulled me from my note taking, and when I looked up, I realized she was standing in the middle of the circle.

A few hands went up, including Jesse's. Our eyes all searched around the circle, gazing at each other as hands went up, looking to see who would raise theirs next. I sat there awkwardly, suddenly realizing that other people had felt a connection during the study that I hadn't. What was just another day at Agape Church for me was a life-changing experience for others.

"Praise God! This is awesome," Mrs. Thomas declared after the last hand went up. "I would like for everyone to close their eyes as I pray with those who've decided to accept God's gift of salvation. If you were too shy to raise your hand, that's okay; God knows the intent of your heart and this prayer is just as much for you as it is for them.

"Father God, we thank you for the sacrifice of your Son Jesus Christ on our behalf. We thank you for your love and for your forgiveness of our sins. Lord, we accept your gift of salvation with gratitude, and we ask that you enter our hearts today and forevermore. In your mighty name we pray, amen."

As soon as the prayer was finished, the circle erupted with cheers and applause in celebration of those who had accepted Christ. Mrs. Thomas went to Jesse first and embraced him with a hug, then made her way around to the others. Hope and Grace jumped out of their seats on either side of me and joined a few others in hugging and congratulating. The emotion in the room was overwhelming—the joy, the tears, the laughs. I was the last one still sitting, watching everyone share a beautiful moment together, and I couldn't feel a thing.

Why don't I feel what they feel? I asked myself. My nose began to burn as tears of frustration welled up at the rims of my lower eyelids. It was like watching everyone open Christmas gifts while I sat there with nothing at all. How were they able to feel a connection to someone who was no longer here? How could they listen to the stories about Jesus and not feel like it was just that—a story?

I wiped a tear off of my nose as I packed up, trying to make my escape before the tears could take over completely. I quickly got up and slung my backpack over my shoulder, which unfortunately caught the attention of Mrs. Thomas. I ignored the blatant eye contact we'd made and beelined my way to the exit.

"Gabby, hey!" she called as she rushed to catch up to me, grabbing my elbow gently when she did. "Are you okay? We were just about to finish up."

"I'm fine. I've had enough for one day, so I'm just gonna head home, now," I sniffled, adjusting my backpack strap on my shoulder.

"Gabby, I really think you should sta—"

"I said I'm fine, Mrs. Thomas! Thank you," I asserted, cutting her off.

She dropped her hand from my elbow and nodded patiently. "Okay. Drive safely. We're here for you if you need anything."

I nodded and walked away, leaving what I had hoped would be another mind-blowing experience, but had proved to be just a Sociology project, after all.

CHAPTER 23

The entire drive home I was fighting tears and fighting myself. Why had I stormed out of the study like that? How could I talk to Grace's mom that way? How could I go back after that? But I was right to feel the way I felt! Right? I could feel just about every emotion except the love for God that I realized I'd been secretly hoping to acquire as a result of these Bible studies. My chest was tight with frustration and my throat felt swollen with a sorrow that I just couldn't seem to swallow.

I'd started going to the Bible studies as a last-minute decision for my Sociology project, but deep down, seeing everyone get along and gather together just to talk about God had given me hope. I'd hoped that maybe if I fell in love with God the way I fell in love with Ryan, my life would be better, somehow. Maybe it would hurt less to have feelings for Ryan if I loved God instead. Maybe if I fell in love with God, Daniel would, too, and his relationship with his father would change for the better. Maybe.

Would I ever know, now? I walked into my house in such a fury that I blew past my mom, not realizing she was in the kitchen as I beelined my way to the staircase.

"Hey! Wait a minute, Gabby!" my mom called out. By the time I turned around she was already close behind me, standing at the foot of the stairs.

"Oh, hey. I'm sorry, I didn't even realize you were there," I sniffled, trying to avoid eye contact, though I knew there was no use in hiding how I felt now that I had turned to face her.

"What happened?"

"More like what *didn't* happen, Mom," I whined.

"Talk to me—I'm not understanding, did something *not* happen with you and Daniel? What is it?"

"When did you know that you loved God, Mom?"

At this question, her posture straightened. She was visibly caught off guard. I remembered her having the same reaction when I'd asked her about church. "Where is this coming from?" she asked.

"Please, Mom, I don't wanna talk about that, I just—when did you know?" I begged, leaning against the wall from the middle of the staircase and letting my tears fall in defeat. My mom quickly pulled me down to sit with her, wrapping her arm around my shoulder so I could rest my head on hers.

"I knew I loved God when I got so tired of trying to hold myself together that He became my last hope. One day I was sitting in church, and all that scripture could've gone in one ear and out the other for all I cared—in that moment, all I wanted was God. The sermon, the Bible verses, the fancy talk, I wasn't there for that. I just wanted to get to Him. I wanted Him to make it all better and I knew He could, and I loved Him because of that. Is that selfish? Maybe. But after one too many heartbreaks, one too many failed friendships, and one too many failed attempts to redefine myself—I was tired. God was my pillow," she said softly.

"Why isn't it like the love I have for Ryan? With him, I remember exactly how I knew and why I knew, but with God, I feel like I'm expected to fall in love with a stranger, Mom. They told me Jesus calls God His father. How can I treat God like a father when I don't even remember my own?" I cried.

I was so caught up in the moment that I hadn't realized that I told her how I felt for Ryan until seconds later. Upon realizing, I sat up straight, hoping she hadn't noticed. Who was I kidding, though? She was my mother, of course she'd noticed.

"Mmm. I see what's happening," my mom said aloud.

"What?" I lifted my head to look at her.

"You've been trying to fill the space in your life left by your father. How about instead, you think about loving God this way: maybe it's not about God filling the place of your natural father, but you making room for Him as your spiritual father. What do you think?"

"I don't know what to think, right now," I admitted, wiping my face.

"That's okay. We don't have to unpack all of that right now. The truth is, Gabby, coming to that moment of loving and accepting God is different for everyone. I don't know what that will look like for you, and I don't want to rob you of your experience by telling you what to look for—but what I *can* say is, you'll know it when it happens—that moment. You might not even fully understand where it comes from, but it'll be there. And hold onto it tight, Gabby, because that love is going to change your life."

"Okay," I said slowly, nodding as I stood up.

She grabbed my hand. "Is there anything else you want to talk to me about?" she asked, and it was the way she looked at me that told me she hadn't missed what I'd said about Ryan.

"No. I'm feeling a little better, now. Thank you," I lied.

"I love you, Gabby," she said before letting go of my hand.

"I love you, too."

The next day, I told Melanie everything: the Bible study, my accidental Ryan confession with my mom—all of it. I of course made the decision to camp out at her house for the day, just in case my mom tried to bring up my slip-up once she got home from work. This meant I had the luxury of being sucked into a random party in the middle of the day with a few of Melanie's Cuban and Mexican relatives.

"You've gotta tell her the full truth, Gabby," Melanie declared, squeezing lime juice over her chips. We were sitting at her backyard bar while her dad prepared food for the grill; Guapo was running around our feet, waiting for the chip droppings he knew would come his way eventually.

"WHAT?! That's like…the complete opposite of what I wanna do. Why would I do that?"

"Because!!! What if she slips up and says something to Ryan or Daniel? Like…in typical parent fashion where they ramble nervously and say a bunch of stuff they shouldn't?"

"I can't imagine my mom being that stupid," I defended, stealing a chip from her plate.

"Suit yourself. I'm sorry about the Bible study thing, though. Did Daniel's dad see you storm out?"

"No, thank God. I don't know what I'm gonna say to him at Daniel's pool party tomorrow." I hadn't even thought about Daniel's dad until Melanie brought him up. What if they told him what happened, and I fell from his good graces?

"Well, maybe no one even mentioned it to him! Then there'll be nothing to talk about except how beautiful his home is. You know— typical parent ass kissing and such," Melanie hypothesized as she poured herself more chips.

"Let's hope so." I handed her my plate so she could pour me some as well.

"I take it you're still not going to tell Ryan how you feel?" She offered to squeeze a lime over my chips and I nodded.

"Nah. It would make things too messy, and it wouldn't be respectful to his or my relationship."

"Right…Daniel. How are things with him, anyway? Do your feelings for Ryan ever get in the way?"

"Things have been really good, Mel. I like him a lot," I swooned. "It's weird because when I'm with Daniel, I don't really think about Ryan, and when I'm with Ryan, I don't really think about Daniel. It's like I've compartmentalized them into different parts of my brain, and it's not until I'm around both of them at the same time that I remember I have feelings for them both."

"That *is* weird… I still think you should tell Ryan. Put it all out there once and for all!" Melanie raised her other fist patriotically, like she was rallying for a greater cause.

"No, you want me to be a homewrecker," I laughed.

"You really think that's homewrecking?"

"You don't?!" I volleyed.

"Let's ask my dad. Hey, *Papá*!" she yelled, sending me into a panic. What was she doing?! Who said anything about involving parents in this?! And of course, I couldn't be rude and shoo him away in his own backyard!

"*Qué pasó,* ladies?" Mr. Reyes asked as he walked over to us.

"Would it be considered homewrecking if a woman confessed her hopeless, undying love for you even though you and Ma are happily married?" She smiled innocently.

"What's this about, *mija*?" he asked suspiciously. "Is there a girl trying to come after Marcus? You better put her in her place, girl. I didn't raise a punk," he teased, punching the air with a couple jabs and an uppercut.

"*Ay*, no! We're just asking, Dad. Stop embarrassing me!" she giggled.

"Okay, well," he sighed, resting his elbow on the bar counter, "a woman can't wreck a secure home. It takes two to tango, but it takes one to destroy a marriage, and that *one* would be me. Let's say a woman does confess her feelings for me; my home would only be wrecked if I do something stupid and step out on your mom. Since I'm the one who lives inside the house, I'm the only one who has the power to mess up what's on the inside."

"But wouldn't the woman still be looked at like…an attempted robber or something?" I asked, trying to get an answer out of him that would get Melanie off my case.

"That depends on what her intentions were, *Gabriella*. If she was trying to break into my house and destroy everything, then yes. But even so, I'm not gonna let that woman try to wreck a marriage I care a lot about, *sí*? So, it's all about the intent behind the conversation," he asserted.

"Do you think it would be pointless for her to tell you how she feels?" I tried again.

"Absolutely. I would tell her she needs to move on. If telling me how she felt was her first step in moving on, then whatever, but it would mean nothing to me because of how I feel for my wife," he said, stealing a chip from Melanie's plate.

"Okay, thanks, Dad, you can go now!" Melanie said, smacking his hand away from her chips.

"Consider this your payment for my wisdom," he ribbed, stealing her entire plate as he walked away.

"There you have it. It's not homewrecking," Melanie affirmed. "Well—unless you want to be a homewrecker. But you don't, right?"

"Of course not, Mel." I paused, analyzing my motives. "At least…not intentionally." When I sat and thought about it, I couldn't honestly say that I didn't want Ryan to leave Indya for me.

"Not intentionally?" Melanie looked at me with a confused expression and then gasped dramatically when I didn't say anything. "No. No, no, no, Gabby! I will not have a homewrecker as a friend! And you know we don't even use the word 'homewrecker' these days! We've shortened it to just the first two letters! I can't be best friends with a ho, Gabby! That makes me a ho by association!" she whined. I loved how this had turned into a crisis over her reputation.

"Oh my God, Melanie, would you calm down and let me explain?"

"Oh, please do! Explain why you waited until the end of senior year to ruin our reputations, Gabby!"

"No one is ruining anything, Mel, that's the point! But you remember when Ryan and I had that argument and he said he liked me *'despite my flaws'*?"

"Oooo, yeah, that was juicy," Melanie confirmed.

"Well, when he said that, I considered telling him I liked him, too, but then I realized that the only reason I'd do that was out of the hope that he'd leave Indya and we'd be together. But that would be…"

"Homewrecking," Melanie finished. "Damn. I see, now. Well, why couldn't you just tell me that instead of having me wait in torment all this time!"

"Because I started to get caught up in how well Daniel was treating me while Ryan was ignoring me. And then I caught feelings for Daniel, too, and decided to give things with him a chance, and…here we are."

Melanie nodded as I laid out the sequence for her. "Right. Okay. So telling Ryan is a no-go… But now what are you gonna do about your feelings for him? Do you really think they're going to magically go away? What happens if Daniel realizes you have feelings for them both?"

"I—I have no idea. I thought moving forward with Daniel would help me get rid of my feelings for Ryan, but it hasn't! And—" I stopped mid-sentence as I suddenly got clarity on what my mom had said the night before.

"You've been trying to fill the space in your life left by your father."

"And what, G? I'm at the edge of my seat here! I feel like I'm watching a Lifetime movie."

"And all this time I've been trying to fill the void left by different men in my life by replacing them with others," I realized out loud.

Melanie stared at me blankly. "I'm sorry, what? Did I accidentally change the channel or something? What happened to my Lifetime movie?" she asked, playfully smacking the remote to the outdoor TV.

"Do you remember what I said about my mom and me talking last night? She said I was trying to fill the place left by my dad, and I didn't get what she meant until now. I've been trying to fill the void of not having a dad with my feelings for Ryan. But then when that wasn't working out, I tried to replace my feelings for Ryan with my feelings for Daniel…but my feelings for Ryan weren't going away so I subconsciously tried to fill the void with God at the Bible studies." *Whew.* I sat back in my seat. "Either way, it all starts with my dad. I really do have daddy issues, and he's not even here anymore."

"Damn," Melanie sighed. We sat together for a moment, processing my realization with the seriousness of someone who'd just found out they had a life-threatening health condition.

"You look like you need a shot," Melanie said sympathetically, stealthily pulling out a bottle of tequila from her dad's stash.

Feeling hopeless, I took the bottle from her hand and knocked back a big sip. I needed more than a shot, but at least it would take the edge off.

CHAPTER 24

The next day, as I parked my car in Daniel's driveway, my mind was racing a mile a minute. Even though I didn't have any proof, I was certain Daniel's dad had heard about my dramatic exit from the Bible study on Wednesday, and that wasn't something I was ready to explain, yet.

On top of that, as if my anxiety weren't enough, my stomach was in knots. Why? Oh, nothing, it's just that Daniel had invited the entire gang to hang out at his pool, and I still had no answer for Melanie. What *was* I going to do if Daniel found out I had feelings for both him and Ryan? How would that turn out? Would it turn into a fight between him and Ryan, or a fight between me and him?

"Hey," said Melanie from my passenger's seat, "you alright?"

"Yeah," I lied. "For sure."

"Things are going to be okay, G. You're just caught up in your feelings right now. Forget about them for today and just have fun." She got out of the car, and I took a deep breath and got out after her.

I could hear the music through the door as we approached his doorstep, and I figured ringing the doorbell would be useless, but I did it anyway to avoid being rude. The last thing I wanted was for

Daniel's parents to think I'd gotten too comfortable. I also *may* have been stalling, but I like my first explanation better.

"Seriously, Gabby? We talked about this. Just walk in," Melanie scoffed, opening the already unlocked door.

As we made our way through the door, Mrs. Ross poked her head into the foyer from the kitchen, and then smiled when she saw us. She was wearing an apron and was covered in what appeared to be flour and seasonings.

"Hey, girls! I thought I heard the doorbell, but I couldn't tell over this loud music. Daniel's in the backyard blowing up the floaties. There's a guest bedroom downstairs for you to get changed in, just keep walking like you're going to the back door, and then hook a left and it's your first room on the right!" she explained warmly.

"I don't think we've met, Mrs. Ross, I'm Melanie, Gabby's best friend," she said, holding her hand out to shake.

"Of course, hi, Melanie! I guess all the best friends will be here today, huh?" she laughed, shaking Melanie's hand. "My husband is around here, somewhere. I'm sure he'll find you guys and say hi. Make yourselves at home, okay? I'm making wings right now, and I'll start on some brownies, later!"

As we walked toward the guest room, we could see Daniel's gorgeous backyard through the giant glass doors and windows. His pool was insane, with a stone waterfall on one edge and color changing LED lights around the perimeter of the pool floor. Across from the pool, a stone path led to a patio with a fire pit right at the center.

I, of course, spotted Daniel and Ryan blowing up the floaties together, talking casually and probably completely unaware of how unbelievably fine they were. It didn't help that they were shirtless, too. *Help me, God,* I thought.

"Where's Indya?" I asked as we passed the back door.

"Right here," a voice rang out as the girl in question walked toward us from what I assumed was the guest room we were headed to. *You've got to be kidding me,* I thought. It wasn't the fact that she was there, it was the fact that now that I could see her in a bathing suit, I realized she had a body straight out of a magazine. Her pure white bikini absolutely popped against her skin tone, and emphasized her figure so perfectly that it was like looking at a living, breathing photoshopped model. My hope was that with Indya there, Ryan would be so far up her ass that it wouldn't be hard for me to focus on Daniel, but now, I was wondering if Daniel would be able to focus on *me.*

"Oh, hey," I said, trying to sound excited.

"See you outside," she said, passing us as she spoke.

Forget your feelings, I told myself as Melanie and I changed into our swimsuits. I'd brought two different options, but after seeing Indya, I pulled out my yellow bikini rather than my go-to, black one-piece. Black was my comfort color whenever I dealt with internal turmoil of any sort, but I couldn't let Indya completely show me up. I checked my reflection one more time before we made our way to the backyard, tugging on my bikini strings to make sure I was accident proof.

"What's this?" Melanie asked, picking up papers that had been slid underneath the door while we were changing. She handed them to me. "I guess it's for you?"

I immediately recognized it as the study guide packet from Wednesday. There was a pink sticky note on the front page that read:

Gabrielle,
Don't worry about Wednesday. Just have fun today.
— Mr. Ross

I let out a deep sigh as I read the note and then put the papers in my bag. "It's the study guide from Wednesday's Bible study. Mr.

Ross must've held onto it for me after I left," I explained. I felt relieved to know that even though Daniel's dad knew what had happened, he was just as eager to move past it as I was.

When we were done changing, we made our way to the backyard to join the others. "THE PARTY HAS ARRIVED!" Melanie announced theatrically as she slid open the back door.

Daniel immediately stood up to greet me.

"Finally," he smiled, pulling my face up by my chin for a kiss. "You look incredible, by the way." He took me by the hand and spun me around.

"Ugh, ok. Time-out!" Melanie announced, making the time-out hand signal. "What we're not gonna do today is over-do it with the lovey dovey shit, alright, guys?"

Daniel laughed, letting go of me. Meanwhile, I still had yet to acknowledge Ryan. "I told you that you could invite Marcus," Daniel objected.

"Marcus-*Shmarcus*. Today is about *friends,* not relationships!"

I rolled my eyes at her *friendship* front. The only reason she was saying this was because Marcus was out of town for the break. She'd practically inhaled the tortilla chips at her family party the day before to keep herself from going crazy over it.

"What's up, G," Ryan said from one of the lounge chairs in front of me.

"Hey!" I smiled, forming a sun visor with my hand as I looked in his direction.

"You alright?" he asked.

"Of course," I half-lied. Even though I felt better, I was still figuring out the whole *"forget your feelings"* thing for the day. I guess, in true best friend fashion, he could tell I wasn't quite all the way there.

Before the conversation could continue, Daniel scooped me into his arms and ran to the pool, jumping into the deep end. I pathetically reached out for Melanie as I screamed, as if she could—or would—save me. In fact, I could hear her cheering Daniel on as we plunged to my demise—that heifer.

"It's cold!!!!" I screamed when I resurfaced.

"You seemed like you needed some refreshment," said Daniel shamelessly as he floated leisurely past me. Meanwhile, I could still hear Melanie over on dry land cracking up. An evil lightbulb turned on above my head, and I swam to the edge of the pool near Ryan and Indya.

"Hey, Ryan," I said casually, not wanting to appear suspicious to Melanie. He got up and walked closer to the pool so he could hear me better over the music.

"I think Melanie wants to join me. Can you help her out?" I winked. He looked over at her; she was tying her hair into a bun in the reflection of Daniel's back door with her back turned to us.

Ryan smiled brightly at my request, then walked over to Melanie. He bent over beside her as if to grab one of the floaties lying next to her and then quickly snatched her up and ran to the pool, dumping her over the edge. "Wait, wait, wait, Ryan, PLEA—" was all she could get out before she felt the cold, sweet feeling of my revenge.

Ryan bent down to dap me up but had no idea that I was planning to get him, too. Right as our fists were about to touch, I quickly grabbed his arm and pulled as hard as I could. He wouldn't budge.

"Damn! Try again!" he mocked, not realizing Indya was creeping up behind him. He was close enough to the edge that when she suddenly jumped on his back, all he could do was fall forward.

Daniel got out of the pool and then reached his hand out to help me get out as well. "Are you alright?" he asked softly in my ear.

"Yeah, why?" I returned. I was starting to get concerned that maybe my emotions were more visible than I thought.

"I just wanted to take the time to ask. I realized it probably wasn't the best idea to throw you in the pool if there actually was something wrong," he admitted.

"Trust me, I'm fine. I just wanna have fun," I reassured him. And I meant it, really. After all the self-induced stress I'd been through during the week, I just wanted to have fun again before we went back to school.

I helped Daniel throw the floaties into the pool, and tried to get back in, but he grabbed my hand and pulled me back toward the lounge chairs with him. "What's wrong?" I asked.

"Nothing, I just want you to myself for a second," he said, sitting down in a chair and patting the space in front of him.

"Hey, Gabbyyyy. Why'd you run away? Are you scared I might get you back for trying to play me?" Ryan teased from the pool. "I thought we were cooler than that, G. I see you were just using me to get back at Melanie, huh?" he taunted.

"YOU SET THAT UP?!" Melanie chimed in the background. "Come in the water, Gabby, I just wanna talk!" she cooed as she splashed water toward me.

"Nah, she won't. She's too chicken," Ryan continued, making chicken noises. Melanie joined in on his foolishness.

I looked back at Daniel, who was staring at me in amusement, but I could tell he still wanted me to sit with him. As hard as his beautiful face was to resist, I felt the pull of my best friends even stronger. "I'll be right back," I told Daniel, running to the pool and jumping back in.

As soon as I resurfaced, Ryan and Melanie began beating me with pool noodles. I snatched Ryan's noodle and began to smack him with it for assuming I was too chicken to own up to my actions. Instead of fighting back, he quickly slipped under the water and began swimming toward my legs. I froze as he got closer, trying to figure out if I should turn and try to escape, or brace for impact.

"SWIM, G. DON'T JUST STAND THERE—" Melanie yelled before I suddenly shot up into the air in Ryan's arms. He had wrapped his arms around my legs and stood up in the water. Because of his height, I was much higher up than I was used to, and it was just as terrifying as it was exciting.

"WHAT ARE YOU DOING!" I screamed as he began walking up the steps of the pool. I was now hanging over his shoulder like a rag doll, secretly enjoying the thrill of not knowing what would happen next.

He stood by the deep end of the pool and then lifted me off his shoulder by my waist so that I was suspended in the air above his head. "Any last words?" he asked.

"Does it even matter?" I replied.

"Good point," he said before he tossed me carelessly into the water.

I made my way out of the pool and headed back over to Daniel, who had his fist held out to dap me up. "You put up a good fight," he laughed.

"Yeah, yeah, whatever. We all know that's the nice way of telling me I lost," I said as I sat down. "Now, where were we?"

"I want to take another picture like the last time you were here," he explained as he spread his legs to each side of the lounge chair and patted the space in front of him again. I obliged, sitting in front of him, and he wrapped his arms around my waist, pulling us back against the seat of the chair. I adjusted myself so that my head lay against his chest, and then wrapped my arms around his waist. Listening for his heartbeat, I closed my eyes to its calm, steady cadence.

"Say cheese."

"Cheeeese," I sang, which was followed by the artificial sound of the camera shutter from his phone. "Let me see!" I sat up and looked at his phone, noting his beautiful smile, and that we looked radiant in the direct sunlight, the beads of pool water shining on our skin like diamonds.

"This is our new signature," he declared.

"Okay," I agreed, smiling up at him. He pulled me in for a quick peck on the lips, and then another, and then—

"YOOO GABBY! DO YOU REMEMBER THIS SONG?" Ryan yelled excitedly from the pool.

I stopped for a moment to listen, and a wave of nostalgia hit me as I recognized the tune. "OH MY GOD, NO WAY!" I exclaimed, sitting upright. It was an Aventura classic, and when Ryan's mom had taught us how to dance *Bachata* during our sophomore year, we'd practiced to this song over and over to surprise her for her birthday.

"Do you still remember the steps?" he asked, making his exit from the water.

"Do I? I still have dreams of that routine!" I got up from my spot in front of Daniel and met Ryan in an open space near the pool. Indya and Melanie swam their way to the edge of the pool to watch.

"Ready?" Ryan asked, placing one hand on my back and holding my hand with the other.

"Of course I'm ready," I almost flirted, mirroring his hand placement.

We jumped right into the routine, starting with a dramatic body roll and turn, followed by a basic side-step sequence from one side to the next. We separated and pulled back together in a series of sharp and smooth motions, all the while maintaining eye contact and a very firm grip on one another. Even though we'd done the dance countless times, doing it shirtless gave us a new level of closeness we hadn't had before. My heart raced each time the routine called for body-to-body contact. Ryan, like Daniel, was perfectly sculpted, so pressing against him was like pressing against a rock-solid, buttery smooth wall.

Our grand finale was a dramatic dip and freeze, with Ryan leaning over me. I held onto his arms for dear life, though he'd never dropped me before—not once. We stared intently at each other as the song faded and then immediately burst into laughter. I let myself fall to the ground gently and looked over at Melanie, who was smiling awkwardly next to Indya, who had disproval and annoyance written all over her face.

"Tough crowd," I whispered to Ryan as he pulled me off the ground.

"Yeaahhhh. I'm never gonna hear the end of this," he muttered under his breath.

I walked back over to Daniel, who also looked far from amused. "What's wrong?" I asked, taking the lounge chair next to him this time.

"What's up with you and Ryan?" he asked, causing my heart to skip a beat.

"What do you mean?"

"I don't know, he just seemed really comfortable touching you like that, and you didn't seem to mind," he explained.

"Daniel, it was just a dance. We've done it like a million times," I asserted. Was it a romantic dance? Yes. But Ryan and I had done it so many times in a non-romantic way that neither of us had considered it inappropriate in the moment.

"Is that supposed to make me feel better? That was practically foreplay, and you've done it a million times?" he pressed.

"Babe, I promise," I insisted, joining him on his lounge chair. "It was just a dance."

"Okay. I believe you," he conceded. "I guess I'm just a little salty that you left me here in the middle of my kisses. Got me over here feeling a little…*clink-clink*," he chuckled, clearly shaking it off.

Clink-clink, I thought. Damn. Even though I felt like what I was doing was harmless, it was making Daniel feel insecure. He wanted me to get on the rollercoaster with him, and I'd left the seat next to him empty to go enjoy a different ride. If the roles were reversed, I'd probably feel the same. Okay, scratch that. I'd *definitely* feel the same.

"I'm sorry," I sighed, fidgeting with my fingers.

"It's alright." He kissed me on the cheek and then stood up. "I'm getting back in the pool. You coming?"

"I'm gonna run to the restroom real quick, and then I'll be back out."

I needed a moment to gather myself so I could, as Melanie suggested, *forget my feelings*. What better way to do so than to scroll mindlessly through social media for a few minutes in the guest bath? I sat on the edge of the bathtub and did just that until I stumbled across the photo Daniel and I had taken earlier. It had been posted a few minutes ago with the caption: *Realizing how much I hate sharing you.* There was no doubt he'd posted it while Ryan and I were dancing.

"What happens if Daniel realizes you have feelings for them both?"

I felt a surge of panic as I thought about Melanie's question yet again. Almost as quickly as I'd had that thought, Melanie barged in.

"I figured you'd be in here. What the hell was that?"

"What was what?" I played dumb.

"You and Ryan! Out there auditioning for *Dancing with the Stars* and shit!"

"Melanie. I get it," I interjected before she could go any further. She was not the best at reading a room, apparently.

"Do you, though? I know I said today was about friends, but that was before you started getting a little too *friendly* with someone who isn't your boyfriend," she argued. Okay. I was officially getting irritated. At least Daniel hadn't cast full blame on me. Melanie, though? I expected better.

"I said I get it!" I stood up. "It's *Bachata*! You know better than anyone else how intimate it is!"

"Uh, yeah! How do you think I got here? My mom and dad danced *Bachata* at the club one night and somehow ended up in the bedroom!" she joked. I couldn't help but laugh with her for the simple fact that it was a true story.

"Look, I'm just saying y'all looked like more than friends out there. That's why I'm on you so hard. I don't want you to mess up what you have with Daniel if you really do like him the way you say you do," she explained.

"Yeah, well, don't worry about it. All I can think about now is the question you asked me yesterday. I really do like him, and I don't want to risk losing someone as sweet as him if he finds out I also like Ryan," I admitted, showing her his post on my phone.

"Awww," she said as she analyzed the photo. "Well, let's go, then, girl. You can't be with him if you're in here feeling sorry for yourself." She started to open the bathroom door, but I grabbed her hand.

"Wait! Did Indya say anything to Ryan about it?" I bit my thumb nail in curiosity.

"Giiiirl yes," Melanie enthused. "I can tell she was trying not to make a scene, but you don't talk with your hands like that unless you're going off on somebody. I wanted to stay and watch, but I had to come check on you, first, so hurry up and let's go before we miss everything!"

She grabbed my hand, and we headed back out toward the backyard, but the show was already over by the time we got there. Indya, Ryan, and Daniel were playing an uneven game of volleyball like nothing had ever happened.

"Ooo! I call referee!" Melanie announced, running to the side of the pool to watch. I got inside and joined Daniel, who was currently fending for himself.

Indya was never the type to assert her presence around us, but that changed drastically once I rejoined the party. For the rest of the day, she made it clear that Ryan was hers by constantly jumping all over him, kissing him, and making sure he never made it within five feet of me. It was clear she was marking her territory.

I even saw Ryan pull her aside and tell her to chill out when he thought I wasn't listening. Had I really been that threatening? If she had even a glimpse of how differently Ryan treated me compared to her when it was just us at his house, she'd know her tactics were quite unnecessary.

"Hi, guys! The food is finished, come get something to eat!" Mrs. Ross called out from the patio sometime later. Ryan, Indya, and Daniel were the first to grab their seats while Mr. Ross got the bonfire started for us to sit around.

"Hi, Mr. Ross," I said as I approached the patio, "thank you for the study guide."

"Anytime, Gabby. You were an excellent actress on Wednesday," he laughed. Once the fire shot up from the bonfire, he stood to face me. "If you ever want to talk about anything, whether it be about the Bible studies, or Daniel, or anything else, I'd be more than happy to listen," he assured me.

I expressed my thanks and then Daniel grabbed my hand from the chair next to me and pulled me around to sit next to him. It was a loveseat and could fit two people. In fact, all the seats were loveseats. Ryan and Indya sat across the bonfire from us, and Melanie sat in her own to our right.

Once we started to eat, I could tell why Daniel's family didn't have a personal chef; his mom's cooking was absolutely amazing. I imagined how hard it must've been for Daniel when she was all over the world translating languages for others. She seemed very sweet, from what I'd seen, but then again, so had Ryan's parents before I found out about…well, you know.

"So…your season is really over, huh?" Melanie asked, breaking the silence. The guys had lost their second game of the playoffs on Wednesday.

"Yeah." Daniel sighed. "I blame whoever messed up the schedule. We weren't supposed to play until *after* spring break, but all the travel expenses and venue fees had already been paid for, so we had no choice but to play this week."

"It is what it is," Ryan added. "I'm just happy I can relax a little, now—spend some more time with you guys before the year ends." He stretched his arm across the back of his seat and winked at Indya.

"Relax?!" Melanie sat up in her chair. "How can you relax when college application deadlines are coming up? I have one left and I'm dreading it because it's the one I really wanna get into."

"I've already finished mine!" Ryan replied.

"Me too," Indya echoed.

Melanie shifted her gaze to me and Daniel. "What about you guys? Gabby, I know you wanna go to community college, but what about you, D?"

"I'm weighing a couple offers for basketball, right now," he told us.

I perked up at his announcement—this was news to me. "I'm sorry, *what*?! Congratulations, babe! That's amazing!" I threw my arms around his neck and pulled him into a big, celebratory hug. We'd only talked about college a couple times, but he'd said nothing about any basketball offers.

"Thank you," he said, tightening his arms around my waist.

"Wait that's awesome, Daniel!" Melanie chimed. Indya followed with similar sentiments.

"I'm not the only one with offers, y'all! Ryan's over there juggling college decisions! Even though he hasn't told me which colleges they are yet."

"I don't want anyone trying to sway my decision," Ryan chortled. I remembered him tell me the same thing.

"Do you know which one you're gonna choose, yet?" Melanie inquired.

"Nah, but now that basketball's over I can spend more time thinking about it," Ryan explained.

I turned to Daniel, suddenly filled with excitement.

"What?" he asked.

"You guys should have a college announcement party!" I suggested. Melanie and Indya also lit up at the idea.

Ryan and Daniel looked at each other, seemingly amused as they contemplated the suggestion. "We'll think about it," Ryan declared, Daniel nodding in agreement.

I sat back and reveled in the fact that the people I cared for most had bright futures ahead of them—it was both inspiring and saddening. I loved that they would undoubtedly go on to do great things, but I was sad at the fact that we would probably never be as close as we were in that moment again. Between the different schools, classes, and basketball games, our quality time would look much different once we'd graduated.

How would I make time for everyone? And how would I choose between hanging out with Daniel or Ryan when opportunities arose? Would I lose one for spending more time with the other? The more I thought about it, the less excited I felt as we sat there. My mood was slowly taking a nosedive.

We finished up the remaining bites of our food, and then Melanie spoke again. "What colors are you guys thinking about for prom?"

"Prom?!" Ryan and I said simultaneously. I avoided looking at him to make the situation seem less suspicious. I'd learned my lesson about seeming *"too friendly."*

"It's barely April," I added. Prom had been nowhere on my mind until she'd brought it up. Then again, I did have a lot going on, so it's no wonder I hadn't thought about it.

"Do girls really think about prom this early?" Daniel asked.

"Absolutely!" Indya sat up. This was the most engaged I'd seen her in any conversation we'd had as a group. "Prom is a big deal. We can't just go shopping for dresses last minute; all the good stuff will be gone by then!"

"Exactly! Marcus and I already agreed on green." Melanie beamed in excitement.

"I was thinking about red, Ry. What do you think?" Indya asked him.

Ry, I repeated in my head. *Ew.* It sounded better when I said it.

"Red is cool."

"What about you, G?" Melanie asked.

"I'm not sure. I haven't been thinking about prom, to be honest," I admitted, looking at Daniel. He glanced back at me and made a silly face. I could tell by the way he discretely squeezed my hand that he'd noticed how uneasy I was becoming. I felt like I was losing control of my own mind. Like I was constantly fighting myself over the smallest things, and I didn't know why.

"Black," I declared after a few moments.

"Black?" Melanie repeated.

"Black," Daniel asserted.

Black. Black like the way I had been feeling. Black like when you're in the dark and can't find your way around. Black with confusion and uncertainty.

If I could summarize how I was feeling—what I was thinking, it would be black, because everything I thought I knew about myself—about what I wanted—seemed to be fading to…black.

CHAPTER 25

I skipped the Bible study that Saturday. How could I show my face around everyone after the last one? I would undoubtedly be the topic of discussion whether I was there or not, so I chose not. I didn't have the energy to pretend not to hear the whispers or see the stares.

Instead, I lay on the couch in the living room and stared at the ceiling as my mom watched a bunch of middle-aged women with rich husbands get into drama that I wouldn't even bother with in high school. Fortunately, she hadn't pressed the Ryan issue. She seemed to be lingering around me in case I was suddenly ready to incriminate myself and admit everything.

I had intentionally left my phone upstairs for the day because, to put it plainly, I just didn't want to be bothered. I'd thrown myself a pity party, but I wasn't aware of it until I'd gotten up to get something to eat and saw that half the day had passed, and I had spent most of it in my feelings.

Now, even though I had unintentionally thrown said pity party, one thing I was sure of was that I hadn't invited anyone else to it, which is why I was confused when the doorbell suddenly rang.

"Did you order anything?" I asked my mom from the kitchen. Food and mail deliveries were usually our only surprise guests.

"No!" she sang from the couch.

I stood on my toes and looked through the peephole of our front door, only to regret it immediately. It was Grace. Not just Grace, though—Grace and her mom. Now, it was one thing to be an asshole at their church, but I had every right to be an asshole from the comfort of my home.

Naturally, though, I didn't have it in me. What had happened on Wednesday was still weighing on me. I couldn't bear adding Saturday to that torment. I reluctantly opened the door and put on the most pleasant face I could muster up in such short notice.

"We missed you at the study today," Grace said softly. Her mom nodded in agreement.

"How do you guys know where I live?" I asked out loud, possibly even a little rudely, still trying to process the fact that they were standing on my doorstep.

"I asked Daniel," Gabby explained.

"We tried to ask if you were home, first, but Daniel said you weren't answering your phone. I hope we're not interrupting anything," Mrs. Thomas added. I snapped out of my rudeness and stepped back so they could come inside.

"Of course not. Come in," I told them. Out of all the days to take a hiatus from technology, this just so happened to be the worst. But knowing they'd tried to be courteous before showing up, I couldn't truly be upset.

Of course, my mom had managed to make herself look presentable in the thirty seconds that it had taken me to open the door and let them in—I turned toward the living room to introduce her and discovered that the TV was off, the pillows were fluffed, and her head was suddenly bonnet-free.

"This is my mom," I introduced in amusement. If only they had seen what she'd looked like just minutes ago.

"Stephanie," my mom added, reaching her hand out for Grace and Mrs. Thomas to shake.

"Éva," said Mrs. Thomas.

"Grace," Grace followed. "We're from Agape Church. Gabby has been coming to our Bible studies, and we just wanted to check on her since she wasn't there today," she explained.

"Oh, well that's sweet of you. Go ahead and make yourselves at home, then!" my mom said a little awkwardly.

"Actually, Stephanie, I'd love to chat with you and let the girls catch up, if that's okay?" Mrs. Thomas asked.

"Sure! We can go on over to my home office. I just got this amazing little couch and I've been dying to put it to use. Maybe you can help me with some decorating ideas…" my mom gushed as they headed to her office.

I'd never really noticed how outgoing my mom was until that moment. It made my heart smile to see her socialize. I couldn't even remember the last time I'd seen her go out or even talk to friends.

Grace and I made our way to the living room and took our places on the couch. She sat in the loveseat adjacent to me, and I sat on the couch where I'd been laying the entire day. Grace smiled at me and looked around, and I immediately cracked.

"I'm so sorry about Wednesday, Grace. I was so rude to your mom, and I probably put you all in an awkward position, and I—"

"It's okay, Gabby! Really!" Grace interrupted, handing me a tissue from my coffee table. I was a complete mess—like a kid who had just scraped their knee outside and couldn't form a complete sentence as they tried to tell their parent what had happened.

"At first, it was really shocking because you seemed perfectly fine the entire time, so it was hard to understand why you suddenly got so upset. I listened to a conversation my mom and Mr. Ross had, though, and he talked about his experience getting to know God. He told her how he had very little knowledge of the Bible and God, very little experience in a church, and how many times he had gotten so overwhelmed that he gave up on God before getting to the place he is today," Grace explained as I sniffled my way back to calmness.

"But that was Mr. Ross," she continued. "I want to understand you, now. I think we got so focused on making sure you understood us, that we didn't realize how little we understood you—how little we know about you. So, Gabby, I guess my first question is: why did you come to our Bible studies in the first place?" This question confused me a bit. I could've sworn I'd told her about my Sociology project.

"I wanted to observe you guys for my Sociology project," I explained.

"Right, you told me that," Grace nodded in agreement, "I guess a better question is: why did you stay? You could've gathered your information and then been on your way, but you kept coming back. Why is that?" she clarified.

"I just… I was hoping to find something about God, or about church, or about church people, that would change how Daniel views religion—or Christianity, at least," I deflected. Even though the Daniel thing was true, I didn't want to acknowledge my recent daddy issues revelation. It's not like I was lying, I just…wasn't telling the full truth.

"Daniel?" she questioned.

I nodded.

"Why?"

"I've heard the irritation in his voice when someone mentions anything that has to do with God. He says it's because of how much his dad tries to enforce religion on him, but I don't want him to write off a bunch of people or even the *idea* of God just because of his dad. I felt like…maybe if he saw that you guys weren't all the same, he would give it a chance. And then maybe his relationship with his dad would get better. And then…" I paused.

"And then what?" Grace continued.

"I don't really know from there. I just want them to have a good relationship," I confessed. I honestly hadn't thought that far ahead.

"And then what?"

I remembered having a similar conversation with Hope where she'd asked me the same thing. I admit my feelings, and then what? It was the same idea right now. I was coming to the realization that thinking far enough into the future was not my strong suit.

Grace furrowed her eyebrows as she listened to my explanation—or lack thereof. "Hmm," was all she said.

"What?" I asked nervously. Was my attempt to deflect the conversation from my own problems failing miserably?

"I can understand where you're coming from, and I think it's really sweet that you want Daniel to have a better relationship with his dad."

Whew. So I'm not failing, I thought.

"It's just…if it was only about Daniel, then why were you so frustrated on Wednesday?" she asked me.

Damn, I thought. *Spoke too soon.* I sat there for a moment, dreading the fact that I was probably going to end up telling the truth—the whole truth.

"I think I know," my mom said from behind the couch, startling me half to death. She walked around the couch to the mantle and grabbed the photo of my father and I—the one I had discovered a week or so before. She placed it on the coffee table at an angle so that both Grace and I could see, and then she took a seat next to Grace. Mrs. Thomas then joined me on the couch.

I blinked away more tears and then quickly wiped the trails of others from my face with the soggy tissue I already held in my hands.

"I was frustrated on Wednesday because it all sounded good, but I didn't feel a personal connection deep down. I just can't wrap my head around forming a relationship with a God I can't physically be around—just like how I have trouble feeling a connection to my own father because I don't remember him. He died when I was a baby."

At this, Grace and her mom were both clearly surprised and sympathetic. I looked at Mrs. Thomas. "You described God as a father figure to Jesus. That just didn't feel possible for me," I explained. I gave up on wiping away tears and just let them roll, but Grace handed me another tissue and then took one for herself.

"That explains what you said about Ryan," my mom added. I looked up at her with dread, utterly shocked that she had indeed planned on talking to me about it—and that for some reason she'd decided that talking about it in front of Grace and her mom was okay. They looked at her in confusion.

"The other night you asked why loving God wasn't like your love for Ryan. Ryan is the first guy you've ever formed a personal connection with, and to be honest, I always thought you and him would end up dating," my mom elaborated.

"Wait, who's Ryan?" Grace asked, probably still trying to recover from my dead daddy issues confession.

"My best friend," I explained. "He's the other guy I was having trouble with that night at your house, but he has a girlfriend. And to be honest, my feelings for Ryan are the reason I kept coming back to the Bible studies. The thing I said about Daniel is also true, but I guess I thought that if I couldn't replace my feelings for Ryan with my feelings for Daniel, then I could replace them with God." At that, I could see the puzzle pieces coming together for Grace.

"So, you have feelings for Ryan, your best friend, and Daniel, your boyfriend, but the root of it all is the unfulfilled connection you have with your dad," she deduced.

"I imagine that's been hard for you to juggle—constantly trying to fill the void you feel with different people," Mrs. Thomas said.

You have no idea, I thought, nodding my confirmation. "I wanted to tell Ryan how I feel, but then I started to really like Daniel. And Grace, when I told you and Hope about this—"

"You weren't sure if you and Daniel were officially together or not. Right. I'm remembering now," Grace said. "Well, if you're officially with Daniel, now, then why not let go of the Ryan thing?"

"I have. I'm not gonna tell him anymore. But I'm still stuck with feelings for both of them, and God isn't solving my problems the way I thought He would."

"Gabby, do you remember what I said to you that night on the staircase?" my mom asked.

"Just that I was trying to fill the space my dad left."

"And then I said, what if it's not about God replacing your natural father, but about making room for God as your spiritual father. Remember that?"

I nodded. "How do I do that?"

"I think the more important question is, do you *want* to do that?" Mrs. Thomas interjected. "Is a relationship with God something you truly want?"

I went silent for a moment. A relationship with God hadn't even been on my radar until it came time to do my Sociology project. "I really don't know," I admitted. I wasn't opposed to the idea, but I also wasn't sure that God was the answer for me. I shifted myself on the couch, trying to analyze how I truly felt.

"Are you okay? It seems like there's more you want to say," Grace prodded.

"It's just that, even if I do make room for God, like my mom said, I just can't get past this empty space I feel from my dad. I mean, on Wednesday, we learned about how Jesus died and resurrected…but then He left. He left His disciples, and I'm willing to bet they felt an empty space, too. It kinda feels like making room for God would be like shifting from one empty space to another."

Grace perked up, which I found a little odd considering the dreary nature of the conversation we were having. "Oh, that's right! You weren't there for the last part of our discussion on Wednesday," Grace remembered.

"I'm guessing I missed something important?" I tried my best to stifle my sarcasm.

"Well, whether or not you think it's important is your opinion, but I think it might help a little. You see, when Jesus left the disciples here on earth, He sent the Holy Spirit, and He promised that the Holy Spirit would never leave them. Rather, the Holy Spirit would be there to help them minister to the world, comfort them in hardship, encourage them in righteousness, and remind them of Jesus' teachings. The list goes on, but that's the gist of it."

"And let me guess, this *Holy Spirit* is somehow also God?" I asked.

Mrs. Thomas, my mother, and Grace all chortled in amusement, and then answered nearly in unison, "Yes!"

"When it comes to the Holy Trinity of God, we try to teach it as simply as possible, but it's a very perplexing concept in and of itself. Consider this, if you left your thumb print, your pinky print, and your index finger print at a crime scene, a forensic scientist would initially recognize three different finger prints. But after running the DNA analysis, all three finger prints would point back to you—one identity. The trinity of God is similar in that there are three persons of God: God the Father, God the Son, a.k.a. *Jesus*, and God the Holy Spirit, all existing at the same time, yet different from one another, but they all have one *essence*. They are God," Mrs. Thomas taught.

"Okay I….strangely understood that, but…what does any of this have to do with what I said about the empty space in my life? I'm still kinda waiting for a solution," I said.

"Right," Grace replied. "The point of my bringing up the Holy Spirit was to show that Jesus may have left, but He sent something even better in return. They had to let Jesus go to make room for what was coming. What are you holding onto that's keeping you from making room for what's to come, Gabby? That emptiness you feel will only ever stay empty because you won't open your hand and make room," Grace preached, standing up before me. I could feel the strength of her voice grow as she spoke.

"You've wrapped your mind around what you *don't* have, and you keep hoping for it to one day be yours, but all it's doing is reminding you of the empty space you can't seem to fill," she continued, taking my empty hands into hers. "You see, when you hold onto something you don't have, it's like closing your empty fist and being upset that there's nothing tucked away behind your fingers."

She formed my hand into a fist.

"You're in your own way by trying to nurture your emptiness, but if you would just open your fist, spread those fingers, and embrace that empty space, you would create the opportunity for something else to be placed in your hand."

She opened my fist again.

"Gabby, you can hold onto the man who's no longer here or, like the disciples of Jesus, you can make room for the Spirit who will never leave. But you've got to want it for yourself. You've got to want to let go. You may feel like you've missed out, but that's nothing compared to what's to come."

The utter power that emanated from Grace's voice had brought me to tears. But I wasn't sad, I was encouraged. For the first time in my life I felt free of the burden of trying to feel that connection with my father. I felt free from the need to substitute his place in my life with a connection to someone else.

I felt open. Open to the idea of a spiritual father. Open to the idea of never being with Ryan romantically. Open to what was to come in my relationship with Daniel. Open to the possibilities that lay before me after senior year. Open because I loved the idea that everything leading up to that moment was nothing compared to what was to come.

We wrapped up our conversation and exchanged hugs—long, heartfelt, genuine hugs. I felt both a sense of relief and the scariness of my newfound freedom all at once. Acknowledging the root of my problems was one thing, but being brave enough to move forward in a new direction was another.

When my initial feeling of encouragement began to settle, anxiousness kicked in again. All I could ask myself was *"now what?"* Being open was scary because it still felt a lot like emptiness, except there was no telling what could fill that space next. As I walked Grace and her mom outside, I realized that we hadn't talked about that day's Bible study at all.

"Oh wait!" I exclaimed as they stepped outside. "What did you guys talk about today at the study?" I asked. They looked at each other, and then looked back at me.

"Grace," they answered in unison before launching into a mini study on my front step.

CHAPTER 26

After spring break, the days blurred into each other like a never-ending cycle of going through motions, but even so, everything was so much better than before.

Seeing Ryan with someone else was no longer the torment it used to be. Melanie and I were the same duo we'd always been, and I was still undefeated in tic-tac-ignore-the-teacher. Daniel and I were in the running for the "cutest couple" superlative in the yearbook, and I knew it was eating away at Tanya, who just so happened to be the head of the yearbook committee. I was even finished with my Sociology project nearly a month before it needed to be turned in.

Senior year was ending off on the right foot, but my anxiousness hadn't gone away. There was a little voice still nagging me inside. *"Now what?"*

After a while, I assumed it was because prom was still three weeks away and graduation a couple weeks after that. Maybe it was the anticipation for how everything would play out—what dress I would wear for prom, prom night itself, and graduation day. Anyway, whatever it was—this feeling—it was keeping me from feeling fully satisfied and distracting me from truly being in the moment.

"BOOM. TIC TAC TOE. That was too easy, Geezy. What's up with you today? You usually put up more of a fight." Melanie smiled like a big little kid as she drew the new lines for our rematch. I snapped back to reality and stared at the paper in disbelief. Four months of undefeated victory: gone. Just like that.

"I figured I'd let you win at least once before we graduate," I lied, trying to nurse my wounded ego. We were supposed to be working on our Sociology projects during class, which is why we were able to goof off so freely. Except, unlike Melanie, I was already done, so I could actually afford to goof off this time around.

"Damn, G. I never thought I'd see this day," Ryan laughed, shaking his head.

"You lost?!" I heard from behind me. Ryan, Melanie, and I jumped at Daniel's sudden and certainly unexpected appearance.

"Yo, didn't we tell you to stop doing that?!" Melanie asked.

"Why are you even here?! Isn't your class like…on the other side of the school right now?" I asked. This had to be senioritis at its finest. Melanie, Ryan, and I weren't doing our work, and here Daniel was, not even in his designated class.

"We finished our work early, so I asked if I could use the bathroom," he said nonchalantly, pulling up a chair.

"Yeah, so you took your whole backpack and dipped. Not suspicious at all," Ryan laughed.

"They probably think you're taking the biggest dump of your life," Melanie added, sending me and Ryan into hysterical laughter.

"Ha. Ha. I see everybody's got jokes today." Daniel rolled his eyes.

"Alright, class, it sounds like everybody's done. Who wants to present first, since we all have so much to talk about?" Mr. Nicholson asked. With the end of the semester closing in, I noticed a few of my teachers growing less patient with us—even Mr. Nicholson.

"Actually, I'd like to get mine out of the way, if that's okay," I offered, raising my hand.

You would've thought I'd sprouted two extra heads the way Mr. Nicholson, Ryan, and Melanie all looked at me. "Uh. Actually, yes. Go ahead, Ms. Perkins. I certainly wasn't expecting this," he commented.

"G, you're finished already?!" Melanie stared in disbelief as I pulled my fully typed project out of my bag, report cover and all. I had planned to just turn it in on the official due date, but with Daniel here, I figured I'd take advantage of the opportunity to present. Part of me still desperately wanted to change the way he thought about *"those people,"* just in case there was any chance at improving his relationship with his father at all.

I stood up in front of the class, and naturally, I had everyone's attention. I doubt it was because they actually cared about what I had to say. Most of them looked shocked. My reputation was pretty strong, apparently.

I opened my report and started to speak, but stopped. I was prepared to condense an entire group of people into words on a piece of paper, but they were more than that—my experience was more than that.

"Everything okay, Gabby?" asked Mr. Nicholson.

"Yeah," I said, closing my report and handing it to him. "I won't be needing this."

He looked at me in confusion and took my report. The class awkwardly stared at me in anticipation of what was going to happen next. I briefly glanced at Melanie, Ryan, and Daniel, who were each giving me their undivided attention.

"I did my project on a high school ministry at Agape Church," I started, fiddling with my fingers. I wasn't completely sure where I was going with this, yet.

"I was gonna get up here and regurgitate a bunch of facts at you, like the fact that the age range was fourteen to eighteen, or that there were six boys and seven girls: 38% Black, 38% White, 23% Hispanic, and so on. I was going to tell you about how surprised I was that they didn't fall into all the preconceptions I'd formed based on my own ignorance. For example, I thought they were gonna be really prude and uptight. I even worried about if my ripped jeans would make me a slut to them," I admitted, gaining a few laughs from the class.

"But they actually turned out to be really…normal. They just happen to love God," I chuckled. I paused for a moment to think about what to say next. How could I tell them about the culture of this group without it sounding like just another school project? Then it hit me.

"Instead of reading you a few lines from my report, I want to tell you about someone. I think telling you about them says a lot about the 'culture' I was supposed to look for." I glanced back down at my fingers and remembered the conversation I'd had with my mom, Grace, and her mom weeks ago. "I want to tell you about Grace," I began, looking up at Daniel.

"Grace treated me like I was a friend when I was a stranger. Grace didn't care that I judged before I understood. Grace was patient with me. Grace was nice to me. Grace took the time to talk to me—and chased after me when I separated myself. Grace knew me before I knew myself. Grace saw my worth and added tax." Now, I was looking at Ryan.

"Grace took insults that *I* deserved and pain that *I* had earned. Grace fought through every disappointment, trial, and storm for me. Grace was beaten for me. Grace was mocked for me. Grace walked with me, and in the times when my own journey was too much to handle, Grace was strong for me." By now, I had gained the attention of students who hadn't been fully engaged at first, and it wasn't until a tear hit my fist that I realized why. I quickly wiped it away and continued.

"The best thing about Grace…Grace doesn't hold any of it against me. Grace doesn't hold it over my head like a debt I have to pay back. Grace forgave me and continues to forgive me when I don't deserve any ounce of it. Grace died for me and rose again, and Grace did it for you, too," I finished, opening my fist, and spreading my fingers.

There was a brief moment of silence before Melanie shot out of her seat with applause. She looked just as confused as everyone else, but I could tell she wanted to interrupt the awkwardness in the air. The rest of the class joined in on the applause, though it was far less enthusiastic. "Thank you, Gabby," said Mr. Nicholson, "I think it's clear you learned a lot from this project."

"Is it okay if I leave early?" I asked him. There were only a few minutes left until the school day was over, but there was somewhere I needed to be—the sooner, the better.

"Yeah, go ahead. I think you've earned it," he complimented.

I rushed to my desk, grabbed my bag, and then quickly left the classroom.

"Whoa, Gabby! Did you hear me talking to you?" Melanie yelled out to me from the classroom doorway.

"No, I'm sorry! I just—"

As I turned around to acknowledge Melanie, I was nearly run over by Daniel, who was right on my heels. He braced our collision with his hands, taking me by the shoulders. "Whoa," he said, "where are you going? Is everything okay?"

"I'm fine," I assured him, turning back to the direction I was headed. "There's just somewhere I need to be."

"What? But you were crying. Why were you crying?" he demanded, matching my pace, though I doubt it was hard for him, considering his legs were much longer than mine. "And Grace? What were those things you were saying about Grace? Did she do something to you?"

I stopped and grabbed his hand. "I promise I'll explain everything later, babe. I just—I need to go right now," I asserted, leaving him in the middle of the hallway.

As I walked to my car, I recalled my conversation with Grace and her mom on my doorstep and how they'd explained to me what they meant when they told me I missed the study on grace.

"So, once we accept Jesus as our savior, our sins are erased, we get the gift of the Holy Spirit, and that's it? There's nothing we have to do to pay God back?"

"That's it. You're saved by God's grace through your faith in Jesus. There's no other requirement for your salvation—no list of tasks you have to perform to earn your way into heaven. Jesus took care of that."

That's it. I had spent so much time being anxious, wondering *now what?* But God gave me a *"that's it."* Sometimes, there's nothing else to a story—nothing else for us to do, and we have to take it for what it is and move forward. We start new stories, new chapters, new moments. Ryan is with Indya, not me—and that's it. My dad is gone, and he is never coming back—and that's it. That's it. And that's okay. I was going to be okay. Life was going to be okay.

Right before Grace and her mom had gotten into their car, she'd called out to me, *"we're having something we call Water Wednesday in the last week of April. It's the day that we baptize anyone in our ministries who gave their life to Jesus. I'd love for you to come and check it out."*

♥ ♥ ♥

The parking lot to Agape Church was considerably empty, and I wondered if I'd run into anyone I knew as I approached the front entrance. I poked my head into random rooms as I walked through the hallway, but each one was empty. As I peeked into the room that we did the Bible studies in, I heard a voice say my name from the hallway.

"Gabby?" I turned to find Mrs. Thomas and another woman carrying what looked like a large kiddy pool box. They set it down, and Mrs. Thomas walked over to me.

"Hi, hun! It's so nice to see you! Are you okay? Is school out early today?" she asked, checking her watch after hugging me.

"I want to get baptized," I told her. "Grace said something about a *'Water Wednesday,'* and I realized it was today, so I left school early because I was scared I'd miss it, but I also left Daniel in the middle of the hallway, and my friends have no idea what's going on, and—"

"Whoa, Gabby, breathe!" she said, grabbing me by my shoulders the way Daniel had. "You…want to get baptized?" she asked. I nodded.

"I just… I've been thinking a lot about what we talked about a few weeks ago—about how I need to let go. And even when I decided to let go, I couldn't get over this obsession with what would happen after that. But today when I was giving my presentation for my Sociology project, it just clicked. I don't have to worry about what's next with Jesus…because it's already been finished," I confessed, wiping a tear from my face.

"Praise God!" Mrs. Thomas said excitedly, pulling me into her chest for another hug. "This is wonderful." She released me and wiped a tear of her own. "It *is* Water Wednesday, but you're early. We're actually setting up out back right now. Did you bring any extra clothes?"

I shook my head. I hadn't thought about the fact that I was going to be soaked when it was all said and done.

"Does your mom know about this—about you getting baptized?"

I shook my head again. "I just decided to do this not even an hour ago," I confessed.

"Tell you what. Call your mom, and let her know what you've decided. I'm sure she'd love to witness this. Plus, she can bring you some extra clothes. In the meantime, you can help us set up," she suggested.

"Sounds good," I agreed.

As we got closer to starting the baptisms, a few familiar faces began to show up, and they were surprisingly happy to see me.

"Yo, what's up, Gabby!" Victor greeted, with Veronica following close behind. "We didn't scare you off?" Veronica joked.

"Nah, Grace hunted me down and insisted I come back, so I figured I'd check it out," I said playfully.

"Yeah. Something like that," Grace laughed.

Suddenly, I felt a hand on my shoulder and turned to find my mom standing there with clothes in her hand. She looked like she'd been crying. "I'm so happy you told me so I could be here," she managed to say.

"Mom, please don't start crying; you're gonna make *me* cry!" I sniffled, trying to suck back tears.

"OMG, now *I'm* gonna cry. Hold me," Victor said, fanning his face and turning to Veronica for a hug.

"Shut up, Victor, you ruined the moment!" Veronica accused, smacking him in the back of his head. My mom and I laughed, and I eyed Veronica and Victor for a second. My suspicions that they were dating hadn't gone away, and at this point I was dying to know.

"What?" Victor and Veronica asked simultaneously.

"Are you two…?" I said, implying the rest of my question by pointing back and forth between the two of them.

"Yes," they answered succinctly.

I knew it! No one on this earth flirted as much as they did.

"Alright, everyone! We're going to start Water Wednesday! Now, I know most of you are here to get baptized, but I quickly wanted to explain what this is all about for anyone who's just watching. We participate in baptism as a public profession of our faith in Jesus Christ; it's a symbolic notion of joining Jesus in His death and resurrection. We submerge our old selves like a burial and come up reborn!"

At this, everyone cheered and got excited. I, on the other hand, grew more and more nervous. I looked around me and saw old and new faces. There were young kids, teens from the high school ministry, and even a couple adults. I also noticed Mr. Ross watching from the back of the crowd.

"I want to start off with a special young lady who originally only stepped foot in Agape Church for a school project: Gabby." Everyone clapped as I walked up to Mrs. Thomas and stepped into the freezing cold water. My mom followed me to the front and stood by with my towel and clothes.

"Go ahead and sit crisscrossed for me," Mrs. Thomas instructed. I did, and then she folded my arms across my chest and placed one of her hands on mine. "I'm gonna ask you a few questions, and you'll answer them out loud, okay?"

I nodded.

"Gabby, do you believe that Jesus is the Son of God?"

"Yes," I said.

"Do you believe that Jesus died for your sins and was raised to life on the third day?"

"Yes."

"Do you confess Jesus as your Lord and savior?"

"Yes," I confirmed.

"Well, Gabby, it is my honor to baptize you in the name of the Father, the Son, and the Holy Spirit," she declared, placing her other hand on my back as she dipped me into the water. Despite the symphony of chaotic and enthusiastic cheering around me, I felt peace as I came up from under the surface—like a blanket of stability had been placed on me. I felt peace in the unknown, because the weight of what I *did* know now filled me with new hopes.

Later, as I left the restroom in my change of clothes, I spotted my mom and Daniel's dad speaking in the hallway. It was only a matter of time before they met, but I would've never believed you if you'd told me they'd meet at church after I'd officially accepted Jesus into my life.

I approached them shyly, not quite knowing what to expect. Had my mom already pulled out unnecessary baby photos on her phone? Was she playing it cool? We may never know, honestly.

"Congratulations, Gabby," Mr. Ross smiled, greeting me with a hug.

"Thank you." I returned his smile nervously.

"Gabby, why didn't you tell me Daniel's dad was a minister here?" my mom asked.

Daniel, I thought. I still needed to tell him what was going on.

"It must've slipped my mind. Hey, do you mind if I head home now? I still need to take care of something," I said quickly, rummaging through my backpack for my keys.

"Gabby," she said, re-acquiring my attention. I looked up to see her dangling my keys in front of me. "Drive safely." I hugged her, said goodbye to Mr. Ross, and rushed toward the parking lot.

It had been a couple hours since I'd left school by the time I headed home. Daniel had to have been worried, considering I hadn't been on my phone the entire afternoon. As I drove, I thumbed through all the confused text messages from Melanie, Ryan, and Daniel anytime I came to a stop.

Sure enough, I pulled into my driveway and found Daniel already parked on the side of the street, leaning against the back of his car. He walked up to my car door and opened it for me, looking perplexed at the sight of my hair, which was no longer in the tame, defined style I'd had it in earlier. He closed the door, and I leaned against it. For a moment, we only looked at each other. It was as if he didn't know what to say, or how to say it, or where to start, so I broke the silence.

"I can explain."

"You don't have a choice. You promised before you took off, remember?" he smirked, resting against my car.

"I got baptized today," I said softly. He looked at me plainly, as if he was trying to understand what I'd told him.

"Wait, so you—"

"I'm one of *'those people,'* now, yes." I nodded nervously. "It was kind of a spur of the moment thing. I was presenting today in class and I just… I knew it was what I wanted," I explained.

"Wow," he sighed, "I definitely wasn't expecting that." He stood up straight and put his hands in his jacket pockets. It was the same jacket he'd worn the first time he took me out. "Are you happy?" he asked.

"I am," I confirmed, tearing up at how strongly I felt about that answer.

"Then I'm happy," he said, pulling me into a hug.

"Really?" I sniffled against his chest.

"Really. You put a dent in my plans, but I'm glad it was for a good reason."

I broke the hug and looked up at him. "Plans?"

"Oh, you thought I skipped class for no reason?" he chuckled. "Turn around."

I slowly turned around, too scared to even ask what was happening. "I wanted to do this in front of your class, but I don't mind having this moment to myself," he explained. I could feel his body press against my back as he moved closer to me.

"Gabrielle Linette Perkins," he continued, sliding one of the most stunning necklaces I'd ever seen across my neck and fastening it for me, "will you go to prom with me?"

I spun around before he could finish saying *"prom"* and tackled him in excitement.

"Yes!" I squealed.

A thousand times, yes.

CHAPTER 27

"Wait, so what's it like? Do you feel any different?" Melanie asked as we headed to lunch the next day. I'd held out on any details about what had happened the day before until we were able to genuinely sit and talk. Not the interruption-filled conversations we'd always dealt with in Advanced Health. You'd think that with May upon us, Ms. Redlich would have developed proper classroom etiquette already—she hadn't.

"Yes and no. I'm still me; I just think about things differently, now. Definitely got a long way to go in the change department, though," I told her.

"Wow, I'm proud of you, G. You've finally found your thing!"

Thing, I thought. I understood what she was implying. Melanie's thing was nursing, and Ryan's thing was basketball—so was Daniel's—but this was more than just a *thing* for me, more than just a passion or a hobby. It was life or death. I'd chosen life.

"Where's Ryan?" I asked Indya when we got to our table. She was there first and seemed to be looking for someone.

"I'm not sure, actually. He said he would meet me here because he needed to do something after class," she explained. I looked around the cafeteria only to realize that Daniel was gone, too. In fact, most of the basketball team was. With murmurs about prom going around, and Daniel's promposal the night before, I figured I might know what was happening.

"I'm sure he'll turn up," I said casually, taking my seat.

"Are we getting food?" Melanie asked.

"Yeah, let's just sit down for a second and let the lines die down," I suggested.

"What? But we never do tha—"

"Just sit down! You'll get it later," I said, yanking her arm down so she'd sit next to me.

"I think you need to get baptized again; they didn't get all the old you off," Melanie commented, rubbing her shoulder. I rolled my eyes and sent her a text message. She looked at her phone, and then looked at me suspiciously before reading it.

I think Ryan's about to ask her to prom, my text explained.

"Ohhh," Melanie whispered. Just then, a basketball rolled across the floor toward our table, with a basketball player chasing after it.

"Sorry about that," he said, picking the ball up from underneath our table. He then backed up a few feet and held the ball in front of his chest so that the name "Indya" could be seen in white paint on the surface.

Right after that, another ball and player came flying toward our table, and he did the same thing. "My bad," he said, picking up his ball and standing next to the other player. He held his ball in front of his chest so that the word "will" was seen.

And then another came. "Whoa!" he exclaimed, "that was close." His ball read "you."

Then another. This time Daniel came sprinting toward us. "'Sup," he smirked, grabbing his ball. His read "go."

By now, students were starting to stop and watch; people crowded around our table to see what was going on. This continued until the phrase "Indya, will you go to prom with" was standing in front of us. We looked around, waiting for another ball to come shooting toward us. Suddenly, Melanie tapped me on my shoulder, and nodded her head toward the right, where the crowd was starting to split open behind Indya. Someone was making their way through—it was Ryan.

"Excuse me," he said, getting the last few people to move out of the way. When they dispersed, Ryan was there with a giant bouquet of roses. He set them on the table in front of Indya, and then helped her out of her seat.

"LOOK OUT!" people screamed as a ball came flying toward Indya's head. She turned to see what the commotion was and recoiled into Ryan's chest, but before the ball could hit her, Ryan caught it in one hand and showed her the word "me?" written across it. She laughed in relief and nodded her head yes, and he pulled her in for a kiss.

And then, of course, the crowd went wild. People clapped and whooped before slowly heading back to their seats. I found myself laughing and clapping along with everyone else, genuinely happy for her.

"How did you figure out what was going on?" Melanie asked as we walked toward a lunch line.

"I've heard a few people talking about prom, lately, so I figured that's what was happening," I explained.

"Has Daniel asked you, yet?"

I smiled to myself and pulled my necklace from underneath my shirt collar. "Yes," I beamed. Melanie's mouth fell open.

"WHEN DID THIS HAPPEN?!" she exclaimed, running her finger across the stones. There were three diamonds: one in the center, one on the left, and one on the right.

"Last night. After my baptism. He was going to do it yesterday in our class, but I stormed off."

"Wow, so that's why he was there! He's smart! I really thought he showed up just because," Melanie enthused.

"Yeah, it turns out not everyone's a delinquent like us," I laughed. "Has Marcus asked you, yet?"

"Nah, I told him I didn't want a promposal. We already know we're going together; I feel like a promposal would just be for publicity at this point." I stopped in place and stared at her. Who was she, and what had she done with Melanie, my dramatic, over-the-top best friend?

"What?" she chirped. "You're not the only one allowed to change, okay?"

She had a point, though. I loved seeing public promposals, but in an era of social media, sometimes these moments just felt like photo-ops we used to flex. I guarantee you there were already countless videos up of Ryan's promposal from different angles, with people coveting over how they were such *"relationship goals."* I liked knowing that Daniel's promposal was just between me and him, so I understood Melanie for not needing one at all.

"Hey, I know this is kinda random," I started, "but do you believe in God?"

"Do I? You're looking at a girl whose family tried to baptize her *twice* as a baby. Once by my Cuban family's priest, and once by my Mexican family's priest," she laughed, grabbing her tray. "My family stopped forcing me to go to Mass with them after middle school, but I believe. I'm just not that deep into it, you know?"

Almost like Ryan, I thought. I felt comfort knowing they had some sort of belief in God like I did. I just hoped that one day, they'd give a relationship with Him a try for themselves. It would make my new journey that much better to go through it with my best friends.

Daniel was waiting for me when we got back to our table, but strangely, he didn't have any food in front of him. "You're not going to eat?" I asked as I sat down.

"By the time I get food, the lunch period will practically be over," he shook his head, "plus…I'm saving room for tonight," he added.

"What's tonight?" I asked, popping a chicken nugget into my mouth.

Daniel looked at me like I was joking. "You serious?" he asked.

"Yes?" I said slowly. "Why?"

"My family is having you and your mom over for dinner tonight? My dad invited her at your baptism. Any of this ring a bell?"

"I left the church early last night so I could get home and talk to you. My mom forgot to tell me when she got home, I guess," I explained. "What's on the menu?"

"It's a surprise." He winked, stealing one of my chicken nuggets.

That night, I'd gone through just about every possible outfit I could think of trying to find the perfect thing to wear. This was more than a t-shirt moment, but not quite a *Sunday's best* moment, you know? As we approached Daniel's doorstep, I focused entirely on not stumbling in my heels. I decided to go with black, high-waisted skinny jeans and a red, off-the-shoulder top that I'd tucked into them. The jeans made it casual; the heels made it dressy. Lastly, the top gave my necklace a chance to be appreciated for the beauty that it was.

"Hi, Mrs. Perkins, come on in," Daniel greeted when he opened the door. He looked incredible, as usual, but it still managed to knock my stomach into oblivion when I saw him. He was wearing a black, satin button-up shirt with the first few buttons undone again, giving a tasteful peak of his chest. If there was anything stronger than butterflies, they were certainly in my gut as I watched him hug my mom and then look at me.

"What?" I asked nervously as I stepped through the doorway. Usually when he saw me, he gave me a smirk, or a big smile, or immediately pulled me into a hug, but this time, he stood there staring at me like he was meeting me for the first time.

"You—"

"Is it too much?" I whispered. "It's the heels, huh? I knew I should've played it s—"

"You're so beautiful," he asserted, grabbing my hand and pulling me toward him for a hug. "Relax, they already love you," he whispered in my ear before letting me go.

And love me, they did. I'd never gotten any unfriendly vibes from his parents at all, but on this night, I didn't just feel welcomed, I felt loved. The smiles were warmer, the hugs were more heartfelt, there was an incredibly comforting feeling about being there. "So, what's the surprise meal Daniel refused to tell me about today?" I asked, taking my seat across from him at the dinner table.

"Mediterranean meatball pitas," Mrs. Ross smiled, setting the dishes on the table. "I learned this recipe during one of my work assignments in Greece."

"Daniel's favorite," I smirked, looking across the table at him. He winked at me and reached for a serving, but his mom quickly smacked his hand.

"Not until we say grace," she scolded as she sat down. Daniel playfully rolled his eyes and held her hand, then reached across the table to take mine. Mr. Ross sat at the head of the table on the opposite end from us and began the prayer.

"Lord, we thank you for blessing us with another meal today. I thank you for Gabby and her mother being here so that we can get better acquainted. Thank you, Lord, for bringing Gabby into your kingdom. It warms my heart to see another soul saved. I'm so thankful that you've placed her in Daniel's life, and I pray that through Gabby you will reach Daniel. Show him your love and your mercy, Lord. Continue to chase after each and every one of us and remind us of your glory. I pray this in Jesus' name, amen."

"Amen," we repeated—well, all of us but Daniel. I looked up at him and saw the irritation in his eyes as he reached for a pita.

There was a bit of an awkward silence as we released hands and passed dishes around to serve ourselves, but Mrs. Ross quickly broke the ice. "Gabby, I just wanted to tell you how happy I am that you've given your life to Christ. How does it feel?" she asked.

"It feels really good," I said warmly, "though, I think I still have water in my ears from the baptism. They didn't have a Bible verse to prepare me for that," I added. Mr. and Mrs. Ross laughed much harder than anticipated, which in turn made my mom and I laugh as well. Daniel smiled at me and shook his head in embarrassment.

"You seem to have made great friends with Grace," Mr. Ross commented.

"Absolutely. At first, I thought she was just being nice because she had to, but when she showed up at my house a few weeks ago, I knew it was genuine," I explained.

"She showed up at your house?" Mrs. Ross repeated.

"Yeah," I chuckled. "I had skipped out on the study that day, and she came by to check on me. The conversation we had then really stuck with me."

It was that genuine, fifteen-minute-or-so conversation on my doorstep about how everything God had done in the past for His people came full circle through Jesus that still stuck with me. It had truly freed me from my misconception that to follow Jesus was to be a prisoner of rules—of religion.

As I'd wrapped my head around the concept of having a personal, unique relationship with God, I'd had multiple conversations with Grace about how to do that. Eventually, I made the discovery that writing my prayers to God felt the most natural. They were like little letters, expressing how I felt, and it was through my new habit of writing prayer-letters to God that I'd decided I was going to let Ryan go through a letter.

I know, I know. You're probably wondering, *What happened to leaving it alone, Gabby? You changed your mind again?* Chill, it's not what you think, I promise. You trust me, right? We've made it this far, so I hope you do. Anyway, I'd decided I would give it to him on prom night, as everything came to an end.

I wanted it to be a grand gesture, but I didn't want to give it to him at graduation, where I could easily slip away for the summer and not talk about it. I would still see him at school after prom, though. I *wanted* to see him after prom—to face him and talk about it. You probably still think I'm crazy, huh? Sigh. Just keep reading, please.

Throughout the dinner at Daniel's place, I talked with his parents about the different Bible studies I'd been part of and what my experience was like, but occasionally, I glanced at Daniel to see his expression. I could tell that he was frustrated but was hiding it behind the occasional, toothless smile he'd give me whenever we made eye contact. The last thing I wanted was for this night to be just about me. Even though I was a guest, I was hoping that maybe the adults would venture off into their own conversation so Daniel and I could talk on our own. It didn't happen, though.

"Thank you for having me." I hugged Mrs. Ross as we began our departure. "The food was amazing, as usual."

"Come back anytime, Gabby. I mean it," she insisted.

As my mom and Daniel's parents wrapped up their goodbyes in the foyer, Daniel and I made our way outside, and he walked me to my mom's car. We stood by the passenger's side and didn't say much. It was obvious that there was something on his mind, but I was scared to force it out of him. Instead, I pulled him into a hug and clung to him, and I noticed his grip around my waist was much fainter than usual.

"Are you too good for me, now?" he asked softly in my ear.

"Of course not," I said back. "I wouldn't be standing here if I thought I was. My seat is all strapped up, and I'm here for the ride," I finished. He chuckled lightly and tightened the hug to standard.

"I love you," he said gently. My heart jumped at the sound of his confession, and for the first time, I felt his heart race against my chest—much different from the strong, steady pace he usually kept. Had it not been for my heels, I would have heard it with my ears, but there was something special about feeling it instead.

"I love you, too," I whispered. And though I meant what I said, I knew that it meant more than what he understood it to mean.

I love you, too, *Daniel*.

CHAPTER 28

Now that we'd all officially been asked, we wasted no time shopping for dresses. That weekend, Melanie, Indya, and I made it our mission to find our prom dresses before all the good stuff was taken.

Some of you may be thinking, *"You invited Indya?"* Of course I did. You know the saying: *Keep your friends close, and your enemies closer…* I'm kidding. We're past the Ryan and Indya thing, remember? The fact of the matter was, we were all going as a group, so we might as well shop as a group! This way, we could all make sure we weren't buying the same dress or dress styles, you know? Nothing's more embarrassing than showing up to prom in the same dress as someone else, even if it is a different color.

Daniel, Ryan, and Marcus already owned tuxedos, so all they needed was for us to buy our dresses so they could get matching ties and those handkerchief thingies they put in the front pocket.

"Are you guys gonna wear a corsage?" Indya asked as she scraped through a rack of red dresses.

"All those roses Ryan got you and you're thinking about a corsage?" Melanie joked.

"No really, though," she laughed, "he's been bugging me about it so he can get one before things start to run out," she explained.

"I personally hate the look of corsages. I don't want to worry about a flower on my wrist all night, and I don't think it's worth buying just for pictures, you know?" Melanie answered.

"Pictures," Indya repeated. "Where are you guys taking your pictures!" She spun around urgently, like she'd been reminded of a homework assignment she forgot to do.

"Do you guys even know any photographers?" Melanie asked.

"I forgot so much went into prom," I sighed. "I'm tired just thinking about it! Whatever happened to the good ol' staircase photos or front porch photos people used to take?"

Melanie shook her head, placing a hideous green dress back on the rack. "One word for you: 'Instagram,'" she said.

Melanie's criticisms of social media were starting to amuse me. She really had changed. She went from the girl who knew social media like the back of her hand for stalk—I mean *researching*—purposes, to the girl who understood its superficial impact on human behavior and no longer bought into it. She had yet another point, though. The capability to go viral because of a bomb prom picture turned what was once a traditional school dance into the Met Gala of high school.

"I guess we have a couple weeks to figure that out, still," said Indya, pulling out a gorgeous, velvet, red dress. It had spaghetti straps, a cowl neckline, and a perfect slit in the side that went high enough to make you look twice, but not high enough to make you look too long.

"You HAVE to try that on," Melanie cheered.

Indya stepped out of the dressing room and Melanie and I let out a gasp simultaneously. If I were still dying for Ryan's affection, this was certainly the dress I'd choose. "This is the one, for sure," Indya confirmed. It had been less than thirty minutes of shopping, and Indya had found her dress; I was starting to think she actually *was*

Cinderella the way things seemed to play out for her in fairy tale fashion.

"Ryan is going to love seeing you in that dress," I smiled.

Indya turned away from the dressing room mirrors and looked at us. "He's going to love taking it off, too." She winked.

Smile cancelled. What did she say? I immediately began choking on my spit. Apparently, even my saliva was shocked and forgot which pipe to go down. Melanie patted me on the back frantically as I gasped for air like an idiot. Nothing's more embarrassing than the cough-choke you experience when you choke on your spit. Seriously.

"Sorry," I gasped, "you caught me off guard," I explained, clearing my throat. Melanie and Indya slowly started to crack up as I regained my normal breathing pattern, and I couldn't help but join in. Even though I wasn't a fan of what Indya had said, I could admit when something was funny.

"So, wait, are you and Ryan planning to…?" Melanie asked without asking.

Indya nodded as she ducked back into her dressing room. "He already got us a room at a hotel," she elaborated. Melanie and I looked at each other. Melanie was amused; I was not.

"Will this be your first time?" Melanie asked. I looked at her like she was crazy—these were not details I cared to know. But she was still Melanie, after all, and details were her love language.

Indya stepped out of the dressing room with her dress back on the hanger. "No, but our first time was really nice, so I'm curious how he'll top that."

Curious about how he'll top that? I thought. What the hell happened the first time? How nice could it be?! We're in *high school* for crying out loud. And what did she mean by it was nice?! Was *it* nice or was the general experience nice? Was it their first time together? Or both of their first times *ever*?

See—THIS is why I never wanted to know in the first place. I had so many questions racing through my head that I had to sit down on a nearby bench to keep from slipping into a pre-midlife crisis. Melanie, on the other hand, saw me take a seat and took it as an invite to get comfortable, sitting next to me as if the interview had just begun.

" *'Top that?'* What happened the first time?" Melanie inquired.

"He was just the perfect gentleman," Indya started, "we hadn't planned on doing it, but we were alone at his house one night, and one thing led to another. Everything just went so smoothly," she sighed as she reminisced. I felt a cold fire run through my veins as she spoke. Letting go of Ryan didn't mean that the feelings had gone away. This was a tough story to listen to.

"Wow. I wish Marcus and I's first time together went smoothly. Ours was a spur of the moment thing in the backseat of his car," she laughed.

"Are you guys planning on doing anything after prom?" Indya asked.

"Maybe," Melanie said mischievously. I looked at her in somewhat of a surprise. This was something *I* didn't even know yet, but she'd told Indya like it was nothing.

Suddenly, both of them were looking at me. "What about you, Gabby? You've been awfully quiet over there," Indya noted.

"I…haven't talked with Daniel about any of that. He *just* asked me to prom two days ago," I told them.

"Wait, have you guys even had sex at all, yet?" Melanie asked.

Yet? Why did she say "yet" like it was inevitable—expected, even? I mean, we almost did, but it was because of a *spur of the moment* feeling, just like they claimed their first times were. Since when did people who haphazardly had sex get to ask other people if they'd had sex—as if doing so would allow you into their club? As much as I'd love to be a part of their little sisterhood, I was perfectly fine with not having had that moment with Daniel, yet. And I wasn't in a rush to get there, either.

"No," I said, getting up. "We almost did, but Daniel wanted it to be special and not a spur of the moment thing," I added. Was that shade? Looking back, it sounded like I was throwing shade. Well, if the shoe fit, Cinderella was probably used to it, anyway.

As we looked for dresses, I wondered if my letter might ruin the hotel plans for Ryan and Indya if he read it before they—well, you know. I was pretty sure it wouldn't, though. It wasn't the type of letter designed to break anyone up. They'd be alright.

Melanie was the next to find her dress, and it was perfect for her. It was a beautiful emerald color with a high neckline and the entire back cut out. Very dramatic, and very Melanie.

I, on the other hand, struggled to find something black on the racks that didn't make me look like I was attending a funeral. I slid a group of hangers to the side in frustration. Whenever I *did* find a dress I liked, my size was nowhere to be found.

"Are you okay?" Melanie asked, walking up beside me. Indya was in the check-out section paying for her dress.

"Yeah, I'm just annoyed that I can't find anything decent around here." I held a dress up to my torso in a nearby mirror and then shook my head and put it back.

"Is that all it is? I know that conversation we had about Ryan and Indya might've been a little uncomfortable. That's my bad," she admitted.

"Oh, that was a *lot* uncomfortable, thank you very much," I chortled. "It's fine, though. Feelings don't go away overnight, but my feelings grow for Daniel every day. So, in a way, it's balancing itself out," I admitted.

I hadn't yet told Melanie about the letter I'd written to Ryan.

I reached for a dress, only to discover another hand reaching for it on the other side of the rack at the same time as me. "Oops." I recoiled my hand. "I'm sorry." I smiled apologetically—until I realized it was Tanya reaching for the same dress. "Oh shoot," I said under my breath.

"Oops is right." Tanya snatched the dress off the rack. "See you at prom," she smirked as she walked away. Had she been listening to Melanie and I talk? There's no way she hadn't been. The question was, how much had she heard? Did she know what we were talking about? *Who* we were talking about?

"Do you think she heard?" Melanie whispered.

"I wouldn't put it past her," I said. I could feel my heart race as "what ifs" began to play out in my head again. It was all I could focus on for the remainder of our shopping. So, about an hour after Melanie found her dress, I was ready to give up for the day—especially because I could tell the other two were starting to grow impatient now that they'd found what they wanted.

"I'm sure you'll find something," Melanie encouraged as we walked toward the mall parking lot.

"Yeah, for sure. There are still a couple weeks until prom. You have time," Indya agreed. I tried my hardest not to roll my eyes. That was easy to say when you already *had* your dress. Plus, the dress was now second on my list of worries. What if that little bitc—I mean *Tanya*—told Daniel what she'd heard? She'd probably give anything to ruin the relationship in the running for "cutest couple," especially when she used to be in my shoes.

Back at home, I sat on my bed and stared into my closet. Out of all the times that I'd gone through this thing trying to find the perfect outfit for Bible studies, dates, and dinners, I don't know why I expected something to magically pop out at me, now—especially not for prom. I just couldn't stop fixating on it, though. Something had to give, eventually.

"Hey, wanna look through some more photos of your dad and I?" my mom startled me by asking. I turned to see her standing in the doorway with the photo album open in her hands, and, at the sight of the album, a lightbulb lit up above my head.

"Mom, you're a genius!" I said, hopping off my bed and making my way to my closet.

"Thank you?" she said with a confused tone.

I slid clothes out of the way until I found it—the black satin dress that I almost wore the night Daniel had dinner at my house. I took the dress out of my closet and held it up to my body, turning to my mom for approval.

"I'm gonna wear this to prom," I told her. Her eyes lit up, and she flipped through a couple pages of the album, then took out a photo and handed it to me. It was the picture of my mom and dad the night she wore the dress that looked exactly like mine.

"It's perfect," she smiled.

CHAPTER 29

How many flat irons does it take to get to the silk-pressed center of a Black girl? Usually one, but prom day called for some extra hands.

Melanie met me at my house the morning of prom to help me tackle my hair in half the time. If there was one thing I hated about doing my hair, it was how long it took, but a great person once said: *With a lot of hair, comes a lot of responsibility.* (It's me, I'm the great person.) Don't get me wrong, I loved my kinky-curly hair, but it had been over a year since I'd last straightened it, so I decided that prom was the perfect occasion to break out the flat irons.

"How are you holding up with this Ryan thing? You think you'll be okay tonight?" Melanie asked as she parted another section of my hair. I glanced at the purse I was going to carry for the night, where my letter to Ryan stuck out from the outside pocket. It was in a standard envelope, with his name across the front.

"I'll be fine. I wrote a letter for Ryan, and I'm giving it to him tonight," I answered. She stopped what she was doing and looked at me in the mirror in confusion.

"Wait, what? What about all that talk about not being a homewrecker?" She set her flat iron down.

"It's not the kind of letter you think it is," I said casually, smoothing my flat iron through a small section on the left side of my head.

Melanie stood there for a moment, mouth slightly agape, waiting for me to elaborate. "Well, what does it say?!" she exclaimed after a few moments of silence.

I laughed and took the letter from my purse and handed it to her. She leaned against my vanity and read through it, then looked up at me with a serious expression.

I started to panic. "What? It's not bad is it?"

"No, not at all, Gabby. This is really…" She stopped, scanning my letter again. "You have a way with words, you know that? This was beautifully written."

"Thank you," I said, taking back the letter. I was sure to put it back immediately so I wouldn't accidentally forget it.

For a little while we stopped talking and let the music fill the silence in the background. To be honest, even with Melanie's reassurance, I was beyond nervous. My letter to Ryan was much more than the confession of love I'd originally contemplated—it was also an opportunity to be rejected, misunderstood, pushed away, or ignored, and the thought of that secretly ate away at me. As I sat there doing my hair I was almost overrun with anxiety, but a text from Daniel lit up across my phone screen and my excitement for prom came rushing back.

"I see you smiling. Who is that?" Melanie asked.

"It's a picture of Daniel and his new haircut," I swooned, showing her my phone.

"I told Marcus not to show me his haircut, or he'd make me want to skip prom altogether," Melanie laughed.

"Wha—Oh, never mind," I said, rolling my eyes when I realized the sexual implications of Melanie's statement. I had almost forgotten about Melanie and Indya's plans to commemorate prom.

"By the way, Gabby, I'm sorry about the whole dress shopping thing," Melanie said. I looked at her in confusion. "When I asked about you and Daniel…" she clarified.

"Oh, that! Don't worry about it."

"No, really. If you wanted to share, you would've. Plus, you just got baptized and all that, so I should've been more considerate about your personal choices before I asked about that," Melanie asserted, looking at me in the mirror.

"I appreciate your apology," I returned.

"Well, look at that," she smiled, flipping my hair forward over my shoulders, "you're all done, *chica.*" My ends were bumped perfectly in a sleek nineties fashion, just as my mom's were in the photo of her and my dad.

"I can't thank you enough!" I beamed, giving her a hug.

"You right! There's not enough *'thank-yous'* in the world. You've got a lot of damn hair," she laughed, gathering her things to head back home. "I'll see you tonight!"

♥ ♥ ♥

I couldn't count down the hours fast enough. This was the first time in a while that I was actually ready without having gone through a mini breakdown trying to find something to wear.

I could already see countless Insta stories and selfies on the socials of other girls getting ready. They all looked gorgeous in their elaborate dresses and makeup and hairstyles—though, there were quite a few dresses that I questioned in terms of the dress code. I mean, I know prom is one of—if not *the*—most anticipated events for high school seniors, but at the end of the day it was still only a dance. I saw dresses that left little to the imagination, dresses that were designed with *quite* the imagination, and everything in between. No matter how many cute dresses I saw, though, none made me feel the way I felt about *my* dress.

"You look absolutely stunning," my mom said from behind me as she fastened my necklace from Daniel.

"Thank you," I whispered. "He should be here any minut—" I started as I was cut off by the doorbell. He always did seem to have immaculate timing. Even when he announced his presence with my doorbell, he still managed to make my heart jump.

I stood on the staircase as my mom got the door, the same way I did the first time he came over to take me out. She stepped aside to let him in, and we immediately locked eyes, like something out of a cliché romance movie. He looked amazing in his all-black ensemble: his suit jacket was lined with satin trim along the lapels, and his button-up matched the rest of the jacket perfectly, all of which was tied together, literally, with a satin black tie.

How can I describe how he made me feel without sounding cheesy? I could say he took my breath away, but that would be too easy. It was more like: he snatched every molecule of oxygen from my lungs and sealed my windpipe shut. I could say something about butterflies in my stomach again, but that would be too repetitive. It was more like: my lungs, now useless, detached themselves from my windpipe and began to flutter like one giant butterfly in the center of my chest. I could say he made me break a sweat, but I'd be damned if I sweat out my edges.

We stood there like two mannequins until my mom spoke up. "Stand on the stairs with Gabby, Daniel, I want to get a photo of you two," she instructed. At that, he snapped out of whatever trance he was in and met me on the stairs.

"You look so beautiful," he whispered into my ear as he positioned himself next to me, placing his hand on my lower back. I felt safe, like he was there to protect me.

After countless photos, my smile slowly began to fade and my annoyance was pushing its way through the makeup I had on. "Mom, we're gonna be late to the restaurant. We still have to take pictures with the rest of the group, remember?" I whined.

"Okay, fine! I'll stop," she conceded. "You two just look so good." I could see the tears well up in her eyes, and it made me think about the photo she'd given me. This had to be a trip down memory lane for her, so I could understand her trying to capture the moment again as much as possible.

We made our way to the door and gave my mom our final goodbyes for the night. "You know the drill," she started. "Don't come back—"

"With nothing we ain't leave this house with," Daniel and I finished robotically.

"Have her back by one o'clock," my mom returned.

"Yes ma'am," Daniel agreed.

In the car, Daniel stared at me the way he had in my house, and I could feel the same tension I'd felt on that picnic table over spring break. "What?" I asked shyly. I was starting to feel flustered and a bit flattered at his attention.

"I really want to kiss you, right now," he admitted.

"What's stopping you?"

"Well…" he started, moving his face closer to mine, "while I was staring at how incredible you look in that dress, and how amazing your hair is, and how gorgeously that necklace lays across your skin, I realized you haven't put your seatbelt on," he smirked.

"Of course. How did I not see that coming?" I sarcastically rolled my eyes and pulled my seatbelt across myself. As soon as it was fastened, he pulled my face toward his and kissed me gently—and almost too quickly for my liking. Did he not feel the same tension I'd felt? Did I not look like a five-course meal at a bougie restaurant? Was I only a snack at a school vending machine?

"What's wrong?" he asked after he pulled away. The frown on my face must've been more noticeable than I'd realized.

"Where's the rest of it?" I pouted.

He chuckled and then started the car. "The way I *want* to kiss you and the way you *should* be kissed don't always line up. If I kiss you the way I want to, we might end up in the backseat and not make it out of the driveway," he added, putting the car in reverse.

"Yeah, my driveway would probably be way worse than a picnic table," I laughed.

Now, before you pass judgement, hear me out. I know premarital sex is a no-no in the Christian faith, and to be fair, I had no intentions of going there with Daniel. But what I won't do, is lie about how I felt for the sake of looking like a "good" Christian. The idea of Christians being perfect, robotic beings who no longer deal with human feelings is what keeps a lot of people from wanting to be Christians today, and I want no part in that. I went through real emotions, real urges, and real thoughts, the same way anyone would. The only difference was I now surrendered those things to God the best I could.

Now, where was I?

♥ ♥ ♥

As if she hadn't already looked good in the mall when she first put the dress on, Indya was absolutely stunning when we pulled up to the restaurant. Her makeup, her hair, the way her leg glowed as it peeked through the slit of her dress—everything was just phenomenal on her.

Melanie was taking photos of her and Ryan in front of a fountain outside of the restaurant. We'd strategically chosen something with a beautiful, outdoor courtyard so that we wouldn't have to drive from place to place the entire night. Ryan was so caught up in his photoshoot with Indya that he hadn't noticed Daniel and I standing off to the side with Marcus.

"Alright, guys, you have enough pictures to last you the whole month on Insta. Get some of me and Gabby!" Melanie demanded, handing the phone back to Indya. At my mention, Ryan finally glanced in my direction, and his face when he saw me was something I'd never forget. It felt like more than just him *seeing* me. It felt like he saw me and didn't brush me off as *just Gabby*. I was *Gabrielle Perkins,* the girl he didn't choose—the girl he usually didn't look twice at until now.

He looked amazing, of course. He was in a black suit, with a red tie that matched Indya's dress perfectly, and his hair was done up with gel, which gave him a suave finish.

"Biiiitch! You look so good! You were right about that dress," Melanie said, trotting over to Daniel and me. I spun around so she could take in my entire outfit.

"Me?! Look at YOU!!!" I exclaimed. Contrary to what I'd done, Melanie actually let her natural curls loose with a pretty up-do and two strands on either side of her face that framed it perfectly.

"Let's take some pictures!" she cheered. I handed Daniel my purse and followed her over to the fountain, where Indya was waiting to take the photos.

As we found our angles, switched our poses, and even changed our scenery, the guys stood a few feet from us and talked amongst themselves. Occasionally, I'd glance over at them and find Daniel watching me, each time with a smile on his face, like he was amused by mine and Melanie's antics. At one point, I caught Marcus taking photos of Daniel, who was posing hilariously with my purse on his shoulder.

"Ryan! Come take pictures with us! *Los tres amigos!*" Melanie waved. Ryan came over and stood between us, with his hands around our waists in a friendly fashion. It felt nothing like having Daniel's hand on my lower back, but I was okay with that.

Habitually, I glanced over at Daniel as we changed poses, only to find that the amusement in his face was gone. He was speaking to Tanya, who was also dressed in black—in fact, it was the black dress she'd snatched off the rack at the mall. It was evident that whatever Tanya was talking about was not making Daniel happy.

By the time Melanie, Ryan, and I finished our photos, my purse was no longer on Daniel's shoulder; he was holding it in his hand like he could care less about it, and that's when I remembered the letter. The envelope addressed to Ryan still peeked out of the outer pocket of my purse, enough so that you could see the letters "R," "Y," and "A." It didn't take rocket science to figure out who the envelope was for, and Daniel had definitely noticed. Combined with whatever Tanya had told him, I had a pretty good idea of what was running through his head

"Daniel, come over here! It's you and Gabby's turn!" Melanie waved him over.

He approached me with a stoic expression, which was honestly more scary than anything I'd seen on his face before. "What side do you want to stand on?" I asked, trying to test his mood.

"Whichever is fine," he said blandly. I stood on his left, and put on the best fake smile I could manage. Daniel lightly placed his hand on my back, like he couldn't be bothered to touch me.

"Smile, Daniel! Act like you've taken a picture before!" Melanie commanded from behind her phone's camera.

Oh God. I began to panic internally. *This is bad. What did she say?* I looked over at Tanya, who was standing nearby with her friends taking selfies. She glanced over at me and Daniel and met my stare with a smirk before walking inside.

"Yoo-hoo! Gabby! Camera's over here, remember?!" Melanie waved her hand to catch my attention.

"Actually, Mel, I think we've got it!" I left Daniel's side to see the photos Melanie had taken, and Daniel walked back over to the side with the rest of the guys and Indya.

"Are you okay?" she questioned, looking at me with confusion. "We were so excited to take phot—"

"He knows," I interrupted. She looked at me in disbelief. "Daniel?" She glanced over at him. "Holy shit; he looks pissed," she whispered.

"And guess who was talking to him a few minutes ago?" I asked, trying to hold my emotions together.

A look of pure irritation washed over Melanie's face. "Tanya."

CHAPTER 30

I approached Daniel but could barely manage a glance from him. "What's wrong?" I asked as we all followed a hostess to our table. I wanted to try and get ahead of things before they snowballed.

"Nothing." He shook his head and stared straight ahead. I looked behind me at Melanie and Indya, whose dates were both showing them affection. Daniel, however, was cold and distant. We weren't holding hands, his hand wasn't on my lower back, his arm wasn't around my waist. Heck, I would've taken an arm around the shoulder so long as he was showing me that nothing really was wrong like he'd claimed.

As we got to our booth, Daniel slid in first, followed by me, and then Melanie. On the other side of the booth, Indya sat across from Daniel, Ryan across from me, and Marcus across from Melanie. To avoid adding fuel to the fire, I sat my purse between myself and Melanie so that the envelope for Ryan would be out of Daniel's sight.

"Look, G, they have chicken fettuccine Alfredo," Ryan said, pointing at the menu. I was taken aback that he even remembered my favorite dish.

"Well, I know what I'm getting," I said, playfully closing my menu and putting it on the table.

"Gabby, I really love that dress. I knew you'd find one!" Indya proclaimed.

"Yeah. Black ended up being a dope color choice," Ryan co-signed.

"Thanks, guys," I gushed. "If I were lighter, I'd be blushing," I joked.

Sitting there and eating with everyone should've felt like any other day at school in the cafeteria, but it didn't. I felt guilty for trying to enjoy myself while it was obvious that Daniel was upset. I wanted it to be like the days at school when everyone would talk and laugh with nothing big to worry about other than an exam we hadn't studied for. Instead, on what was supposed to be a special night, I was more than worried, and not just about one guy, but two—just like I'd been for majority of the semester.

I was worried about how the one in *front* of me would react to what was inside the envelope, and worried about the one *next* to me thinking the envelope was something it wasn't. This wasn't how I'd planned for the night to go. I'd thought I would be worriless. I'd thought my boy troubles were finally behind me.

I had yet to figure out how I would give Ryan the envelope, and the more the night progressed, the less sure I became of what my approach would be. I did manage to save face during dinner, though, cracking jokes here and there and contributing to the conversation when I could. Daniel spoke a little bit, but he was nothing like the energetic, silly guy I was used to.

As we began to make our way out of the restaurant, Melanie took my hand and headed in a different direction. "We're going to the restroom! We'll meet you outside," she announced. The way she was pulling me with her told me this was *not* an actual potty break.

When we got into the restroom, Melanie checked under the stalls in routine fashion, as if anyone who might've been there would have any idea what, or whom, we were talking about. Then again, that's what we'd thought at the mall, and look how that turned out.

"Are you still going to give Ryan the envelope?" she asked.

"I mean, I want to! But there's no doubt in my mind that Tanya told Daniel that I have feelings for Ryan, too," I explained, pacing back and forth. "How am I supposed to give Ryan the envelope without sending Daniel over the edge? If I try to sneak it to Ryan, it'll only confirm whatever Tanya told him, and if I do it directly, it'll seem like I don't care about Daniel altogether!"

"Shit!" Melanie said, putting her hands on her head in frustration. "I swear to God, if it weren't prom night—"

"I know, Mel. I know," I sighed. "But we can't give her that satisfaction of knowing she got under our skin."

"Yeah, well, we also can't give her the satisfaction of ruining your relationship! Some bitches are just so miserable that they have to drag everyone down with them," Melanie huffed.

"Hey," I said, grabbing her by the shoulders. "We are going to have an amazing night, and everything is going to work itself out. It's prom night. We've waited so long for this," I breathed. The truth was, my heart was racing, and I wanted to cry, but I couldn't let my drama bring my best friend down with me.

Melanie nodded and then wrapped me into a tight hug. "I love you. I'm so sorry this is happening."

"I love you, too." I exhaled with disappointment. It was clear that giving Ryan the letter that night was no longer happening; reconciling with Daniel was far more important. It's not like I *had* to give Ryan the letter that night. It's just that I'd pictured my night going so much better than it was.

When we walked outside, everyone was talking casually except Daniel, who was slightly off to the side, not saying anything. "See y'all at prom!!!" Melanie yelled as we split up into our separate vehicles.

Daniel still opened my door for me but wasn't making any eye contact, and it was starting to frustrate me. It was so blatantly obvious that something was off. If he was going to lie like nothing was wrong, he could've at least treated me like nothing was wrong. Of all the nights to have an attitude and blow me off, this wasn't the one.

For the first few minutes of driving, we sat in silence, but eventually, I couldn't take it anymore.

"Are you gonna tell me what's wrong? I saw you and Tanya talking."

"What's in the envelope?" Daniel asked instead of answering my question.

"I knew that's what this was about," I sighed, shaking my head.

"Let me see it," he demanded, glancing at my purse in my lap. His voice had much more audacity this time around.

"Excuse you?"

"It's for Ryan, right? Your so-called *'best friend?'*" He was getting far more fidgety, like he had the urge to jump across the seat, and not in the same way that he did when the night had first started. I started to feel unsettled.

"Yes, Daniel. It's for Ryan, but it's not what you think. What is wrong with you?!" I pleaded.

"It's true, right? You like him?" I didn't say anything, and he scoffed. "You know, I thought something was up a while back at my pool party, but I shook it off like the idiot I am. But then lo and behold, Tanya comes up to me today and confirms everything I suspected," he finished, gripping the steering wheel tighter.

"Daniel, I'm with *you!* I love *YOU.* Tanya wasn't even there for the whole conversat—"

"You were cracking jokes with him back there right in front of me like I didn't even exist!" Daniel yelled, interrupting me. "Here I was trying to give you the love he was too *PUSSY* to give you, and you still want him, anyway," he accused, glancing at me. The endearing, sweet look I was used to seeing in his eyes was long gone.

"That's not true, Daniel, I don't want to be with him," I cried. "Why won't you listen to me?"

"Give me the envelope." He reached into my lap with one arm and tried to take my purse.

"No, Daniel! You need to focus on the road!" I said, clutching my bag and moving it to the far side of the passenger's seat.

"DAMMIT, Gabby! Give me the fucking envelope!" he yelled, still reaching for my bag with little regard for the fact that he was driving. "If you had nothing to hide, it wouldn't be an issue, but I'm right, aren't I? AREN'T I?"

"STOP IT!" I yelled, pushing his hand away from me. "Why are you doing this?" I sobbed. I was absolutely terrified. This wasn't Daniel. This was someone else who looked like Daniel with a satin-trimmed suit on. The love was gone. The gentleness was gone. All I saw there was pain personified.

I looked ahead of us as I fought his arm away from my purse, noticing a four-way stop sign that we were about to blow through. "DANIEL, STOP!" I screamed, no longer fighting to keep him away from the letter. He ignored me and continued to reach for my purse like his life depended on it.

"DANIEL, PLEASE!!!" I begged at the top of my lungs. He slammed the breaks and we slid into the intersection, his tires screeching from the friction. The momentum of the stop sent me flying face first into the dashboard. It was only upon the excruciating pain coming from my nose that I became conscious of not having my seatbelt on.

I screamed out in pain, grabbing my nose in hopes of keeping the blood from getting on my dress. There was no use; there was too much blood to control, and it dripped from my hands like a feeble attempt to hold water.

"Oh my God, baby, I'm so sorry!" Daniel panicked, reaching out toward me to see the damage he'd caused.

"Don't!" I turned away from him and cried. Why was this happening? Why now? Melanie and Marcus were riding behind us, and Ryan and Indya weren't too far behind them. We were still stopped in the middle of the intersection, and it wasn't long before they'd caught up to us.

"Oh my God, what happened?!" Melanie ran up to my side of the car and swung the door open. I hopped out and immediately grabbed ahold of her, accidentally smearing blood on her arms.

"Is it broken? Is my nose broken?" I sobbed.

"NAPKINS! I NEED NAPKINS!" Melanie yelled to Marcus, who had stopped right behind us. Ryan and Indya were pulling up to us now, as well. "How did this happen?!" she asked, but all I could do was cry when I tried to explain. I was still in shock, and couldn't quite believe what was happening.

"WHAT DID YOU DO?!" Melanie demanded as Daniel tried to approach us.

"It was an accident, I swear! Gabby, I'm so sorry—" He reached out to me, but I pushed him away, staining his shirt and jacket with blood in the process.

"Just take it," I managed to say, holding out my purse so he could retrieve the letter. Now, he refused to take it. We were starting to attract attention as traffic began to go around us, people staring as they drove by.

"Did he hit you?!" Melanie asked, bringing napkins to my face. I shook my head no as she examined my face for other injuries.

"I would never—"

"I ASKED GABBY," Melanie snapped, cutting Daniel off.

"We were fighting over the letter, and—" I stopped my explanation at the sight of Ryan and Indya running up to us. The last thing I needed was for him to see me like this, but I saw the blood drain from his face as he realized there was blood leaking from mine.

"Gabby, what happened?" he asked me. I shook my head as a new wave of tears kept me from answering. As wrong as Daniel was, I knew if I told Ryan what had happened it would turn into a fight between him and Daniel, and there was already enough bloodshed from me alone.

"She said something about them fighting over a letter," Melanie said, still wiping blood from my face. "We need to get you to a hospital, *mija*; I think your nose is broken."

Ryan turned his eyes to Daniel and made a beeline for him.

"Did you touch her?" Ryan asked through his teeth, inches from Daniel's face.

"Bro, you need to back up off me. Of course I didn't. I would never do that," Daniel defended, standing his ground. My heart began to race as I watched them come toe-to-toe. *Please, God, don't let them kill each other.*

"Why is she bleeding?!" Ryan yelled. I had never seen either of them get this angry, and it was starting to feel like everything was my fault. None of this would be happening if I hadn't brought the letter—if I hadn't written it at all.

Why did I have to write the stupid letter? My breaths began to quicken.

"We were arguing over a letter she wrote to you, and..." Daniel looked at me as he explained and began to get emotional.

"And what?!" Ryan snatched Daniel by his suit jacket. "I swear to God if you put your hands on her..."

"I already told you I didn't!" Daniel yelled, yanking his suit from Ryan's grip. "I didn't see the stop sign so I slammed on the brakes, but she wasn't wearing her seatbelt! It was an accident, like I keep trying to say, but no one's FUCKING LISTENING!"

Somebody make them stop, I thought, but I couldn't get the words to come out of my mouth. Cars began to honk as congestion from our stopped cars began to build up.

"Where's the letter?" Ryan demanded.

"What?" said Daniel.

"I said, *where's the letter?*" Ryan shoved Daniel in the chest. "Since it was so fucking important." He shoved again.

"You've got one more time to put your hands on me," Daniel threatened.

I can't breathe, I thought, turning away. No matter how many breaths I took, I couldn't seem to actually take in any air.

"Gabby, are you okay? Look at me," Melanie instructed.

"I can't…" I panted, clutching my chest in pain. It was as if it was caving in on itself despite my efforts to inflate it with my lungs.

"I'm on the phone with 911 right now, they have an ambulance on the way, Gabby," Marcus reassured me.

"GUYS, STOP IT!" Indya yelled suddenly as fists started flying between Ryan and Daniel.

"Make it stop," I cried softly, though no one could hear me over the commotion. I clung to Melanie as flashes of darkness threatened my vision. I could hear the echoes of shouting become quieter and farther away, until finally, there was nothing.

CHAPTER 31

I awoke to the sound of sirens and the subtle bumps and shakes of a moving vehicle and slowly realized I was in the back of an ambulance, propped up on a stretcher, a paramedic to my left digging through a bag of supplies. I was immediately reminded of the excruciating pain of a broken nose as I attempted to inhale but failed miserably.

"Here's some ice for your nose," the paramedic said, gently holding an ice pack on my face until I took over. "Can you tell me your name?" he asked.

"Gabby," someone said in unison with me from my right side. I turned to find Ryan sitting next to me, his blood-stained letter in hand. My heart nearly jumped out of my chest. *He read it,* I thought. There was no way he hadn't. It was addressed to him, after all.

"Ryan," I sighed. "None of this was supposed to happen." I choked back tears.

He slid closer to me and grabbed my right hand, and I noticed the bruises and scratches on his knuckles from fighting. "Are you okay?" he asked.

I shook my head. "I should've never written the letter. If I hadn't, we'd all be at prom right now." I relaxed my head against the stretcher and let the tears spill from my eyes.

"What did the letter say?" he asked.

I looked at him in confusion.

"What do you mean? It's right there," I replied, eying the paper.

He turned it toward me so I could see the blood and ink smeared together into an illegible cluster of words and letters. If you tried hard enough, you could probably still read it, but why bother when he could just ask me himself?

"It's about love," I sighed, looking straight ahead. I knew the letter by heart. I had rehearsed it out loud a million times to make sure it sounded right, but I'd never intended for the words to actually come out of my mouth. Writing it down was my safe way of letting it out while holding it in.

"What did it say about love?" he asked gently.

"I can't." I shook my head in protest and wiped away more tears. I could feel a ball of resistance form in my throat from trying not to cry.

There were a few moments of silence before he spoke again. By now, the sound of the sirens had stopped, though we were still moving.

"Does it say you…love me?" he asked again, a little softer this time.

I returned my gaze to him to find him looking down at the paper, bracing himself for whatever I'd say next. "No," I started. I could see a slight tinge of disappointment settle on his face. "Even though I do," I admitted. At that, he looked up and met my gaze with his own. He was crying, now, too.

"What does it say?" his voice broke as he asked one final time, dropping his head again, a move I suspected was meant to conceal his own tears.

This was it. This was the time to redeem myself for all the years I'd gone without sharing my heart with Ryan; only now, my confession of Love was much different, and hopefully, much better.

"Hey," I started.

He looked up at me again.

"I know this is weird…and maybe even random, depending on when you get this. But I've wanted to talk to you for a while…and now I finally know what I want to say—or at least how I want to say it.

"I want to tell you about a Love. A Love that sees every bit of you and appreciates every detail. A Love that hurts when you hurt and smiles when you smile. A Love that listens. A Love that understands.

"I know life can be tough, and we don't always understand why we go through the things we do, but I assure you that there's a Love like no other that will walk you through it. This Love is jealous, and it can't stand to see you with anything or anyone less than you deserve. It cries, 'I'm right here!' and longs for the day that you realize it so you can experience all it has to offer.

"And I know this sounds sweet, so far, but I have to warn you. This Love is crazy. It's radical. It knows no limits. This Love doesn't hold back. It tells you how it is, and it tells you how it isn't. It's a Love that fights for you. A Love that cares for you. A Love that says nothing—not my bloodied body, not the pain I endured, not even death—could ever keep me from you.

"If you take nothing else from this letter, take this: in the middle of the storm, listen carefully, and in the heat of every battle, pay attention. Despite the trials of this life, Love is calling for you, ordering your steps, and showing you The Way. So, promise me one thing, and I'll promise you another. Promise me that you'll give Love a chance, and I promise you, you won't regret it.

"Love loves you. More than you know."

ACKNOWLEDGEMENTS

Thank you to Lily Choi, my developmental editor; Kim Haulena, my copyeditor; Serena Connell, my book cover artist; and my cousin April, my graphic designer—you all made publishing my first novel a dream come true. Thanks also to my friends and family; your unending support throughout this process encouraged me deeply. Most of all, thank you, God; you have blessed me and kept me, and I'm forever grateful.

ABOUT THE AUTHOR

Jazmine Harris is her given name, but her friends and family simply call her *Jaz*. Over the last ten years, Jazmine has established herself as a digital creator on many fronts, obtained two STEM degrees, and written her first novel—but she would argue that none of these things matter. When it comes to her identity, Jazmine has found herself searching for something beyond her occupation or her accomplishments to define herself by. She hopes to one day fill this page with descriptions of how she experiences herself and how others experience her. When that day comes, she hopes those descriptions boil down to one word: *love*.

Jesus replied: "'Love the Lord your God with all your
heart and with all your soul and with all your mind.'
This is the first and greatest commandment.
And the second is like it:
'Love your neighbor as you love yourself.'
—Matthew 22:37-39